Chronicles of the Bear: Volume I

By

Remy Morgeson

Chronicles of the Bear: Volume I
Revised Edition. August 2, 2023.
ISBN: 978-1-7367161-0-6
Written by Remy Morgeson.

The Bear is Born
Left for dead by the demon beast of the Northern Forest, a young boy turned into a man sets out on a path to avenge his slain father. But will the old saying about digging two graves ring true for Asbjorn just as it has for so many others? And what might an old witch know of the creature the Northerner seeks? And is it worth risking more than just his life to find out?

The Bear Awakened
Continue the tale of Asbjorn as he now faces the coming of a new threat. A tide of black steel is sweeping up from the far south, putting everyone in their path beneath their merciless blades. But what interest does a single Northman have for such an army, and why have they been sent to claim him for the dark power they serve?

The Bear in Shadow's Grip
It has been weeks now since the razing of Asbjorn's home. He and his pursuers alike have been pushed to their breaking points by the long chase that's followed. But Asbjorn still has one chance left for him as the enemy closes in, the Blade Mountains that rise high and divide the great north from the sprawling south. But despite the promise of safety, the jagged peaks may hold their own share of perils, a danger that might leave Asbjorn and the forces on his trail all dead before everything is finished.

To Kill the Stars

Asbjorn's home was destroyed at the hands of the black steeled legion but that is not the only place in the world to have felt the touch of their dark master. The lord of the obsidian citadel's grasp reaches far and wide, his wrath known by more than just the scattered people of the frigid north. Tomek Antal's home of Marsax was enslaved and brought to ruin nearly a decade ago. The oppressed villagers were slaughtered during a failed uprising. Accompany Tomek as he treks across a blasted land in his own bid for retribution, leading him to a confrontation with the master of the black citadel, one that will show just how terrible the dark lord's power can truly be.

The Bear is Born

I

The sun had just peaked in the autumn sky when the stag lifted its head. The animal grazed lazily in the secluded clearing deep within the woods. They had picked up the beast's trail earlier this morning before first light, tracking it ever since to reach this moment. The boy could hear his father's rhythmic breathing from just over his shoulder. The two crouched in the tree line as they watched the animal feed. The thing looked so massive and towering to his young eyes. Its antlers swept up to what seemed to be innumerable points. This was his first hunt after his coming of age over the summer months. The stag was to be his first kill on his way to manhood, and he could not stop himself from shaking.

Slowly, he lifted his father's bow. The grip of it trembled in his hand. The tension was so great on the string that he struggled to pull it back. It bit into his fingers which were having difficulty keeping hold of it and the arrow at the same time. For the large man that knelt just next to him, handling the weapon was second nature. He was a hunter and trapper by trade and the bow had become almost an extension of himself. But for a boy of only twelve years old, it was proving to be no easy task. The pressure of finally being in the moment was truly setting in. He'd practiced for hours over the spring and summer out behind the small longhouse where he and his father lived, sending countless arrows streaking into the targets the big man had erected in the fields for him. But being by himself and in the calm of sunny days was one thing. It was completely different in the wild wood and having his quarry mere yards away.

He prepared to take his shot as he tried to gather himself. His breaths came short and rapid as his heart thumped. He took an unsteady aim as a single bead of sweat ran down his cheek. He was petrified before the animal that was yet unaware of his presence. His body went rigid, and his fingers locked like a vice. The string started to slip from his grasp to nearly let the arrow go early. His mind raced at the thought of what would happen if he missed. He would surely spook the stag so that it bounded off to leave him with nothing. How would he ever face his father and the other boys back at the village again, and what would they do for meat for the coming winter. It was one thing to endure the laughter and teasing of the others who'd already brought down kills of their own, but to go hungry and shoulder the disappointment of his father was another thing. He knew he couldn't miss.

His arms began to judder the more his worries raced. Everything went blurry for a moment as the stag drifted out of focus. Then he suddenly felt a strong hand fall upon his shoulder. His father's firm touch brought him back to where he was. The man's breath was warm on the back of his neck. The words that were whispered in his ear were steadying and reassuring.

"Calm down, Asbjorn," his father softly said. "Breathe in, and then exhale slowly, just like you learned back home. Remember what I've told you and what you've practiced out in the fields. See the arrow take flight. Watch it in your mind as it sails through the air to strike the target. And then let it go."

Asbjorn let his eyes close in response to the calming instructions. He did as the man had said and pictured the large stag that stood in front of them. He imagined himself taking a sure aim and then freeing the arrow. He saw it streak straight towards the majestic creature to pierce its heart. An instant later, his eyes flicked open to come to lock with those of the beast. Its nostrils flared as it sniffed at the cool air to just pick up their scents. It started and turned to run just as Asbjorn went to release his fingers. The string flicked out and the arrow flew directly toward the fleeing creature.

The world around the boy suddenly seemed to slow down and drag in that moment. Time itself had almost stopped to take notice of what he'd done. He watched wide-eyed as the arrow flew forth. Its fletching caused it to spiral as it cut through the air. The shot managed to strike home just behind the creature's right foreleg. The wooden shaft penetrated deep into the animal's flank. There was a slight spray of red with a wild spasm and a burst of leaves and sticks. The beast jumped and took a few faltering steps through the trees before falling. It tumbled headfirst into the dried underbrush that was strewn over the forest floor. Asbjorn was able to see it moving for only a second after. When it had finally ceased, he and his father carefully came up to find it lying motionless on the ground. Its eyes were open but there was no trace of life left in them. His father had him stay back as the man went up to make sure the animal was down and would stay that way. He waved him forward only when he was certain.

Asbjorn came to his father's side to take in the beast. He saw that it was even more splendid up close. Its antlers seemed an even larger crest than they did when it first raised its head from grazing. The tips looked to span from fingertip to fingertip should he stretch out his arms. He glanced up at his father who regarded the deer with a flat expression. The stern look worried Asbjorn that he may have done something wrong. But then a slight trace of approval came across the man's features. He glanced down to give a small nod and a half smile. With a firm hand, he gave Asbjorn a stiff slap to the back. The boy stumbled forward and was almost knocked off his feet. Asbjorn looked up to give his father a grin of his own. He held himself as tall and straight as he could. In comparison to what the big man had often brought down, the boy's stag was nothing special. It had probably only been away from its mother for a year or two judging by its size. But to Asbjorn it was everything that he'd hoped for and more. His first hunt was over and done with, and that was enough for him, at least for now.

It was just turning dusk as father and son trekked back to their camp at the edge of the woods. The small pitch was nestled in a grouping of trees near a twisting stream. Jurgen carried the dead stag over his shoulders for his young son who followed behind. The boy had tried it for himself for a few hundred yards but still lacked the strength to manage on his own. They did not speak a word to one another about the hunt on their way back. The look on Asbjorn's face said enough to tell his father just how elated he was. It didn't matter that the deer was by all accounts a scrawny one. It would have more than likely been passed up by a more seasoned hunter to let fill out for another year. But truth be told, Jurgen was even having a hard time hiding his expression. He struggled to maintain his stoic exterior so as to not give away his feelings.

Jurgen periodically glanced over his shoulder as Asbjorn hurried to keep up with him. The two moved steadily through the choked underbrush. Even with several hundred hounds over his back, the experienced woodsman was able to easily traverse the dense landscape. His long strides carried him swiftly in and around the thick trees. He stepped over the broken logs and dead branches that littered their path with incredible ease. He'd done so for so many years he thought nothing of it.

But such was Jurgen's gait that Asbjorn was having difficulty staying up with him. The boy found it challenging to navigate the scattered debris like his father. He tripped more than once as he trudged through the thick leaves. He badly skinned his knee on a fallen branch and then fell to bang his chin a few steps later. But all of that mattered little to Asbjorn with how high his spirits were. His mind shut out the discomfort as he was determined to not be left behind. Jurgen could have sprinted through the scrub and the youth would have found a way to keep up, pushing himself over the treacherous terrain to maintain his father's pace.

At last, the pair reached their campsite that sat in the lap of the secluded grove. The night birds were just beginning to come out as the sun dipped low. Asbjorn immediately went to work at building a fire to stave off the cold. Jurgen strung up the deer in a nearby tree to keep it off the ground and away from forest scavengers. Father and son settled in around the glowing warmth once the flames had crackled to life. They wrapped themselves in soft furs as they took a late meal. The salted venison and dried berries they ate silenced their rumbling stomachs. The water from the nearby stream cooled their throats.

Jurgen stretched out and relaxed on his bedroll as he enjoyed his supper. He lay back to gaze up at the stars that were just beginning to emerge. He let out a deep breath as he just finished the last of his berries. He spit out a small seed as he took in the view.

The same could not be said for Asbjorn. The boy's enthusiasm was still running high from the day's events that he was having trouble winding down. He consumed his meal with a ravenous vigor. He took in large mouthfuls of meat to puff out his cheeks as he chewed. In between bites, he would continuously glance up to where his kill gently swung from the tree. He was unable to remove his eyes from the deer for more than a few moments at a time. He couldn't help but anticipate his next hunt, looking forward to it even as he took in the sight of his last.

"You keep eating like that and you're not going to have anything for tomorrow," Jurgen suddenly spoke. Asbjorn's head snapped around with a half-eaten bit of venison hanging from his mouth. "You best pace yourself and save some for later."

The surprised youth glanced down. He saw his remaining rations and realized his father was right. He'd become so distracted that he'd eaten more than half of what was there in a single sitting. He had only a few strips of meat and a handful of nuts left, and that had to last him through the next day and the morning after. Red-faced, he bit off the chunk that still dangled from his lips. He replaced it in his food bag before tying off the strings and tucking it away.

"I'm sorry, father," Asbjorn sheepishly responded. "I was just thinking."

Jurgen couldn't help but smile as his son apologized to him. He sat up on his bedroll to come around and face the boy. The big man tied back his wild blonde hair and scratched at his chin through his beard. He tried to remember just how he'd felt so many years ago when his father had done these same things with him.

"Have I ever told you about when my father took me out on my first hunt?" he asked in a soft voice.

Puzzled for a moment, Asbjorn thought it a strange thing for his father to suddenly say to him. It was a rare instance when Jurgen offered to talk about himself in any kind of personal way. The big man was often guarded and rarely spoke of such things. Asbjorn was not at all expecting the like to happen out here. But when the mood did take the other, the boy found that he could not help but hang on his father's every word. He inched in closer to the fire so as not to miss out.

"I must have been about your age," Jurgen began, seeing his son move up. "Maybe a little bit older. I'd been pestering him all summer and well into the game season to teach me how to shoot but he always said he was too busy tending to our fields to be pulled away. Every day I would ask him and every day he would give me the same answer. It left me wondering if I'd ever learn how to handle a bow. I remember that by the time my mother got fed up with it I was just lucky enough to be able to hold the thing, let alone actually hit anything with it. After days of nagging, he finally broke down and gave me a lesson. If you can call ten minutes of grumbling about how I wasn't doing anything right a lesson, that is."

Asbjorn could not stop himself from breaking out into a broad grin. He thoroughly took in the tale about the days when his father was once a boy like himself. He often forgot that the big man had once been young, too. Jurgen hardly ever dropped his hard exterior for very long. It had always made Asbjorn slightly anxious and on guard around his father. He often felt like Jurgen was always watching and judging his every move. But hearing the man talk of his youth in such a way somehow revealed another side of him, one that Asbjorn just now found himself able to relate to.

"So," Jurgen said, seeing that he had the other's attention. "After my less than impressive display, my father finally resigned himself to taking me on my first hunting trip. He wasn't at all happy about it in the least. I remember that we came to these very woods," he said, "probably not too far from where we are now. It was so late in the year that everything that hadn't been brought down had pretty much been scared off. We had to camp and trudge through the fallen brush for nearly two days before we caught sight of anything. We finally tracked it to a small clearing in the middle of nowhere. Thinking back, it must have been about the saddest, spindliest looking little buck I've ever seen. There was hardly enough meat on it to waste an arrow."

At the recollection of it, Jurgen couldn't help but chuckle and shake his head. He was lost in the memory of his younger days. He hadn't brought these thoughts to mind for what seemed like ages now. He was never one to be taken by melancholy but in this instance, he couldn't help it.

"Did you kill it?" Asbjorn asked. "With your bow, I mean?"

"Be patient, boy," Jurgen responded, remembering he was still in the middle of a story. "You're getting ahead of me. Settle down and I'll tell you."

Asbjorn settled back on his bedroll to do as his father said. He did not take his gaze off the man as the firelight reflected in his chestnut eyes. Jurgen could only smile again as he picked up where he'd left off. Asbjorn was obviously excited to hear what happened next.

"Now," the big man went on, putting a dramatic tone in his voice. "As I was saying. My father and I had tracked this scrawny stag to a clearing that was encircled by tall trees. We stayed low in the brush as we carefully inched up. We watched this tiny thing grazing on the dry grasses. It just nibbled at the tops that hadn't already been claimed by the cold. I was so eager that I wanted to go in and just take it straight away. But my father said no, hoping that something better might happen along. After a while, I finally heard him curse under his breath. He realized that it was probably going to have to be this or nothing. I remember that my hands were trembling so much that I could hardly get the arrow on the string when he handed me the bow. And the look on his face did nothing to help my confidence."

Softly, Jurgen once more let out a snort. He ran his fingers through his hair as he looked into the fire. It was almost like he was deciding if he really wished to go or not. Or perhaps he just wanted to leave it there, sparing himself from having to say how it ended.

"Well," he finally sighed, carrying on after a long pause. "I must have made a noise or something when I drew back the arrow. Because when I did, that little stag looked right at me. Our eyes came together for just an instant. He saw me and I saw him, and then everything stopped. So," he said, bringing up his hands as if holding a bow. "I took a careful aim, yanked the string back to my cheek, and then—"

"And you shot it straight the heart!" interjected Asbjorn. The boy nearly fell into the fire as he jumped with elation.

"No," Jurgen quickly said. "I was so damn nervous that I kept hold of the arrow and let go of the bow by mistake. It snapped back and cracked me right across the bridge of the nose. Blood went everywhere!"

At his own story, the big man suddenly burst out in a raucous laughter. His adulation almost tipped him backward as the memory of it all came flooding back. Asbjorn could only stare with a baffled look on his face. He was not quite sure how he should react. Gradually, his own expression spread to a wide smile, until both father and son were soon doubled over in amusement.

"So that's how you got that scar," Asbjorn managed to say between gasping breaths. "I always thought that it was from fighting bandits or raiders or something."

"Nope," Jurgen laughed even louder. "The damn bow hit me right in the face!"

"What happened after that?" asked a panting Asbjorn.

"Well, we didn't get the stag that's for damn sure," answered Jurgen. "We had to eat stale potatoes and sour mutton all winter long. My mother was so angry that she made him sleep out with the goats for a week. He wouldn't even let me touch his bow again until next spring. It was miserable."

With their eyes both watering, Asbjorn continued to laugh along with his father. The two of them shared in a rare moment of levity. Gradually, though, Jurgen's laughter died away as he looked back into the flames. A hint of sadness came to his face as he wiped a tear from his cheek.

"I haven't thought about my father like that for years now," he said. His voice fell low. "He was never really someone to endear himself to anybody for very long. I know that when I was a boy, I always felt like more of an afterthought to him than anything else. We were never really able to connect or see eye to eye. It only got worse as I got older. I don't think I ever really meant all that much to him," he remarked. "The feeling became mutual after a while."

Jurgen let out a long exhale as he stirred up the embers of the fire with a stick. He threw it into the flames before turning towards Asbjorn.

"You know I'm very proud of what you did today, my son," he said. "You'll grow up to be a fine man one day. I'm sure of it."

In that moment, Jurgen looked at his young son with a warmth and respect in his eyes that the other had never seen before. Asbjorn was again a little uncertain of what he should say or do. He tried to think of something, but nothing immediately came to mind. The two just sat quietly together in the warming glow. Then suddenly a horrific sound boomed out in the dark. It rolled over the forest to shake the trees like a distant thunder. Jurgen and Asbjorn's hearts both came to their throats when the resounding roar hit their ears. The blood in their veins ran cold as the echo faded.

"What was that?" Asbjorn asked as he sprung to his feet. His voice was no more than a shivering whisper.

"Just a bear," answered Jurgen, "that's all. No need to be worried, though. It won't come near the fire. Now sit back down."

Asbjorn knelt back to the ground next to the jumping flames. His eyes were wide and still gazed into the blackness. He'd heard many a bear call before back on the outskirts of their village of Brekka as the colder seasons set in. He'd even seen a few from a distance as they fished along the riverbanks. But never had the boy heard such a savage bellow that had just split the night. The fearsome sound seemed to carry on the wind to linger much longer than it should have. Even now, he thought that he could still hear it reverberating over the countryside, darkening the moonlight that shown through the autumn clouds. As Asbjorn tried to once again settle in, he drew even closer to the flames. He anxiously scanned the trees as he did so.

Jurgen eyed his son and was able to sense the restlessness coming off the boy. He saw the unease that was written over the lad's face. In truth, he had concerns of his own after hearing the blasting call. He did his best to maintain his composure without alarming the other.

Casually, he pulled his large hunting pack over and undid its straps. He brought forth from its lining his large axe that he'd brought along just in case. The weapon had been presented to him by the village smiths years ago. It was a gift for rallying the men during the bloodiest bandit raid the people had ever seen, the same one that had tragically claimed the life of Asbjorn's mother. The man had rarely brought it out over the time since. He preferred to keep it stowed away along with the memories that went with it. But every now and again he found he would have use for it, with Asbjorn being captivated every time he caught a glimpse. The boy's gaze would follow down the axe's broad, sweeping head, tracing over the etchings that adorned the steel to stop at the blunt hammerhead on the back end. The weapon was a superb piece of northern craftsmanship. It was truly a deadly thing in the hands of someone who knew how to use it.

"We'll get a good night's sleep," said Jurgen. He reclined on his pack and laid the axe across his lap. "And then head back home in the morning. It's best to be wary with bears about."

"But, father," Asbjorn protested, "we were supposed to go back out tomorrow. Didn't you say it wouldn't come near the fire. And you do have your axe. Besides, it'll probably be gone by dawn, right?"

"I said no, Asbjorn," Jurgen sternly responded. "There are far worse things than just earthly beasts in the deep parts of the north woods and sometimes they're not content to stay there. This could be nothing but then again maybe not. It's best if we don't tempt fate. No," he reiterated. "We head back tomorrow. Now lie down and get some sleep."

Asbjorn crawled back to his bedroll without saying a word. He wrapped himself in a heavy fur to hunker down and keep warm. He wanted to argue against his father's decision further but part of him knew the big man was right. It was better for the two to head back home in the morning, showing caution and returning to the woods to hunt another day.

But that was only a small part and was lost in the fervor of a boy who'd just experienced his first taste of manhood. Deep down, Asbjorn wanted nothing more than to be in the dense forests on the trail of another stag. Gradually, he drifted off where he lay beneath the stars. He dreamt of stalking his prey as a wave of sleep crept in. The twinkling dots in the sky faded and gave way to slumber. He rested well as his father watched over him.

II

Asbjorn awoke just as the sun's rays began to scatter away the nighttime shadows. A thin dew clung to the trees as a fog hung in the air. The woodland birds were just starting to greet the dawn with a chorus of chimes. He was enchanted by their chirping and the other sounds of the forest. He looked over to see his father near the remnants of last night's fire. Jurgen's hands still clutched around the handle of his axe. The man breathed steadily as he reclined on his hunting pack with a heavy cloak draped over him, not yet roused as was his son.

He surely didn't stay awake all night, did he? Asbjorn wondered, rubbing the sleep from his eyes. *No,* he thought, *he must have dozed off shortly after I did, once he'd made sure the bear had gone.*

As he chased away the last traces of sleep, Asbjorn tugged his blanket tighter around himself. He stood and moved on stiff legs to wake his father so that the two could start breakfast. It was going to be a long walk back to Brekka if Jurgen was indeed set on returning home today. They would need a hearty meal before packing up and heading out. Asbjorn's hand was almost on his father's shoulder when he glanced down to notice the bow that was resting at the man's side. He stayed his touch for a moment before he could disturb the lightly snoring woodsman. A risky notion suddenly crept through his head. It was one that he should have instantly dismissed but listened to, nonetheless.

"Perhaps there's still time for one last outing after all," he said with a smile. He was certain his father would be proud of him if brought something back he got all on his own. And he was itching to make the other boys in the village jealous once they found out.

Carefully and quietly Asbjorn shrugged off his heavy furs. He snatched up his father's bow and slung the quiver of arrows over his shoulder. His heart raced as he left the campsite behind and crept through the mist-shrouded forest. A feeling of exhilaration and nervousness ran through him at the same time. He knew that he would have to be quick about what he'd set out to do if he wished to be successful. He hoped that he could make it back before his father woke up and had a chance to become too angry with him. He was risking a more than certain punishment for willfully disobeying Jurgen's instructions. But in his mind, it would be worth it if he could snag something good.

Asbjorn soon managed to come across what he was searching for. It was a wide trail that cut its way through the trees like a farmer's plow carves through the fields. Splintered branches that had been crushed and snapped like twigs lay scattered on the forest floor. Thick limbs had been broken off from their trunks to litter his way as far as he could see. It looked as if some kind of giant had trampled a path straight through the heart of the wooded landscape, leaving only a battered trail behind before vanishing without a trace.

"What could have done something like this?" Asbjorn whispered almost in awe. His feet took him lightly along the decimated path. "This couldn't be a simple stag, could it? Maybe a whole herd of them? Or something else?"

With is heart still pounding, he slowly followed the sweeping trail that had been razed through the woods. His breaths quickened as his eyes darted about the further he went. If his own pulse had not been beating so loud, he would have immediately noticed that something amiss. The sounds of the forest had long since faded around him. An eerie quiet had come to settle over the landscape. The birds no longer sounded or even a leaf rustled in the wind. Every instinct inside of him began to scream to stop and head back toward the safety of his

14

father but the urge was unwisely ignored as he banished his inner protests. He was being spurred along by the irresistible curiosity of youth and a need to prove himself, not to mention a desire to make all the other boys back in Brekka envious of his accomplishments. He continued to force himself to follow the path for what seemed like hours. He found not a single discernable track within the slew of downed vegetation. He still had no idea at all of just what kind of creature he stalked. His mind started to run away with itself the longer he followed the trail. Was it man, deer, beast, or something else he pursued? His anxiety rose with every step, but he was determined to find out.

At last, Asbjorn came to a thick wall of interwoven pines. The twisted branches brought him to an abrupt halt. He poked and prodded at the tree limbs with the tip of his bow to try and find a way through. He saw no sign of how to penetrate the barrier of prickly greenery.

He let out a dejected breath as he gazed up at the trees. The trail ended here but there was still no trace of whatever it was that had made it. He was just about to turn and head back when he suddenly heard something. It was a snapping of twigs and a crunching of earth on the other side of the branches. He slunk closer with his ears open and his eyes wide. He noticed the veil of pine needles thinning in a spot that he'd not seen before. As he squinted, he could scarcely make out a lumbering movement through the obscuring limbs. He could only discern that it was a large shape that swayed back and forth, so far seemingly unaware of his presence.

This is it, he thought in a blind excitement. *This is my moment! This is what I've been trailing since sunrise!*

Carefully, Asbjorn reached to take an arrow from the quiver that hung at his back. He quietly nocked it against the string of the bow. He stalked onward to push his way through the pines as silently as he could. The dried needles poked at him but not so much that he couldn't proceed. Just as he was about to emerge from the far side, he pulled back the arrow. He took a deep breath and held it in as his foot fell for a final time. He put the last bit of tension on the bowstring with a shaky hand. He went to step out from the covering foliage ready to loose the projectile.

Just as he moved into the open, there was a sudden, violent flurry. The trees around him exploded in a shower of splinters and snapping branches. The impact sent Asbjorn up and off his feet to come slamming down to his back. The wind was knocked from his lungs to leave him gasping for air. The great bear had come bursting through the thicket of pines with an unearthly force. The massive animal towered over him as he fought for breath. The giant beast was unlike any of the natural creatures whose form it appeared to wear. It was of a char black pelt and showed eyes that blazed with an infernal fire. It lumbered towards the horrified Asbjorn with jagged claws that dug into the earth. A frothing slaver hung from teeth that were every bit the length of daggers. The creature had a hellish aura that flowed from every inch of it. The very air around the thing seemed to grow hot despite the abundance of cold.

Asbjorn somehow scrambled back to his feet terrified beyond measure. His panicked breaths came in rapid succession as the monstrous creature closed in on him. The black beast roared the same deafening cry that he and his father had heard the night before. The thunderous sound was enough to nearly burst his eardrums.

With a massive foreleg, the demonic thing took a powerful swing at the boy. Claws that were long and sharp enough to rend him in half flashed in the morning light. Amazingly, the fear shocked Asbjorn had just enough sense to throw himself backward at the last instant, sparing himself from being totally torn apart by the bear's nails. But as swift as he was, he was not quite swift enough. The sweeping blow still managing to connect to send him spinning through the branches and crashing back to the ground. A pain greater than any he'd ever known before came to shoot through him. The blood flowed freely from four deep gashes that had been carved into his side.

In a daze, Asbjorn propped himself up to see the hazy outline of the great bear move over him. The thing blotted out what little sun snuck through the trees and surrounding fog. The forest spiraled in his vision as he turned over to his belly to try and drag himself away. The beast was upon him before he could make it more than a few feet. Its eyes were like pinpricks of fire that glowed in the misty gloom. It exhaled a stinking breath that was hot on his face as it inched closer. He tried to breathe but all he could do was tremble. The thing stepped down on him to nearly crush him underfoot. Then there was another shape before him. It was one that was much smaller but still no less imposing. From the surrounding mist, he heard the onrushing battle cry. His father streaked in with axe in hand.

Jurgen rammed himself into the titanic bear with a furious charge. He cleaved wildly with his blade as he drove forward. The sharp edge bit deep into the beast's muscular hide. The man that swung it bellowed a vicious shout with every stroke. But despite its sharpness, the axe only seemed to enrage the creature. It left hardly anything more than scratches in the beast's flesh. The great bear bawled in rage in response to Jurgen's assault. It brought itself up to its hind legs to utterly dwarf the man that stood between it and his son. The thirst for blood shown in the monster's searing eyes as bright as hellfire. The taste for fresh meat was on its tongue as it gazed at the meal before it.

"Run, boy!" Jurgen shouted to Asbjorn. He firmly stood his ground and refused to back down. "Move it dammit, now!"

But regardless of his father's urgings, the groggy Asbjorn could barely make out what the man was saying. The pounding in his head drowned out the other's persistent screams. He could see his father's mouth moving but there was nothing but muted sounds coming out. He struggled to his feet despite anything that Jurgen might be yelling. Once up, he

17

managed to stumble along only a few yards before collapsing back down. He was unable to will his shaky legs to take him any further. He rolled over and looked back to see where his father still hopelessly fought against the bear. The burning eyed monster flung the frantic Jurgen around as if he were a toy. The man's body collided with the surrounding tree trunks one after the other. His mane of blonde hair slowly turned to a crimson mop.

With a single hand, Asbjorn reached out towards his father's blurred shape. The boy's shaking arm quickly fell limp to his side as his remaining strength left him. Try as he might, the last sounds he heard were those of his father's muffled shouts, followed shortly by the bellowing roar of the mighty beast. As the blackness rolled in, something stinging and warm flowed into his eyes. The unconsciousness washed over him as all went silent.

Asbjorn came to with a violent start. He stared into the wide blue eyes that met his. The curious face behind them was framed in honey locks as it oddly regarded him back. He wasn't sure what to say or do at first as he did the same. He could swear that he knew the young girl that watched over him so intently, or at least he thought he did, but it was hard to tell between the waves of dizziness in his head. He was almost positive that her name was Magdalena, and that she was the daughter of Jarl Manus, the current head of his home village of Brekka.

"Hello," said a weary Asbjorn, forcing out the word in a voice that was little more than a whisper.

Despite only saying a simple utterance, the boy felt like he must have tumbled down a mountain. Just pushing out the breath was nearly all he could do. Every inch of him was sore with a battered stiffness. The act of speaking only a single word almost made him nauseous. The girl in front of him only smiled back with a strange little grin. She tilted her head before hopping down and quickly scurrying off. She disappeared through a half-opened door as she began shouting, the sound of here racing steps taking her away.

"Poppa, poppa!" Asbjorn could hear her call in excitement. "Hurry, he's awake!"

Asbjorn slowly sat himself up after the girl took her leave. He found that he was in a dimly lit room illuminated by only a single candle. He rested in a soft bed of warm furs and heavy blankets. The straw mattress beneath him helped to sooth his aching bones. He tried to pull the covers off and swing his legs around and over the edge, but a sudden jolt of discomfort prevented him from doing so. He felt to find that his left shoulder and upper chest were both wrapped in thick bandages. The smell of strong herbs and potent balms came off them. It was a cloying aroma that made him woozier than he already was. His fingers brushed against the linen to cause him to wince from just the slightest touch. Then, from outside the room, he could hear the approach of booted footsteps coming his way, not knowing what to expect as they drew near.

"You really are awake this time, aren't you?" said a gruff voice as the door creaked the rest of the way open. Jarl Manus came into the room. Asbjorn had only ever seen him up close perhaps on a handful of occasions before. His rough-hewn face was framed with a greying beard of heavy thickness. His deep brown eyes appeared almost black in the dimness of the interior. The man brought up a chair that rested at the foot of the bed to take a seat.

"I do apologize for the enthusiasm of my daughter," he said in a deep tone. "But she's been watching over you night and day for more than a week now. She hardly ever left your bedside for very long unless we made her. She'd run to fetch one of us every time you so much as twitched. It was hard to tell that she actually meant what she said this time."

"More than a week?" Asbjorn questioned hazily. He gazed up at the jarl.

"Yes," answered Manus with a nod. "You've been unconscious for more than eight days. When you and your father didn't return when expected, a group of us went out searching for the two of you, not really sure where to start looking. It was only by sheer luck that one of us heard your voice out in those woods. You were delirious with fever when we found you. You mumbled incoherently about the burning eyes and a great devil bear. We had little hope that you'd actually live through whatever it was that happened to you out there, but it appears we were wrong."

For a long moment, all that Asbjorn could do was stare blankly at the jarl. A puzzled expression played across his face as he tried to recall what the other was talking about. And then, in an instant, it all came rushing back to him. He suddenly remembered tracking the stag through the forest, the wall of trees, and then the furious charge of the great bear. The monstrous beast had been a thing of unbridled rage when it came at him, with eyes that flared as if they were made of burning coals and from hell itself. He could still fell its claws carving into his chest. His side throbbed at the mere thought of it. The infernal creature would have surely killed him if it had not been for the fierce onrush of his father. The man stormed out of the mist at the last possible moment to confront the thing head on. Jurgen had barreled into the beast with his axe flailing and chopping. The blade carved into the creature as the man screamed his war cry. It was only by his father's hand that Asbjorn had made it out of those woods at all, but then if he was here, where might the other be?

"Jarl," asked Asbjorn in a soft voice, "where's my father?"

At first, Manus did not bring himself to answer the boy. Instead, he only looked grimly to the floor as he let out a long sigh and rubbed the crown of his head. He looked like a child that awkwardly squirmed to avoid responding to an unwanted question. His face hid an obvious severity he did not wish to vocalize.

"What's important is that you're safe now, my boy," he said at last. "You're here, and that's what matters."

"Please," Asbjorn pled to him after hearing the vague answer, "where's my father?"

Letting out another breath, Jarl Manus's eyes regarded the distraught boy. A grave look dwelt behind them that leaked out to his creased features. He got up and slowly walked from the room. He returned a few moments later with something wrapped in a soft hide, placing it across Asbjorn's lap.

"It's all we found of him, I'm afraid," the jarl said somberly. "There was nothing else."

Pulling back the supple covering, Asbjorn revealed his father's axe. The heavy blade glimmered in the flickering candle flame. It was scratched and nicked now from the fight with the great beast. A red smear in the shape of clenched fingers still marked around the wood of the handle. As he held it, tears began to roll down the boy's cheeks. They fell on the steel that he cradled in his arms. His fingertips traced over the etchings and markings on the head. His hand wrapped around where it showed the last place that his father had held it.

"It's all my fault," Asbjorn whimpered meekly, unable to lift his head. "I thought the bear had gone. It's all because of me."

As the young boy wept, Jarl Manus remained next to him the entire time. He knew there was nothing that he could adequately say or do to console the grieving youth. Asbjorn was filled with the sorrow of a child who had just lost his only family. The feeling was far too great for the jarl to understand having never experienced such for himself. In the end, all that was in his power was to place a comforting hand on Asbjorn's shoulder, letting him know that someone was still by his side. He sat with the boy as he listened to the other's stricken sobs. Asbjorn's tears still fell over the blade that he clasped in his hands. The spots where they landed shimmered in the candlelight.

III

The air was still in the small glade as the wolf crept through the underbrush. The animal slunk low to the ground as it moved out to the open. It sniffed cautiously at the air to take in the irony scent of fresh blood. Its nose twitched as the heavy aroma enticed it onwards. Just across the clearing, it could see the object of its ravenous desire. The carcass of a small deer had been split down the middle and hung from a low branch. The creature remained tentative in its shaky approach despite what dangled before it. It inched a single leg forward at a time ever so slowly.

It had not been an easy few months for the predators of the Northern Forest. The numbers of their usual prey had grown scant by the overhunting of the men that lived in the surrounding villages. The scrawny wolf was just pushing the edge of starvation when it'd picked up the smell of the kill drifting on the winds. It had followed it for nearly a mile in hopes of finding an easy meal. It fought against its own bestial instincts now as it edged closer to the swaying meat. Its gaze was locked as it watched the carcass shift back and forth. Its tongue licked at teeth that were ready to sink in, but still it maintained a wary distance.

From above, a pair of narrowed eyes observed as the beast neared the suspended kill. The young man behind them stared with a mix of both disdain and disappointment. He scowled as the half-starved creature could resist its baser instincts no longer. The thing's flared nostrils drew in the now overpowering smell. With caution no longer a concern, the wolf finally tasted what it had come so far to find. It bit into the waiting flesh to lose itself in the long overdue feeding frenzy.

Asbjorn looked on from his perch high in the tall pine. The beast beneath him fed as it gnashed its teeth and ripped away large strips of venison. Where its pack was, the Northman had not a clue. He hadn't picked up signs of any wolves in the area or heard any howls to indicate they were near. From the looks of it, perhaps it had been left on its own, abandoned for fear of slowing down the others or lack of food to spare. Or it might be the last one that was left. The huntsmen were known to take more than just deer for their supper, although wolf was a gristly meal, but its pelt could still be useful.

The hidden Northman drew back the string of his bow. The wolf below voraciously swallowed down bits of the dangling deer to remain distracted. He took aim at the creature with the arrow he pinched between his fingers. It would be a simple thing for him to take the beast now. Even a boney one such as this could bring him something for its fur back at the village. He knew it wouldn't be much but in times like this every little bit helped. But then he suddenly hesitated. He stayed his hand to spare the creature for a few moments longer.

The young Northerner eased the arrow from the taut string as he lowered the bow. He carefully hung it from a stub of a tree limb just next to him. He'd brought down the deer that the wolf feasted on earlier this morning, cutting it open and hoisting it up in an effort bait in a much bigger prey. He'd done this same thing now so many times since his father's death that he'd lost count. He'd ventured out season after season in hopes of once more encountering the hulking devil bear. But each time, he had to settle for something far less. The constant frustration of failure was beginning to weigh heavier year after year. In disgust, he glared down at the skinny wolf as it continued to gorge itself. His hand moved over to close around the handle of the old huntsman's axe that rested in the crook of the tree by his side. This miserable creature was once again not what he'd come out here to find, but it was better than nothing. He supposed that would have to do.

23

Carefully, Asbjorn moved to position himself just above the animal. He stole between the branches with a gentle grace that belied a man of his size. The wolf below gave pause in its feasting for just an instant as he poised himself. The creature's head came up and its ears perked as it seemed to sense the hidden danger. Then the big Northman leapt from his place in the tree with a savage cry, bringing down his blade into the hard earth just in front of it. Asbjorn could have taken the thing for himself anytime that he'd wished to. His mark would not of had the slightest notion of his presence until it was too late. But his turbulent spirit yearned for a fight. The creature here was sure to give him one. Whether it lasted long or not was another matter.

The wolf jumped back and let out a snarl in response to the man's sudden appearance. It bared its teeth at the one who'd just come between it and its half-eaten meal. Its ears lay back flat, and its muscles tensed as it circled around him. Its front shoulders hunched high as its head hung low.

In most normal circumstances, the lone animal would have simply retreated back to the forest when confronted by such a threat, taking the quickest route of escape to search for an easier kill elsewhere. But game was in such low abundance thanks to the scores of greedy hunters this year. The beast was reluctant to pass up such a ready dinner for fear of not finding another later. Besides, it had already tasted fresh meat. It was not about to back down now, and there was suddenly a far fresher supply available.

With a wild lunge, the animal came at the waiting Asbjorn. Its jaws snapped wildly at the areas of his exposed flesh. Swiftly, he fell back to stay just out of reach of its yellowed teeth. He deftly avoided the mangy thing's bites to keep inches away. As it continued to charge in, he swiftly batted it across the face with the flat of his axe. The arcing swing nearly split its head open from the force. The hard steel connected to knock it aside and send it rolling across the ground. Asbjorn pressed in with his advantage as the beast slowly picked itself up. As he moved towards it, the wounded animal came back at him with a lurching pounce. It was a desperate effort aimed straight at his throat. But the young man easily smashed the thing down once again with the butt of the axe handle, driving it headfirst into the forest floor.

As it lay near motionless at his feet, the spent wolf meekly growled at the youth that stood over it. The animal puffed and panted as a thick foam frothed from its cheeks. It still tried to snip at Asbjorn's toes with what little strength it had. It crawled along to try and get at him. With a strong leg, he put his boot firmly on the squirming beast to keep it from moving. He raised the axe and then brought it down yet again. With a single blow, he finally put an end to it. But it was almost too easy, just as it had been so many times before.

Asbjorn stood over the fallen animal to yank the blade free. The sharpened edge had cleaved into its body to put it down clean and do minimal harm to its fur. The young man took no pride at all in slaying the beast as he just had, finding not the least bit of satisfaction in its death. It should have been more than capable of putting up a struggle should it have wished to. Especially after having just tasted blood and being lost in its feeding frenzy. But this one had proved to be too weak from the previous lack of food to display any such temperament. It had failed to be any kind of challenge for him and left a bitter taste in his mouth.

Asbjorn let out a long sigh as he lingered alone in the glade. He stared down at the dead animal and then glanced back to the strung-up deer. Though dissatisfied, it might not be a total loss for him after all, unlike several other years when he'd missed out on getting anything larger than a hare. With a quick motion, he planted his axe in an old tree stump that jutted from the ground. He cracked his knuckles and rolled his neck to ease his tensions.

"No sense in letting anything go to waste I suppose," he grumbled to himself. He pulled his sharp knife from his belt. "Might as well get something out of this."

By the time Asbjorn finished skinning his catch it was far too late to begin his trek back to Brekka. The sun was already heading toward the west to fade dim. The big youth preferred to not be stumbling through the darkened woods with fresh pelts and his bow and quiver strapped to his back. He was wary of catching his foot or twisting an ankle on the uneven terrain during the day let alone after dark. He was able to make it back to his small campsite just after dusk. He staked out the skins fur side down so that they could dry out a bit overnight. He then set about building himself a small fire to help chase away the growing chill, resigning to ride out the rest of the night here after another disappointing day.

Asbjorn found that he did not rest well under the northern sky on this night. The memories of his father were running rampantly through his thoughts. They always seemed to come to him more vividly out here in the wilderness, particularly when he ventured into this stretch of woods. In fact, it was not far from this very spot that the two of them had been set upon by the massive bear some eight years ago. His father's final cries still came to his ears on the worst of nights to keep him awake. His thoughts drifted back to that time and remained there as he stared into the fire. He was unable to stop himself from fixating on the past. But gradually, the tired Northerner managed to drift off to an uneasy sleep. The taste of the day's failure was still fresh in his mouth to keep him tossing and turning, along with other things.

Asbjorn awoke early with it still being dark. He broke camp just before the first rays of dawn emerged to begin his journey back. He moved swiftly through the littered forest even being laden down by the two pelts and his other equipment. He reached the outskirts of the village just as the other residents were emerging to set about their day. Most paid the big man little attention as he went amongst them. They too preoccupied with the drudgery of their usual tasks to show much notice. They headed out to their fields or to tend to their animals without casting an upwards glance. Asbjorn did the same as he passed them by.

There were others, however, that watched him move along with a cautious eye. They were wary of the quiet youth that often kept the people of the tightknit community at arm's length. Since his father died, he had not engaged much with the other villagers. In a small place like this many took it as a snub and looked unfavorably upon him. It also didn't help with the many incidents that he had been at the center of. The residents here did not like their peace being disturbed nor did they tolerate those that raised a ruckus.

Once he'd returned, Asbjorn's first stop was the village tanner. He was hoping to offload the hides from yesterday's outing to earn himself what little coin he could. He'd never really thought much of the old leather worker that ran the place. He found that the surly man was always quick with a biting comment or an insensitive dig, not to mention the smell was horrendous and made his stomach queasy. He just wanted to conduct his business and go but it was never that simple when coming here. When he reached the place, he found the elderly gentleman out back and busy at work, stretching a fresh hide across a wooden frame to put it off to the side along with several others.

"Oh, it's you," the wrinkled fellow grumbled. He glanced up from his work when he heard Asbjorn approach. "What have you brought in with you this time?"

"Nothing much really," answered Asbjorn. He unstrapped the furs from his shoulder. "Only two. A small deer and a scraggly wolf."

"That's it, eh?" snorted the old tanner. "I've seen children bring in better than that. You know your father was one of the best hunters this village has ever seen back in his day. Don't know what went wrong with you."

"So you've told me," Asbjorn sighed. "Just have a look at them, will you?"

Asbjorn unrolled the pelts and spread them out in front of the old tanner. He tried to fluff up the fur and make them look bigger and better than they actually were. He didn't like to exaggerate but he could use all the coin he could get this time around. His purse was depressingly empty as was his coffer back at home. But unfortunately, the old man hardly bothered to show them any interest, giving the skins barely a sideways glance.

"Neither of those look very bearish to me," the gruff man mocked. His creased face gave a snide smile. "When are you actually going to bring me the big one?"

"Eventually," Asbjorn answered in a deflated tone. "But what about these?"

The tanner just halfheartedly eyed the two. His gaze went from the skins, up to the youth, and then back down again. Asbjorn could tell that the old man was deciding if they might be worth anything. He hoped the payout would at least amount to something for his trouble.

"Three bits for the scraps," he finally said. "Take it or leave it."

"That's all?" the big man responded. "That's not even half of what you paid last year."

"They've been bringing these to me in droves this season, boy," the old tanner replied. He went back to his work. "I've got plenty of wolf and deer inside. You're just lucky that I'm feeling generous today and offering that much. Like I said, bring me something bigger, then we'll talk. If you can ever find it, that is."

"Just give me the coin," said an annoyed Asbjorn, "and spare me the lip."

With a grunt under his breath, the old man dug into a small purse that hung at his belt. He plucked out three thin pieces of silver. Asbjorn begrudgingly accepted the small payment he'd been offered. He was honestly glad that it was even that much if he were being truthful. He turned to leave without saying anything more. The surly tanner just shook his head as he watched the big youth go.

"You keep chasing ghosts like this and you're gonna lose that place of you and your father's out there," the tanner hollered after him. "That or starve to death. Whichever comes first."

Asbjorn gave no response to the other's comments. He simply trudged away. He didn't even bother to glance back as he found himself slipping further into a brooding mood. The mouthy shopkeep only reinforced the reasons he preferred to keep to his own company. This was certainly not the first time the local merchants or his fellow villagers had treated him in such a way. He knew that it sadly wouldn't be the last. The past had taught him that when one started in there would more than likely be others, regardless of if they were around one another or not.

Asbjorn was well aware that most people in Brekka looked at him as if he were some kind of a deluded fool. To them he was someone who brought trouble along, or possibly an obsessed madman depending on who one talked to. He had spent the last eight years fixated with finding what he believed to be the great devil bear of the Northern Forests. It was a hellish creature of lore and legend that was said to stalk the woods for the blood of men. Most believed that the beast was nothing more than a myth. It was a frightening tale to scare and excite as they gathered with one another around a fire, but nothing more. But Asbjorn thought much differently than that. He believed that he'd encountered the demon up close and all too personally and sought to do so again.

The big Northerner knew that he'd seen the creature with his own eyes when he was only a boy. The monstrous thing had set upon him in a bloodthirsty frenzy. They had all tried to say that it was only a large brown bear that had wandered down from the lands farther towards the mountains, seen through the eyes of a terrified child that was about to die, but he knew better. It had been no natural creature that had taken his father from him that day. No sign or trace of it could ever be found by the other villagers who'd come upon him in the woods. He would not relent in his pursuit until he'd found the beast once again, felling it so that it was slain and broken at his feet. But for the time being, all that Asbjorn could do was meander through the streets of Brekka, wondering how he would find the means to pay for what he needed to make it through the winter.

In past years, Asbjorn had always managed to at least bring in enough skins to meagerly support himself. He had to scrimp and scrape, but he was still able to make it through relatively fine. But this season had proven to be a particularly difficult one for him. The forest game was too thinned to provide much of a bounty. Thanks to the work of the other hunters, Asbjorn knew that he had to come up with something, or it was going to be a long, miserable stretch once the snows finally arrived. But right now, he suddenly realized that he had not taken breakfast before leaving camp and heading back home this morning. And no good idea ever came to anyone with an empty stomach.

With his belly protesting, Asbjorn gave pause in the middle of the way. He stopped and hesitantly glanced toward Brekka's only tavern. The lone Northerner was typically a rare sight at the place at any time of the day or year, again preferring to avoid the disparaging looks and offhanded remarks of the other villagers. None of them were really someone that he would consider a close or even distant friend. He sometimes found it hard to ignore their comments that would drift far enough to reach his ears. But his stomach was empty, and he also remembered how horribly sparse his own cupboards were. The few bits of silver he'd earned were just enough to buy himself some meat and drink with a little left over for later. With a heavy sigh, the big youth hung his head and made his way in. He hoped for once that he might actually have a decent meal here in peace.

Asbjorn did his best to slip in unnoticed. He thankfully saw that the tavern was not too crowded this time of day. The few men that did sit at the tables were too absorbed in their own drinks and conversations to notice his entrance. It was a stroke of good luck that he would gladly take for once. He found a quiet corner at the far end of the large drinking hall, away from the slanted glances and annoying chatter of the other patrons. He asked for a simple meal of sausage with spiced cabbage and crusty bread. They were some of the cheaper offerings that were prepared at the tavern, so they did minimal damage to his funds. The food tasted good enough to the big man who'd not partaken of a hot meal for himself in quite some time. He washed the bites down with a pint of clove mead to clear his throat. Asbjorn was just halfway through his breakfast and in deep thought when the front door of the place suddenly swung open, with trouble walking in to once again find him here.

The group of four young men strode in out of the morning air. All of them boisterously carried on with one another as they thumped their way inside. They were led by a cocky youth named Dorn. He was the dark-haired, loud-mouthed son of Brekka's most well-off woodsman.

The bothersome brat was never shy when it came to flaunting his status thanks to his father's pull with the village elders. He often used it to his full advantage, getting his way and having what he wanted whenever possible. Asbjorn and Dorn had never been ones to have the warmest of feelings towards each other. The woodsman's son had always been terribly jealous of the big Northerner. The dark headed youth deeply resented the physical superiority of the other. And he particularly despised all the attention that Asbjorn received from Jarl Manus's young daughter, Magdalena. To his credit, Asbjorn did his best to remain inconspicuous in his secluded corner and hope that the four would not take notice of him. But unfortunately, they spotted him nearly straight away. One of them pointed him out to the others almost immediately.

Asbjorn let out a long breath as they headed his direction. He took a swallow of his mead as they drew closer, rinsing out his mouth as he prepared himself. With the lingering disappointment of yesterday's hunt still on his shoulders, this was the last thing that he wanted to deal with right now. But deal with it he would, in whatever manner was fitting.

"Well, well, boys," said Dorn. He strutted up to stand at the edge of Asbjorn's table. "Look who's here. Where you been keeping yourself, As?" he asked. "We haven't seen you for so long we were beginning to think you didn't like us anymore."

"I've been busy, Dorn," Asbjorn said flatly.

"Still a man of few words I see," Dorn said. He rested his hands on his hips. "After not talking to us all summer and that's all you have to say for yourself, 'I've been busy.' I'm beginning to think that you're not happy to see us."

"I bet he's been out looking for that big bad bear again," one of the young men with Dorn put in. He threw up his hands to resemble mock claws. "I wonder how he did this time?"

"Oh, that's right," said Dorn. "How's that been going for you anyway? Any luck yet?"

"Like I said before," Asbjorn answered again. "I stay busy."

"Ah, don't be like that now," remarked Dorn. "Come on. What'd you find this time? I bet it was something really terrifying like a man-eating chipmunk. Or maybe even something worse, like a giant squirrel."

At that last dig, Dorn and his three friends burst out in a snickering laughter. The entire group delighted themselves in the cutting quip and teased with a juvenile satisfaction. For his sake, Asbjorn simply sat in his chair unmoving and quiet to try and let it roll off his back. He clenched his fists under the table to bulge the veins in his forearms. He wanted nothing more than to shoot up and fling his chair aside. To teach Dorn a lesson that he felt was far overdue. But he'd promised the jarl that there would be no more incidents after the last time. The previous occasion the two boys had scrapped ended very badly, particularly for the woodsman's son. Dorn, however, continued to push it further, not relenting despite the other's silence and unwillingness to act.

"Well, maybe it's good that you didn't come across the thing," Dorn managed to say between grating laughs. "It might have wanted to see if you tasted just as good as your father did. It's probably best if you didn't give it indigestion again."

The next few moments were a near total blank for Asbjorn. His vision tunneled in straight on Dorn. He could still see the other laughing to be sure. But the sound had been drowned out by the reverberations of his own pounding heartbeat. He slowly slid the small table in front of him aside, raising himself from his seat to come up to his full height. He glared down at Dorn as the amusement of the youth and his three friends gradually began to taper off. The spiteful braggart still smirked at the demeaned Northerner with everyone else in the tavern looking their direction.

"Now come on, Asbjorn," Dorn said in a dismissive tone. "You're not gonna let a friendly little jab like that get to you, are you? I thought you had thicker skin than that."

"I think he might actually be a little angry this time," said one of his cohorts. "Maybe we should just get our drinks and sit down."

"If you're itch'n to do something, take it outside, boys," the old tavern keeper called out from behind the bar. "I don't need blood stain'n my floors or you break'n my tables and chairs again."

"Shut up, old man," Dorn yelled back as he continued to smirk at Asbjorn. "He's not going do a damn thing. Not after what my father said he'd bring on him if he did. Are you, big boy?"

Dorn hardly had a chance to finish his sentence when bits of wood and splinters went flying everywhere. In a sudden rush, Asbjorn picked him up to drive him hard through the front door of the tavern. His muscled shoulder was planted squarely in Dorn's midsection. The powerful Northerner slammed the unfortunate fool back first to the ground outside. Asbjorn brought down his full weight on top of the woodsman's son. He quickly mounted him to come up and rain down a hail of blows. Dorn's friends and the few other men in the tavern flooded out behind the pair as quick as they could. The boys ran over to frantically try and pull the furious Asbjorn off. But the three of them were simply no match for the infuriated Northerner's raw strength. His still pounding arms and fists fell in rapid succession. He threw them aside like they were nothing more than a minor annoyance. The anger inside of him reached a point that was far beyond anything he'd ever felt before or could control.

As he lost all restraint, Asbjorn found that it was impossible for him to rein in his emotions. The frustration of the constant mockery and the mention of his father finally pushed him well past what he could take. He unleashed all the pent-up wrath that had been boiling up inside of him on the poor soul he'd pinned. He didn't care at all if Dorn were to live or die and everyone that stood watching could see it.

The other men that had been inside the tavern came rushing over to assist Dorn's friends now. They grabbed and pulled to halt the torrent of Asbjorn's pummeling fists. But he shrugged them off just as easily as he'd done with the others. His mind was lost in the fury that had overtaken his senses.

At last, everyone came surging back at him at once. They piled their combined mass on top of him like a tidal wave to try and hold him down or pull him off. Despite the number of bodies, Asbjorn continued to struggle with everything he had under the heap of humanity. He tried to pry his arms free to get a hold back on Dorn. He made one final lunge as the battered youth desperately tried to drag himself to safety. His grasping hand just closed around the other's ankle to nearly snap bone and tendon alike. As he yanked the panicked Dorn back, he heard a rise of voices and even more rushing footfalls. What sounded like the whole of the village was headed his way. With the shouts increasing, more men raced over to join in the pile. He could feel more weight force him down and something slip beneath his chin. He shouted one last time but it was cut short. He lost his grip on Dorn amid the frantic assault. He bellowed a thick foam from his lips as the pressure increased around his throat. And then the day turned into night. All suddenly went black for the still struggling Northerner.

IV

Asbjorn awoke to the sound of dripping water echoing between the walls. The pungent smell of moldy refuse and who knows what else clung in his nose. His eyes fluttered open to find himself in an all too familiar cell. He'd spent more than his share of days and nights here in the past. He pulled his aching body up to sit on the edge of the wooden cot he'd been tossed on. The uncomfortable thing was lined with dirty straw and tattered furs not fit for a dog. Wringing his sore hands together, he let a long breath slip from his lips. His chestnut eyes traced along the lines of filth that were caked between the stones. They followed up the walls and stopped at the small, barred window that was just near the ceiling. Just enough light and a hint of a breeze slipped in to make the place tolerable. With the sun where it was, the bars cast a depressing shadow over the opposite side of the room. The position told Asbjorn the day was just about finished.

The young Northerner knew very well that things had gotten far out of hand this time. He'd completely lost his senses in the seething fire that he could usually keep in check. Asbjorn had nearly beaten Dorn to death after their exchange this morning. His anger fueled a thrashing the likes of which he'd never unleashed before. It was true there was certainly no love lost between the two. Neither one cared to be around the other for any longer than it took a second to pass. But that certainly didn't mean that the big man wished the spoiled oaf dead, just shut up for once and put in his place. But for now, all that he could do was sit and await the inevitable repercussions that were sure to accompany his actions. He stared into the sky on the opposite side of the bars to take in the blue that was steadily turning a reddish orange.

In a way, Asbjorn usually took an odd comfort in always finding himself in the same cell after these kinds of incidents. The four walls had seen him so many times they almost greeted him like old friends. He'd counted the stones on numerous occasions that he knew their number and pattern by heart. A few even showed an odd scratch or scribble he'd left during his more extended stays. But he was beginning to grow weary of their repeated company the more he saw of them. It was becoming a more regular occurrence for him to find himself in their presence. It wore on him now much more so than it ever did. The time he spent here now passed by slower and slower. After waiting for what felt like hours, he finally heard the clicking of a heavy lock, followed by the unmistakable squeaking of a door swinging open. The jailor was letting in the same person that always came for him when he was thrown here and Asbjorn was preparing himself for the scolding that was sure to come.

"You know where he is," said a rough voice. "Just head to the back. Same place as always. He's beginning to make this like a second home for himself, wouldn't you say?"

The sound of booted footsteps moved towards Asbjorn's cell. He was not at all ready for the coming conversation in the least. Stepping into view, Jarl Manus stood tall and silent in the hall outside the barred door. An expression of grave disappointment was etched on his face as he regarded the young man. Never enjoying when the jarl looked at him as such, Asbjorn could not bring himself to meet the other's gaze. He instead kept his head down with his sandy hair hanging in front of his face. The older gentleman just glared at him like a disapproving father getting ready to discipline a rebellious son. Manus cleared his throat once he'd decided how to begin.

"I just don't understand you sometimes," he softly uttered, shaking his head as his eyes also went to the floor. "I thought that after last time we'd reached an understanding that this was not to happen again. You promised me that you would control that temper of yours, Asbjorn. Was there any truth to that or were they just hollow words?"

The jarl gave pause to await a response. He glanced back to Asbjorn with a mournful expression. He had seen the other in here too many times than he cared to remember over the past few months. He was running out of things to tell the village council in order to secure the other's release. But unfortunately, Asbjorn did not so much as twitch or attempt to mumble a syllable in his own defense. The jarl was met with nothing when it came to the big youth providing an explanation. Letting out a heavy exhale, Manus wished he had more to say than what he was about to. But there was nothing else. He thought it best to just get on with it.

"You know," he continued with a sympathetic tone, "when I brought you back to the village that day, the one after your father was killed, I felt a strong sense of obligation towards you. But I just don't think I can do it anymore. You've become a grown man over the years that I've taken care of you, Asbjorn, of age now long enough to stand or fall on your own merits. As you know, I think a good deal of you. But I've grown very weary about speaking up on your behalf. It's worn thin not only on me but on everyone else as well, and it's time to put an end to it. This was the last time I could do this for you," he said. "It won't happen again in the future. I just thought that you should know that."

As the jarl finished what he had to say, the silent Asbjorn still had not shifted or uttered a peep. His head remained down with still nothing to voice. Once more, Manus was hoping that he would receive some kind of a response. But his patience was nearly pushed to its end when he was again met with none. His next words were laced with a growing annoyance that he couldn't mask. The expression on his face showed much of the same.

"Don't you have anything to say for yourself," he asked, "or are you just going to sit there like a pouting child?"

"So, why did you then?" Asbjorn suddenly spoke. His voice was muffled, and his head remained down.

"Why did I what?" responded Manus.

"If you're so tired of it, why did you speak up for me again to the council?"

"Why do you ask questions to which you already know the answers," the jarl replied. "It's the same as last time, and every other time before that. But I've told her the same thing that I've just said to you. I won't do this again, no matter how many times she asks me.

"Magdalena is my only daughter," he went on, "and there's very little that I would say no to her about. But I have obligations as the village leader that I just can't ignore any longer and seeing that proper justice is meted out is one of them, even when it concerns you."

The Jarl again gave a long pause in his speech. He searched his thoughts carefully for the next words that he wished to say. His and Asbjorn's eyes still had yet to meet in the dinginess of the musty jail. Manus wished that the other weren't so stubborn and would at least give him an upward glance. But faced with more of the same, he could only let out a solemn sigh, deciding to simply go on with himself as he'd done before.

"I know that you were only defending your father's honor today," he said, holding a great amount of empathy in his voice. "And I know that you desperately want to find and bring down the bear. But it's time that you realize it's just not out there, my boy. It's only a legend and it always will be. Now please let this hunt go before it goes too far. Move on with yourself and let your father rest while you still can.

"I'm afraid my time is short and that I must leave you now," he added. "You know I wish you nothing but luck in whatever you're searching for, the same as I always have. I only hope that you'll think hard on my words and what I had to say and bury the past before it buries you. May you find your peace, and may it treat you well, Asbjorn. I hope the sooner it comes your way the better it is. Goodbye, son."

With that said, the jarl was gone, leaving the young man once again on his own in the dank cell. Asbjorn sat motionless on the cot for quite some time afterwards. He

39

continued to listen to the steady dripping before he finally raised his head from the floor.

He's right, dammit, the big youth thought. He brushed his sandy hair back and out of his face. Asbjorn knew that he had wasted a great deal of time pursuing the mythical bear over the past years, with many of his actions putting Jarl Manus and the few others that he cared about at odds with the other villagers more than once. The jarl had stuck his neck out for the young man on too many occasions to be counted. Asbjorn always promised that things would be different but never seemed to follow through. But he also knew how to do nothing else with his life. His consuming obsession had stolen the last years of his boyhood only to follow him into becoming a man. And then there was her to consider as well. The jarl's daughter, Magdalena, had always been there for him. Out of all the people in Brekka, she had taken it upon herself to watch over him the most, ever since the day he'd been brought back to the village after being found near death. She had stayed by his side then just as she did now. What she ever saw in him he would never fully understand.

Eventually, Asbjorn heard the locks of the heavy door clank open again. The jailor came to escort him out and gather his things that'd been brought over from the tavern. After collecting his possessions, he dolefully headed home with slouched shoulders and a hanging head. The autumn twilight was just beginning to creep across the sky as the sun had nearly set. The young man once again did not glimpse up to meet the looks of the other villagers that he passed. He avoided their glances just as he had with the jarl's. He was already well aware of what expressions their faces would hold for him. He could feel the scornful eyes and angry scowls that were cast in his direction. He could hear the bitterness in their low murmurs they thought would not make it to his ears but did. The sharp slurs cut him deeper today more than he would usually allow.

Brekka had been Asbjorn's home now for all his life, but he still often felt like an outsider amongst the others and the close-knit families of the area. More than once he had considered just packing up and leaving without so much as a word. Every year felt more difficult as the village seemed to further disregard him and push him to a distance. As he headed up the old trail that would take him home, he was grateful to leave the stares and spite filled comments behind. His small house sat empty and awaited his return on the far outskirts of the community. He was ready to be home and once again in his own company. He'd had quite enough socializing for one day. Then, just as he neared the edge of the village, he heard the sweet voice call out. It was almost like music carried on the breeze just as it always was.

"Making trouble again, I see," it said in a soft tone. "Don't you ever learn from your mistakes?"

Asbjorn looked up to see Magdalena standing just off the path. Her honey-colored hair was curled around her fingers as she waited for him to come by. She gave him a little half smile as she walked toward him. Her deep red dress swayed around her. To Asbjorn she looked like a vision from a dream. Things almost slowed down for him as she approached. But behind her crystal blue eyes he saw the concern that she always carried for him. It was pronounced even more so today than the last time they'd spoken, which seemed to always be the case as of late.

"They started it," he answered. He forced a slight grin of his own as he awkwardly scratched his head.

"That's what you said last time," replied Magdalena. "And the time before that. And also the time before that I think. I wish you could get a grip on that temper of yours and learn to let things go. I don't like seeing you get hurt like this."

"I think that Dorn came out a little worse off than I did," Asbjorn said. "He never was very good at backing up that mouth of his, even with his friends around."

"You know that's not what I meant," she responded as she circled around him.

41

"I know," the young man replied. "But they just...they insulted my father again."

"I know they did," Magdalena said. She came to stand close to him. "But you have to learn to just put their words aside and try not to listen to them. My father told me how angry everyone was with you this time. He said that he's not going to be able to speak up for you in front of the council anymore."

"He's already told me about it," Asbjorn admitted. "And he's spoken for me enough as it is. I know that whatever happens is on my shoulders now. I can accept that. And it's long overdue. I'm thinking about just leaving so that no one else has to worry about me anymore, let alone what I might do next. I seem to be a big enough problem as it is."

"Now you're just being silly," replied Magdalena. She stepped even closer. "Just promise me that from now on you'll put what they say aside," she asked, gently brushing his cheek. "And be better than they are. They only like to get a rise out of you, and you always seem to give them just what they want."

"I know," the big man nodded. "And I'll try," he said, touching her hand. "I promise I'll try."

"Good," Magdalena replied with a smile. "Now I have to get back before it gets too dark, and father notices I'm gone. And judging by the smell you could use a bath before you attract every fly within ten miles. Now go and get yourself cleaned up," she added, "and I'll try to come and see you tomorrow. It depends on how easy I can slip away from another music lesson again."

Magdalena turned to head back to the village. She gave him a small peck on the cheek that she'd just brushed her hand against. As she went, she cast him one last smile over her shoulder. Her eyes fluttered and stayed on him for just a moment before she was off. He watched her go from where he stood on the path until she was well out of sight. The feeling of her warm lips on his stubbly face lingered even as he turned to make his way onward. It always seemed to bring his spirits up whenever he was able to see the enchanting young lady. She awakened a feeling that he never quite knew how to express. But his mood was a very different thing on this evening despite even the brightness of Magdalena, burdened by a weighted melancholy that he couldn't seem to shake.

The dejected Asbjorn plodded slowly back to his home as the sun fell. His mind was a tangle of thoughts and emotions as he went along. For the most part, he strongly regretted his actions at the tavern this morning, resenting both Dorn and himself for letting what was said get so far under his skin and kindle his anger. Asbjorn was also deeply disappointed that he was again unable to draw out the bear. He'd returned empty handed after another frustrating hunt. Every time he came back into the village without it, he had to weather a bevy of mocking looks, always feeling that he'd shamed his father's memory not just to himself but also to everyone else. Perhaps he should do what Jarl Manus and Magdalena had urged him to and just let it go, moving on with it and starting anew. But deep down he knew he could never truly put his father to rest without slaying the beast. A large part of him did indeed yearn for it all to just be done but his need for satisfaction ran too strong.

As Asbjorn came around a bend in the path, he could just make out the silhouette of his small longhouse. The place looked deserted save for a strange light shining from within. He knew that he had not left anything burning when he'd left several days ago. He was not fool enough to have an unattended fire going before setting off for the woods. After everything that had already happened today, he was in no mood for guests, and woe to any trespasser who happened to be unfortunate enough to be inside.

The big youth pulled the cover from the old woodsman's axe he carried. He cautiously crept up to the strangely quiet structure. The house had an odd air about it tonight. It was as if an eerie dread almost seeped from the gaps in the rough timbers. He carefully peeked through the cracks in the shuttered windows with a single eye. He spied a crackling fire that burned in the hearth and a hunched shadow that lurched in the glow. He quietly went around to the front door and took a deep breath to set himself. He reared back before bursting through to nearly tear it off its hinges. Within, the only intruder to be found was an old woman standing before the table. Her shaking hands moved to place down two bowls and a pair of spoons.

"Welcome home, Asbjorn," the wrinkled crone greeted. She did not seem to be alarmed by his entrance. "I've been waiting here quite some time for you to get back. You may not realize who I am, but I've known what it is you've been seeking for years now. My name is Heggra," she said, "the witch of the north woods. And we have much to discuss."

V

Asbjorn took a seat at the table that Heggra had prepared. A large kettle bubbled away from where it hung over the fire that crackled in the hearth. He could smell the meat and herbs that simmered away. His stomach rumbled and his mouth watered at the thought of the sustenance, but he didn't let it show. He had not eaten since trying to take breakfast earlier this morning when first returning to the village, being rudely interrupted by the loudmouthed Dorn and his friends before he could have his fill. To say that Asbjorn was hungry was a gross understatement. The aroma of stewed venison came to his nose to entice his appetite. But the big youth also did not trust this woman who had so easily made her way into his home. After all, only a great fool would knowingly drop their guard in a witch's company.

For her part, Heggra simply continued to go leisurely about herself as his eyes followed her every move. She ladled out a bowl of broth and chunks of meat and vegetables. She sat it down before him as the steam rolled off. He warily regarded the dish as she took a seat across from him. He'd heard several stories before about Heggra from his fellow villagers when he was younger. The outcast witch of the north woods as she was sometimes referred to. Many thought of her as nothing more than an eccentric medicine woman. She was someone to seek out when the more conventional remedies of Brekka had failed to cure an ailment. But there were others that whispered far darker things about the old woman. That to reach out for her aid was to enter into a pact with the worst kinds of demons. Asbjorn had always suspected that the truth lay somewhere in the middle. But at the moment neither mattered that much to him. He simply stared at the old crone that had intruded into his house. He had still not made a move to touch the bowl that she'd sat on the table.

"You should eat, you know," Heggra said in a screechy voice. "Someone like you needs their strength. It's not poisoned if that's what you're afraid of."

"Prove it," Asbjorn responded. He pushed the bowl of stew towards her.

"Oh, fine," she said, picking up a spoon with her gnarled fingers. She scooped up and swallowed down a mouthful of broth along with a hunk of meat. She smacked her lips together once she was finished to help drive the point home.

"There, does that put you at ease?"

In response, Asbjorn slowly brought the bowl back towards him. He smelled it as he continued to eye her. Heggra's sunken face showed back at him to display an odd grin. The strange, twisted smile revealed the few nubby teeth that still poked from her gums. He'd attempted to ignore it at first but now that it was so close, he could resist it no longer. He forsook a spoon to simply guzzle down what was within. It had been quite some time since something this good had been cooked in these walls. Asbjorn typically got by on dried, salted game and whatever else he could easily prepare or remembered to keep on hand. The young man had missed partaking of meals such as this in his home, even if it had been made by a stranger who was said to be a witch. As he finished off the last gulp, he became aware that he had momentarily forgotten about his uninvited guest. He was embarrassed that he'd let his composer slip, even for an instant.

"There now," said Heggra. Her grin widened. "Isn't that better?"

"Yes," murmured Asbjorn. He was half red-faced as he wiped his mouth with the back of his hand. "Thank you. Now, why are you here?"

"I'm here to help you, boy," Answered Heggra. "Or should I say, to help you again."

"What do you mean, 'again'?" said Asbjorn. His brow was furrowed. "We've never crossed paths before."

"Of course, we have," the old woman said. She rose from her chair to pour him a flagon of mead. "You were just half-dead at the time and don't remember it is all."

"I don't understand," he questioned. He took the mug from her trembling hands.

"Who do you think mended your wounds when they carried you back here all those years ago?" Heggra replied. The smile vanished from her face. "Certainly not those fools, do you? You were barely hanging on by the time the jarl sent for me. Not even I was sure that you could be brought back from how far you'd slipped. You were delirious with fever when I arrived that night. Babbling to yourself about all manner of things. But there was one that was always consistent," Heggra went on. "The bear, Asbjorn. You kept speaking about the great devil bear that had come for you. Giant, you said it was, with eyes of burning fire and claws as sharp as steel. They all thought that you'd gone mad in that moment, but I knew the truth about what you spoke. I knew that you'd seen the beast for yourself the day you almost died. The same as I have."

"You've seen it, too?" Asbjorn asked in a low whisper. He leaned in closer to the old woman.

"I have," she nodded. "Many years ago."

An intense glint came to his eyes. "Tell me what you know about the thing."

"More than you do, Northman," said Heggra. "I know that it's a creature of fury and death, a vengeful spirit of the forests brought about by man's arrogant encroachment into the wilds. It walks the night in search of those that it might vent its wrath upon. It appears where it will before vanishing back into the surrounding woods. But I also know how to bring the monster to you, if you're not too afraid to die."

"Why would you want to help me?" Asbjorn asked. He leaned back. "You owe me nothing."

"Because it's you that owes me, boy," the old woman hissed. Her eyes narrowed to make her look every bit the witch that others said she was. "And I want the beast dead, the same as you do.

"I wasn't always like this, you know," she continued. A trace of deep sorrow ran through her tone. "I was once young like you, if you can believe that. Young and beautiful. But then that demon happened upon me and in one terrible instant took everything I held dear. The monster butchered my husband in our small home that rested within the forests not far from here and then fell upon me to cost me the child that grew in my womb. I awoke nearly dead and broken days later. There was no one nearby to answer my cries or come to my aid. You'd be surprised at the bargains that one is willing to make with the dark things when all has been taken from them, Asbjorn, ready to trade their very soul to cling to life for just a moment longer. But not even I can persist forever, and I've paid far too great a price and spent too many years chasing vengeance not to see it done. Perhaps we can help each other in getting what we want. What say you, Northman?"

Asbjorn did nothing but silently stare into the bottom of his mug for a moment. He wondered if trusting the old woman would be akin to making his own deal with the devil. His heart wanted revenge just as much as Heggra's seemed to want hers but was a chance at it worth dealing with a witch such as she was said to be. But he had taken so many risks in the past what did it matter if he took one more. He was more than likely bound to die or break himself sooner or later in his hunt for the beast. He swallowed down what little was left in his cup. He stared Heggra dead in her squinted eyes.

"Tell me how to summon the thing," Asbjorn said, "and I'll take its head for the both of us."

The old woman smiled another, almost toothless, grin. She shuffled over to gaze into the flames that danced and popped in the fire pit. The light fell on her wrinkled flesh even harsher than it had before, showing the ancient woman's age now more than ever. The flames reflected in the milkiness of her cloudy eyes. Her shaking fingers working in the air as if she were knitting or sewing at something that only existed to herself. She seemed half lost in a long dead memory. Her body was here, but her far off stare was lost in the blaze.

"Three nights from now," she responded at last. "There will be a red moon. A blood moon. That's when you can call it to you.

"Venture out to the beast's lair in the Iron Throng Hills far to the northwest of here. The opening can be found dug within the rocks and surrounded by a grove of black trees. Dwelling nearby on the flats of those hills are the grey stags, Asbjorn. Their ashen pelts are as soft and delicate as fine smoke and when they move, they look to be made of a waving mist. Slay one of them. Spill its lifeblood and hang its carcass in the demon's den. And when the moon turns red it will come to you, drawn by the scent of its most elusive of prey.

"But be ready, Northman," she said. "For the devil bear's rage is bottomless and its strength from another world. To face it is to face a thing of pure power the likes of which you have only felt a small part of, and you will be all alone against its might. I wish you good fortune in your hunt whether you topple the creature or not. You're going to need all that you can get by the time it's finished."

The old witch turned and made to take her leave after her last words. The hem of her tattered skirt swished around her. Her feet scraped over the floor in an awkward gait. She offered nothing further as she trundled to the door. She did not pause or look back as she moved to pass into the night.

"Wait!" he called out before Heggra was out of sight. "I have to know more than that. I've seen how strong this monster is. What can I possibly do to fight such a thing?"

"I said that I could tell you how to bring it to you," the old woman answered. "I never said I knew how to kill it. You are full of great fury, Asbjorn. I can see it bursting in you even now. Most men that have hunted the beast were bold, but there was always fear in them. Their spirits shrank the moment they saw it and they had lost the battle before it began. Remember how you felt when your father died and have ever since. Do not follow in Jurgen's footsteps or so many others that went before him. Use your rage to strike the demon down or your fight is already over. Beyond that, you are on your own, boy. The same as you've always been."

With that, the old witch was gone. Asbjorn was left staring out into the blackness as his door softly swung back and forth on its hinges. He slowly walked over to pull it closed. He leaned heavily on it as he thumped his fist against the wood.

Three nights, he thought. *Only three nights after so long.*

As his mind drifted off, he rested his forehead on the doorframe. His sandy hair spilled down his back and over his broad shoulders. He'd waited so long for this time to finally come he was almost at a loss. It had been a nearly eight-year quest that had consumed his thoughts night and day since he was a boy. The question now, was not how he would fight the bear, but if he would finally reap the satisfaction he'd sought or simply meet his own death, just as his father had?

In an instant, his feeling of trepidation fled from his mind as quickly as it had come. It was replaced instead by one of grim resolve. He turned and marched across the room to fling aside a dusty deer skin. He cracked open the old chest that had sat beneath it. From within the trunk, he carefully lifted it out. He unfolded the soft cloth that was wrapped around its head and handle. It was quite a bit lighter in hands now than it used to be, ever so much more than when he was younger. He rarely brought himself to remove it from the chest anymore, however. He honed and oiled the heavy blade every year only on the eve of his father's death.

The axe gleamed in his hands as he turned and examined it in the firelight. His eyes followed along its hard contours and curved edge just as they did when he was a boy. Compared to this, the blade he'd used to fell the wolf yesterday was only a toy. It still sat where he'd left it after arriving home to find Heggra here. It was the sharpest of edges that this axe held, keen and deadly enough to slice through the flesh of the devil if it had to, and with what he was planning it just might. He swung it through the air with his muscled arms. The heft of it felt so at home in his grasp as if it always belonged there.

Once again, Asbjorn looked into the steel of the etched blade. He was almost able to see the reflection of his father's face looking back at him for an instant and then it was gone. Alone in his home, he let out a long, deep breath, ready to claim the retribution he knew was his after so many years.

"It's time," Asbjorn said, almost as if he were addressing the weapon itself. "Three nights, and it's time."

VI

Asbjorn wasted little time in preparing for his journey after Heggra had gone. He took only a scant amount of provisions and his bow, arrows, and father's axe along with him. He did not bother to tell anyone where he was heading, let alone mention a word of it to Magdalena. He knew that the girl would only try and talk him out of his grave endeavor. Perhaps she would even go so far as to have her father intervene to prevent his leaving. They may know him well but neither of them could ever understand what he was about to do. He thought it best this way as he swept from the village. If he returned alive to see them again then so be it. But if not, they could all believe whatever they wished, either assuming he simply left or that something worse had occurred.

It was an arduous excursion for Asbjorn over the rugged countryside that lay between him and his destination, marked by dense woodlands, rocky ridges, and sloping valleys. He had traveled east before many times. He'd traversed through the dense forest and even to the sprawling plains that lay on the opposite side. But this was as far to the northwest he had ever dared to venture. The deserted region held nothing that the people of his village or their closest neighbors cared about. The place was a jagged and harsh landscape where no crops were able to take to the soil. Any livestock that was brought here was sure to die for lack of anything to graze upon. He'd heard that it had once been a prosperous and lush territory many centuries ago, but war had swept through the region decades back to forever taint it with death. It was now known for being a haven for bandits and raiders. Thieves and killers sought refuge here when not engaging in their foul livelihoods. Other things were also said to dwell in the countryside, roaming the night after being drawn to the area by so much bloodshed and they'd remained ever since.

As the big Northerner went, he did manage to catch a glimpse of the turbulent Northern Sea from time to time. It was a sight that he had only ever heard about and did not leave the best of impressions on him. The waters were rough and almost like an undulating hell that stretched all the way to the horizon. The waves were every bit as tall as the biggest longhouse of Brekka, and in some instances even taller. It was said that his people and their neighbors had originally come from a distant shore that lay far across the turbulent expanse. They had long ago left behind their native lands in search of something better for themselves. But with tides as violent as these, Asbjorn had his doubts about how anyone could brave them and not end up at their depths. The surges were strong enough to tear even the sturdiest of ships apart.

At last, he arrived at the distant hills that he'd been seeking. He reached the outskirts a little before the sun had hit its height on the second day. He wished that he could take just a bit of time to rest and recover himself after his journey. His aching legs and his back and shoulders were killing him. He'd also had to remain vigilant as he'd traveled. He had seen a pair of distant campfires burning in the night to remind him he was not alone out here. There was even one instance when he swore that he'd noticed something shifting in the dark. He'd not caught a good glimpse of it but thankfully a waving torch and a harsh shout had spooked it back into the shadows.

But Asbjorn also realized that the hours that were left to him were fleeting and precious. The time of the crimson moon quickly drew near the longer the days dragged on. He pushed his body through throbbing muscles and the weight of his own weariness. His thoughts were firmly focused on the task at hand. He knew that he could rest as much as he'd like to when all was done, or even more if he ended up dead, whichever came first.

It did not take Asbjorn long to locate the black grove once he arrived at the edge of the rocky mounts. He was seemingly drawn to where it lay on their eastern fringe almost by instinct. He did not venture to within the tangled trees when first reaching them, however. He instead chose to make camp a short distance away before heading into the rough stretch of hills. He hoped to find the dwelling place of the grey stags as quickly as possible, bringing one of them down before all the light had faded from the sky and he was left with nothing but darkness.

Asbjorn carefully crept through the jagged rocks and narrow passes. He doubted how any creature at all could make this place its home. There was not an inch of land he'd seen so far that looked even somewhat hospitable. The Throngs were a hostile, barren terrain, with little in the way of vegetation or freshwater to sustain anything. The scattering of woodlands that surrounded the small range mostly consisted of leafless, bark-stripped trees. The streams and brooks that crisscrossed the territory were more akin to muddy creeks and fetid marshes than rivers. There were more than enough tales passed around that told of the perils of visiting this remote place, ones that spoke of more experienced hillmen than he who'd lost their lives in the twisting ravines or to gods only knew what else. But the big Northerner cared not about any of those things. This is where he was told to go, so this is where he went.

Moving deeper into the hills Asbjorn found that the mounds became even tighter and more choking the further he pressed. The paths became an almost impossible maze to navigate. He had to suck in his chest and midsection more than once to even barely slip through the narrowest of rock formations. At one point his foot became so stuck between two stones he had to wiggle it free with the help of his axe handle. Once loose, he thought of turning back to perhaps find a different route to take, one that seemed less like a suffocating coffin compared to the one he was on. But then, to his surprise, he saw something that made him reconsider. His hand went to the rock to pluck it from the granite.

Between his fingers, Asbjorn held a wisp of the duskiest fur. The strands were even thinner than the finest of thread. Looking around he began to see bits of moss and traces of greenery stuck to the stone. He cautiously moved along to continue to follow the confining gorge. As he went, he came across even more tufts of the greyish hair. He also noticed that much of the sparse plant life he'd seen grew thicker here and appeared to have been torn away in spots. Following a steep incline, he finally came to a point where the path widened. The slant led upwards to escape the smothering pass. Slinking up as quietly as he could, he just poked his head over the edge. His eyes came up just enough to get a glimpse.

What he saw on the top of the small plateau was a strange sight for a lowland youth. His expression turned to puzzlement as he took it in. They were small, sleek animals the like of which he had never heard of before, built narrow and long in body with a silky coat and multi-pointed antlers that followed the curve of their head. They licked at the mossy clumps that were strewn between the dark crevices that separated the stones. It was a tiny herd, still unaware of his presence so far.

These can't be the same animals the old witch told me about, Asbjorn thought. His eyes narrowed. *They're no bigger than a pony. Nowhere near the size of the stags that roam near Brekka.*

But then he took a closer look at them. Their ashen pelts and delicate fur seemed as soft and smooth as mist. He noticed their fine coats made them look as if they were almost wrapped in a moving smoke. One almost seamlessly blended into the other should they cross paths.

These must be the grey stags that Heggra spoke of, his mind said to him. *They have to be. They have to be, dammit!*

Ever so slowly, Asbjorn slipped his bow from over his shoulder. He eased an arrow from the quiver to carefully nock it against the string. He brought the weapon up to draw back the projectile that rested between his fingers. He steeled his nerves and took the steadiest aim he'd ever taken in his life. He knew that should he miss, he would more than likely not get a second chance at this. Tomorrow would come and go before he could track down the herd again or another like them. He had come too far and waited too long to be denied now. The feeling of his very first hunt with his father rushed back to him.

With his arm steady, his hand reached his cheek. His eyes focused in so that all he saw were the animals in front of him. He picked out one that had the broadest part of its flank facing towards him, giving himself the widest target to lessen his chances of failure. Then the bowstring went taut. A tiny groan sounded from the stretched fibers so that Asbjorn could hardly notice it for himself. But the stags' ears suddenly perked as their heads raised and they all looked his direction. The herd began to scatter as they undoubtedly knew he was there.

Asbjorn sprung from his hiding place in the stones with all the urgency he could muster. He sprinted forward and dropped to one knee to brace his aim. For an instant, all the animals blurred together. They may have appeared like a wavering mist at first but when they moved it was like a billowing fog. He lost track of which was which as they bounded in, around, and amongst each other. They used their own kind as cover as they darted away to disorient his vision. Then he thought he saw a singular shape just at the edge of the fleeing turmoil. Without thinking, he sent the arrow straight towards the closest of the animals he could still make out.

For a brief moment after he released the projectile his heart sank. The streaking arrow looked to miss its mark. It appeared as if would sail just wide of his fleeing quarry, refusing him the kill that he needed and had come so far to obtain. But then, as if by fate, the stag leapt right into the path of the arrow's sharp tip. The shaft found its way into the animal's flesh to bring it down almost where it stood.

The other animals were gone and well out of sight by the time this one hit the ground. Its body still twitched as a small smearing of crimson spread across the plateau top. Asbjorn walked over to stand above it as the last bit of life seeped from its crystal black eyes. He left the arrow in the wound to avoid losing any more of the blood than was necessary. He tied its legs together and heaved the dead beast up and across his shoulders. He was beyond tired as he turned to carry the carcass back through the narrow passes and to his campsite to get what little rest he could. One part was at least over and done with, but the real task still lay ahead and waiting for him. His mind now focused on felling a much larger prey. It was one that had eluded him for far too long but if he had his way tomorrow it would soon be his. If only he could now avoid becoming the prey himself and bring down the beast that had claimed the lives of his father and so many others.

VII

The last bit of light had long faded as Asbjorn crouched in the darkened cave. The irony aroma of the stag's blood was heavy in his nostrils. He was almost thankful for the clinginess of the metallic smell. The odor helped mask the stink of decay from other dead things that were rotting around him. It had already been nightfall by the time he'd made it back to his campsite the evening before. The half-exhausted youth strung up the slain animal before allowing his body to rest and recuperate in front of his fire. He'd slept much later than he had planned to the following morning, waking with a start to work out his stiff muscles as the sun steadily rose. After limbering up his extremities, he'd eaten a quick meal. After that, he'd hastily collected his things and shouldered the stag before venturing into the black grove.

Struggling through the twisted trees, it hadn't taken him long to decide that this was not a place he ever wished to return to. He could safely conclude that once was enough for anyone. Gnarled branches reached out in all directions like grasping claws. The rough trunks that marked the landscape appeared to be covered with screaming faces that were there one moment and then gone the next. He wondered how something the size of the great devil bear could make it through this interwoven mess without leaving the slightest trace of its passing. His own footfalls still showed clearly in the deep mud behind him. But then he thought that it was best to not question the comings and goings of demons. The way of such things were not meant for men to understand.

The sharp twigs that stuck out scraped at his exposed skin as he pressed on, leaving dozens of tiny scratches down his arms and across his cheeks. His boots had quickly become slogged down in the thick muck by his own weight and that of the stag. He was finding it difficult to keep his sense of direction in the hazy bog. More than once he became turned around and had to back track, following his trail back to where it looked a bit more familiar, or at least he thought it did. A few times he even passed an odd skull or other trace of remains that jutted from the mire. He wondered how many others had trudged to a halt and been trapped in the filth attempting to do the same as he.

At last, he had managed to push through the web of ashen limbs. He emerged into a marshy clearing that spread out before a jagged mouth in the rock face. The cave entrance was like a screaming maw of stone. It opened wide to ward off any who thought themselves brave enough to venture within. There was a draft of air that spilled out to nauseate the world. The stench reminded him of the old leatherworker's back at Brekka, but he doubted if even that surly oaf would tolerate this smell. It carried with it the stink of a hundred dead and their silent urgings to turn back and flee. Any sane individual would have instantly listened and turned to run.

Asbjorn had trudged through without hesitation. He plunged into the shadows that awaited him on the other side. As he made his way into the bowels of the earth, his eyes gradually started to adjust to the dim interior. The darkness was broken only by a few shafts of light that managed to sneak through the cracks in the stone. He'd followed the dank passage back and downward for what felt like miles, finally coming to a wide cavern at the end of the lonely tunnel. The high chamber was ringed by a small ledge above. Droplets of water fell to land on the scattered and crushed bones of all manner of creature. He saw deer, wolf, man, and even other bear skulls strewn about, some with decomposing strips of flesh still clinging to them. Asbjorn could not help but wonder if his father's remains might be buried here somewhere, mixed in with the countless other skeletons that littered the floor.

That doesn't matter now, he'd thought. He threw the dead stag at his feet as he chased away the sentiment. *All that's important is the kill. And I will kill the bear, father. For you, for me, and for everyone.*

Asbjorn had snatched his hunting knife from where it hung at his waist. He set about to do what the old woman had instructed. With the sharp blade, he split the smoky coated stag down the middle. He flung the animal's blood over the cavern walls and the scattered remains that lay throughout the cavern. He next impaled the carcass on one of the pointed stalagmites that rose from near the center of the floor. He climbed up to take a hidden perch on the narrow ledge overhead, anxiously waiting for it to come.

Asbjorn had been sitting here now for most of the day and well into the night. The rays of the sun that filtered through the rocks were long ago replaced by shafts of silvery moonlight. His backside throbbed and his muscles cramped from being hunched over for so long. He shifted every so often to try and relieve the stiffness in his spine. He'd been thinking about what the witch had said to him before she'd departed his home. He considered what she mentioned about his own feelings towards the beast and wondered if the moon would really turn the bleak scarlet she said it would. His spirit yearned for the creature to come, ready to finally face it again but only this time with himself being the one to walk away.

But another part of him still questioned if he could actually take the monster. He'd seen the ease with which it dispatched his father years ago. He'd wanted this for so long that he could practically taste it but would the strength of a single man be enough to fell the thing when so many others had met their end? And that's when he felt a slight tremor vibrant through the rocks. The dust and the few pebbles he could see in the darkness shifted ever so much. It was followed shortly by another shudder that had grown slightly stronger. Then even more as bits of stone began to fall from the ceiling.

As his eyes fixed themselves on the tunnel, Asbjorn's heart pounded in his chest. His breath quickened as the sweat started to bead down his face. Around him, the silvery streams of light faded away, replaced instead by shafts of deep red that bathed the blackness. As he stared wide-eyed, a crimson glow grew from the cave entrance. The walls quaked as a massive form was silhouetted in the light. Then he saw the thing step into the cavernous space from the mouth of the tunnel. The great devil bear, with eyes burning like two perfect pearls of fire just as they had when he was a boy. Its muscular girth lurched across the cave to where the remains of the stag hung on the spike. The earth continued to shake with each of its footfalls. It sniffed at the dead thing for just an instant. Asbjorn hoped that his scent did not linger on the pelt of the slaughtered animal. Then, with the snapping of bone, the beast gnashed its teeth into the dangling carcass, nearly devouring it whole with a single bite.

Asbjorn watched as the hellish creature voraciously fed upon the dead stag. The terror that he'd felt so many years ago suddenly rushed back to take over his mind. For a moment, he was only a boy again and could do nothing else but tremble. His body went cold despite the heat that rolled off the monster. But then he saw his father's face before him. He heard the man's dying screams ring out in his ears. He remembered what Heggra's final words to him had been before she'd left, about not seeing the fear in him and his own rage that had brought him this far. There could be no doubt or hesitation for him tonight. The anger that dwelled inside would have to be his fuel to overcome the exuded terror. If it didn't, there would be one more set of nameless bones to join the rest. And from the looks of it, the pile was already big enough.

The fire that he'd pushed down for so long suddenly came to Asbjorn in that moment. It was the fury of a young boy turned into a man who had seen his only family be torn away from him. The feeling was greater than his dread. It burned even hotter than the paralyzing fear that held him. This creature below was a blight upon the land and its people and Asbjorn would purge its presence from the world, once and for all.

Asbjorn rose from his hiding place with bow in hand. He rained down a hail of sharp iron and wooden shafts upon the beast. Arrow after arrow found their way into the devil bear's thick flesh. The monster was surprised for an instant but quickly retaliated with a deafening roar. The blasting sound shook the hillside and nearly rent the Northman's eardrums to shreds. The splitting pain came close to spiraling his mind into oblivion. But despite the agony, he forced himself not to waiver, forsaking to even clap his hands to sides of his head to find relief. Instead, he came back to bellow a savage cry of his own. He continued to release his onslaught of piercing projectiles. But it would take far more than that to begin to slow the beast down. Its anger was now kindled and its ire raised.

In response to the Northerner, the bear came to its hind legs. The enraged creature slammed its claws on the stone rim. Bits of rock went flying everywhere as Asbjorn narrowly managed to escape. The spot where he'd been a second ago was pulverized to dust less than an instant after. He leapt to his belly more than several lengths down the rim. A loud snap accompanied his hard landing when he came down. His desperate dive out of the bear's way had saved his life for the moment but the haphazard act had cost him the use of his bow. It was broken in half and now in splinters.

Asbjorn was back to his feet in less than an instant. He cast the useless weapon aside as he pulled his father's axe from where it hung on his back. The giant bear lurched after him still on its hind legs. It leaned on the rocky ledge as it swiped at him with its claws. With each swing, he was able to stay just out of harm's way. He hacked at the creature's reaching forelimbs with his blade. His sharp steel left deep wounds where it bit into the monster's flesh but still the beast seemed undeterred and came for him. With another bellow, it roared at the Northerner again. Its searing eyes flared as its steaming breath blew around him. The monster reared itself up even higher this time, bringing all of its weight down to collapse the ledge in a shower of stone and rubble. As the rocks cascaded down, Asbjorn fell with them. He tumbled over the beast's back to crash to the cave floor just behind it. Scrambling to his feet, he was immediately up and carved into the bear's backside. He came around to its right flank to press his assault. It whipped its head back and forth to shake away the dusty debris. The axe only angered it further despite Asbjorn's efforts.

The big Northerner screamed in vengeance as he continued to furiously chop. The grievous injuries left by his hewing arms still did little to impede it. It slammed its weight into him to pin him between its side and the hardness of the cave wall. It crushed the breath from his lungs with its massive girth. Again and again the beast smashed itself into him, until the cavern quaked and rocks from the ceiling were crumbling down. In a showing of desperation, the winded Asbjorn dropped to the floor just as it tried to ram into him again. He crawled through its legs to stagger to the far side of the rumbling cave. The great devil bear came around to face the young man one more time. Its char black coat was now soaked red as it eyes still burned for his blood.

"Come on, you demon!" he bellowed in defiance. A scarlet spittle flew from his lips. "Come and finish it, then!"

The bear finally appeared to sway on its tree trunk like legs. The creature's breaths came labored and heavier than they did before. Its side and haunches were marked with deep lacerations that had slashed all the way to the bone. Its back was peppered with the broken off shafts of no less than a dozen arrows. It pulled in a great lungful of air and let out another ferocious roar, nearly crumpling the man that faced it to his knees this time. It threw itself into a full-on charge. It came straight at him, aiming to finish him for good this time.

Asbjorn could feel the stone beneath his feet tremble. The beast's great mass picked up speed as it rushed towards him. It looked to plow headlong into him to pulverize him to paste, battering him to the ground and then devouring whatever broken bits were left, but only if it could catch him.

At the last moment, Asbjorn flung himself aside. The devil bear rammed full speed into the rock just behind him. The earth itself moved under the force of the beast's impact. The shock of the collision caused the ceiling to at last give way and come plummeting down. Asbjorn ran for the tunnel that led back to the black grove as tons of stone dropped from above. The bear and any sense of his whereabouts were lost within a cloud of choking dust. He managed to throw himself prone just as he passed into the safety of the tunnel. The sound of the last few rocks toppling down and settling into place came to his ears. His arms covered his head to shield himself.

The dust slowly began to settle as Asbjorn pulled himself up on wobbly legs. The fine particles that swirled around him clung to his blood and sweat. Gradually, the red glow that had heralded the bear's coming died away, replaced once more by the crystal moonlight that crept in. He leaned his back wearily against the cool stone. He reclaimed the breath that had been crushed from his lungs. As he rest on the handle of his axe he stared at the fallen rocks that buried the beast in its own den. It was a bittersweet victory for the Northerner not having struck the killing blow himself, but it was a victory nonetheless, and he would take it.

"For you, father," Asbjorn exhaled. He clutched the axe close. "For all of you."

He turned to make his way out with fatigue nearly overwhelming him. He had to brace himself on the walls of the tunnel to avoid toppling over. He'd made it only a few steps when the fallen stones suddenly exploded around him. The great bear lunged after him with its jaws gaping wide and one free claw that was not pinned down. In an instant of surprise, it took a vicious gash from his side with its raking nails. Asbjorn went to the ground as blood flowed freely from four jagged wounds. It was a pain that he'd felt before long ago when he was much younger but it did not stop him then and it would not stop him now.

Asbjorn launched himself at the trapped monster with a frenzied cry. He cracked the thing across the side of the head with the blunt hammerhead of his axe. He brought the weapon back around to connect with it again, torquing all his strength behind the strike to nearly bludgeon the beast unconscious. Barely hanging on, it made one final effort to get to grips with him, but he kicked the thing's listless foreleg aside with his boot to bring the axe high over his head. For just a moment, Asbjorn gave pause to stare into demon's blazing eyes, the same rage that coursed through himself reflected in kind within those fiery orbs. And then, with a fall of his blade, the devil bear was slain. A wafting of steam drifted up from where his axe had embedded itself.

Asbjorn nearly collapsed on top of the thing. The once searing light was now gone from its dim sockets. It was finally done after so many long years, and for the first time in a long time, his heart felt still.

As he stood, he gripped the handle of the axe to help him steady himself. He'd struck with such force he had to use his foot to pry the blade from where it had cleaved into the side of the creature's skull. With the flip of his wrist, he went to flick away the glistening gore that clung to the steel but found that the scarlet was stuck fast to the blade. The beast's viscous blood had stained the once vibrant axe a dark crimson. The same steam that had risen from the killing stroke lingered around the steel. As his fingers tightened around the handle, his forehead bowed against the blade. A somber satisfaction rushed over him.

"It's finished," he said with a long exhale. "This time, it's finally finished."

But then his gaze once again fell upon the bear. The darkened tunnel was silent and completely at rest in the scant moonlight. There was still one more thing for him to do before all was said and done, and then they would all see for themselves what it was that he had hunted, and they would know.

VIII

It had been nearly two weeks since Asbjorn's brawl in the streets. The huntsmen were arriving with their kills and the men of the surrounding lands were bringing their goods to barter for the winter. Not a single man or woman had seen the big youth since the jarl had once again secured his release from jail, not that any of them were actually going out of their way to look for him. The last stretch of days had been a rather tranquil and uneventful time since his disappearance. A peace of mind had come to settle over the residents of Brekka following his parting. Most were fine with the fact that he was gone and hoped that he would remain so. His violent outbursts had upset the village more than enough over the years, especially as of late. But there was still one that worried about him and yearned for his return, not knowing what she would do if she were never to see him again.

Magdalena sat before a warming fire in her father's home. She ran a comb of varnished cedar through her golden hair. She stared quietly into the skipping flames with a sullen expression. Her thoughts were firmly centered on the missing Asbjorn. She had tried to visit him several times over the past days out at his home on the outskirts of town, sneaking away when her father and mother were too preoccupied with their duties to notice. But each time she ventured out she had found the place quiet and empty. It was as if the big man had just gathered up a few unnoticed items to depart without a trace. The young girl had tried to speak with her father about her growing concern for the absent Asbjorn. Her mind had been running away with itself and thinking the worst. But each time the jarl had simply said that perhaps it was better this way.

He'd asked her to put it aside and let the restless youth seek whatever peace he could find elsewhere. But Magdalena had the stubbornness of her mother running through her. She was far from the type to forget those that she cared about. It was especially true for the one she'd never fully realized just how deep her feelings ran for until now, when he wasn't here to share them with.

As she sat before the hearth, Magdalena wished that she could see him just once more. If for nothing else than to at least tell him goodbye before he went. There were so many things that she wanted to say to him since he was no longer here. Words that she had kept locked away deep within her heart, even from herself. But now it seemed the chance to voice all that had remained unspoken would never come. The feelings were only a lingering reminder of something that might have been but now couldn't. As the young lady gazed into the flames, she let out a long sigh, still lost in her thoughts and the glowing fire.

"What troubles you, my daughter?" asked a tender voice from just behind her. Magdalena's mother came into the room. She was an elegant woman of poise and almost statuesque beauty. The resemblance between her and her daughter was more than apparent to anyone in Brekka. Where the jarl could many times come off as gruff and hard, she was very much the softness that stood behind him. She was a calming word that helped sooth away the village's woes.

"I'm sorry, mother," Magdalena answered after a moment. "I didn't hear you come in. I was just thinking."

"About him again, I expect," her mother said. She sat next to the girl and took the comb in her own hand.

"Yes," nodded Magdalena. "I'm worried where he might be. It's not like him to be away this long without at least returning for a short time. It doesn't look like he's been back home for days."

"I thought that you might have gone out there a few times," her mother smiled, running the smooth cedar through

Magdalena's locks. "You always ran after him, ever since you were children. Helping to get him out of trouble and sometimes in it. Why should that change now?"

"Forgive me, mother," Magdalena responded. "But I just have to know where he is. I can't believe he'd just go and not come back like that. Do you think that I should just forget about him like father says, even if it hurts to do so?"

"That all depends, now doesn't it, my dear," her mother answered.

"Depends on what, mother?" she asked.

"It depends on whether you believe he'll come back or not," the woman said. She gathered up her daughter's hair to work it into a long braid.

"Asbjorn has always had a great unease in his spirit, ever since the day his father was killed. It's like a storm that refuses to settle. It grows calm for a moment or two only to rage up again without warning. Perhaps whatever he's doing is his way of trying to quiet that storm. I doubt his leaving has anything to do with how he might feel about you, though. But rather it may just be something he has to do for himself.

"I remember that your father was a lot like Asbjorn when he was younger," she went on, "always disappearing to run off on some adventure. There were times when I wondered if he ever really cared for me at all. But he did. More than I ever realized at some points. What you have to ask yourself now is, do you feel that Asbjorn is worth waiting for, or is it time to let him go and move on?"

There was a long silence before Magdalena let a reply slip from her lips. Small tears welled up in the corners of her blue eyes. She gazed through the front window that was cracked open just enough to let the cool air from outside creep in. She wished that she would see him walking towards her home on the opposite side. Her mother continued to weave the young lady's thick hair together. She already knew the answer her daughter was about to give.

"I know he is," Magdalena finally said. She wiped her eyes clear.

"Then you must let that thought be your guide, my dear," her mother replied, tying off the end of the braid. "And never give up hope."

After that, the two of them embraced one another for a long moment. The woman's comforting arms were wrapped around her daughter as the logs crackled in the hearth. She knew all too well the turmoil the young lady felt inside but also realized that these were not her decisions to make. In the end, Magdalena's heart was her own and she must respect that, come whatever her daughter may want from life, even if it was the difficult route.

As Magdalena's mother pulled away and smiled at her, the two of them suddenly heard a loud banging at the door. The grumbling Manus stomped from his private chamber at the back of the house to investigate the pounding. He mumbled annoyed curses under his breath about how he was far too busy to deal with any more trade or merchant disputes today, gruffly remarking that this better be important or someone was going to pay. He threw back the heavy door to find a wide-eyed young man from the village standing in front of him. The stunned youth's hand was raised in mid knock, just about to fall again.

"What is it this time!?" Manus barked out. "I have pressing things to attend to!"

"I'm, I'm sorry to disturb you, jarl," the young man almost whimpered. "But coming into the village, there's something you should see."

"Fine," the jarl huffed. "Magda, Magdalena, I'll return shortly."

"To beg your pardon, sir," the youth interjected. "But I think it might be something they wish to see as well."

Mother and daughter both just glanced at one another with puzzled expressions. The pair looked back to the annoyed jarl as the man nodded a hasty approval. It was not uncommon for Magda to accompany her husband on official matters from time to time, but the request of Magdalena's presence as well was quite a rarity. The three of them threw on light furs over their shoulders to help guard against the midday cold. They followed the nervous messenger as he led the way.

As the jarl and his family trailed behind the youth, they could all see a large crowd approaching. The men and woman all gathered around a broad figure that marched at their center. The people gave the man a wide birth as they walked cautiously by his side, almost as if they were terrified to pass within arm's reach. In his hand, he carried a heavy axe whose blade showed a deep red. The steel glimmered with a sharp crimson in the midday sun. Around his frame was draped the blackened pelt of a massive bear. The head hung from his shoulder to sit like a skewed crown. He looked like a conquering warrior coming in from a great battle. The masses parted in his wake as he strode through their number. He came before Jarl Manus and the two women that stood at the village leader's side. His chestnut eyes looked into those of Magdalena and then to her father. He pulled the bear's pelt off to show it to the man that stood speechless in front of him. He presented the dead beast's hide so that the whole of the village might see.

"You told me that the devil was only a myth, jarl," he said. "But I saw it come and take my father from me all those years ago. I looked into its eyes of fire when I was only a boy and I was afraid, but then it found me again and this time I did not look away. I have slain the demon beast of the Northern Forest and taken its head as my own. The bear is finally dead. The long hunt is over."

And with those words, Asbjorn was home. Every resident of Brekka was struck aghast by what he had brought with him. They may not have missed his presence but not a single one would dare dispute his return, for the demon beast had been real, and he had just laid it low for all to see.

IX

An ocean of stars churned and roiled in the heights of the obsidian chamber. The walls of black glass reflected the movements of the planetary bodies and celestial heavens above. The massive room was like an expansive void that rose ever upwards. A portion of the infinite cosmos appeared encapsulated within its confines. Galaxies spiraled in the deep blackness that went on and on. The trails of streaking comets cut through the ether, their tails of blazing gasses crisscrossing the heights. Suddenly, the scattering of stars flared bright. They coalesced together to form the constellation of the great Ursa that hung in the northern sky. Below, iron doors of the chamber slowly swung open. A grizzled man in black steel and trailing cloak swept past the similarly clad sentries that stood guard. Their eyes did not dare raise or follow him as he entered. The guards simply remained stoic and unmoving at their posts.

General Zantz strode down the center of the lengthy chamber. The golden trim of his ebon armor shined in the reflected starlight above. A forged broadsword hung from his hip. A helm in the image of a leering death's head was carried under his arm. He walked confidently along the path of lush indigo that stretched from the entryway, following it to a throne of bronze that sat upon a raised dais. The seat seemed as if it had been twisted and pulled from a metallic liquid. The tarnished metal flowed up to a spire that resembled outstretch claws. A solitary figure in the shape of a man rested upon the dreadful chair. The being's body looked to be made of the same star-flecked night that swirled in the heavens. It was draped in a violet satin, with two horns cresting from its brow to follow the curve of its head. Its visage was a featureless hole in space, save for two golden orbs that burned where eyes should have been, watching the general approach.

"You summoned me, Lord Xiphactinas?" the general said. He stopped and bowed his head before the great throne.

"Yes, Zantz," responded the figure that sat upon the bronze. Its voice was a hollow resonance that came from both itself and the void above. "Those that dwell beyond the stars have spoken to me again. They send a grave foreshadowing."

"How may I be of service to you, my lord?"

"Look above you, Zantz," answered Xiphactinas, motioning with a hand whose fingers ended in dagger like tips. "And tell me what you see."

"I see the heavens as always, my lord," Zantz replied. "And the image of a great beast in the blackness."

"It is the great bear of the north, general," whispered the star flecked being. "And I have been told that one of his kin shall come to strike me down. This cannot be allowed to stand, Zantz. I will not be destroyed by the likes of such filth."

"Command me as to what I must do, my lord," the general said. "And it shall be so."

"I charge you with this, Zantz," spoke Xiphactinas. "You are to take two companies of my black steeled warriors to the lands at the top of the world. Over the cutting mountains that separate those chill climes from the rest of civilization. Once there, put every man, woman, and child of that region under your blade. Leave none of them alive to draw so much as half a breath once you have finished. But this Son of the Bear is not to be killed, general. Bring him back to me in chains, broken in both will and spirit."

"Why not just let me put him down for you, my lord?" Zantz asked. "It would be my pleasure to do so."

"Because it is I whom he destined to kill," replied Xiphactinas in an unsettling softness. "And I wish to put an end to such a life personally. It has been far too long since I have satiated my baser desires. I look forward to it."

"The north is a far-off place, my lord," said the general. "It may take some time to reach those lands."

"Time has no meaning for me, general. I am forever, so long as such a foe is dealt with."

"Then how shall I know him when I find him, my lord?" asked Zantz.

"There will be no mistaking him, general," Xiphactinas replied. "Those in the darkness have shown me that he wears the visage of the great animal itself upon his shoulders and that his fury in battle shall be unlike any that you have ever faced before. He sleeps within himself for now but to awaken the beast inside is to rouse the spirit of rage itself. Take one of the seeing stones with you and be swift in your task, Zantz, and offer mercy to none that stand in your path. Now go, general, you waste yourself here."

"Your will shall be done as always, Lord Xiphactinas," the general responded. He bowed his bare scalped head. "The people of the north shall be put to a swift end and the man you speak of brought before you so that you may take satisfaction in his death personally. There is no power greater than yours and all shall soon realize that. Until I return, my lord."

General Zantz turned on the spot with his instructions. He took his leave of the celestial chamber of his master. He exited the same way that he had come, striding out with his cloak billowing behind as he passed into the endless halls of the obsidian tower. From somewhere outside, unseen horns trumpeted a deep tone, summoning his black clad warriors to make ready for the task ahead.

With the general's parting, Xiphactinas once again sat in the solitude of his inner sanctum. As always, he watched the cosmic bodies above follow along their age-old path. The golden orbs that were his eyes rested upon the outline of the starry Ursa. They narrowed as he stared up at the fierce constellation.

Are the heavens correct in their portent? his unfathomable mind thought. *Is this truly the form of my destroyer?*

"No," Xiphactinas whispered to himself. He scattered the image with a wave of his hand. "My power shall be challenged by none. I refuse to be brought low by a mere man such as this. Hear me fate, destiny or not, the Son of the Bear will die. So swears Xiphactinas!"

The Bear Awakened

I

The grass swayed with the coming of the morning breeze. The light of the rising sun reflected in the droplets of dew that clung to the tall brush. A small herd of deer lazily grazed across the wide-open flatlands. The dawn sparrows stretched out their wings to ride the chill winds into the air. As the creatures of the north rose, the villagers of Stonewatch were just beginning to set about their morning routines, waking with the sun to work out stiff muscles and clear drowsy heads. Men hurriedly went around tending to their flocks and opening their small shops. Women bustled about inside their homes to ready the day's breakfast and rouse the children from their beds. It was a quiet scene that played out every morning as it always did. It was one that spoke of long, tranquil days for the people of the remote hamlet.

Stonewatch was a small place when compared to the more developed settlements that lay over the rugged mountains. It was a mere speck on the world if one cared hard enough to look for it. The clustering of homes and merchant dwellings sat open and bare along a spacious stretch of the Northern Plains. The people formed a tightknit community that worked hard to take care of their own and support their neighbors.

But despite their isolation, the locals here suffered for little when it came life. The nearby forests and rolling plains provided them all they needed to get by. Game was often quite bountiful for the hunters and trappers, while the dark soil was rich and fertile for the farmers' small collection of crops. When not struggling with the land, the people here took their pleasures with simple things. They found their leisure in a lively horse race or with a spirited game of hurling or wrestling when not toiling away. Some would spend their hours doing nothing but waiting outside their homes just on the edge of the village, scanning the distant horizon with watchful eyes for any sign of an incoming traveler.

But such was their locale, that visitors from the outside were often few and far between. Word was carried only by the rare soul who thought themselves brave enough to be heading further into the harsh Northlands. Stonewatch was one of those places that sat where one world was just ending and another began, seeing the best, and sometimes worst, of both.

Today had started out like any other for the residents of the tiny village. The sun's rays had broken over the horizon the same way they did every morning at this time of year. The tasks that had remained unfinished from the evening before were picked up from the exact spot where they'd been left off. Not a beat was missed between a night's rest and the freshness of the day. The early rising farmers were out in the fields when they first took notice of it. Flocks of birds scattered from the surrounding woodlands to take flight and flee in all directions.

It began with a gentle rumbling that shook the ground. It was just enough to cause the livestock and beasts of burden to anxiously fret in their hitching. The men that were out with their carts and plows glanced about in nervous confusion. The sound rapidly increased in volume as the earth continued to shake. It was a noise like thunder but with no clouds to darken the day. Even the people within their homes and the small village proper felt and heard the quaking after a time. Men and woman gazed from windows and came to open doors to see what could be happening. Their children poked their heads out to have a peek. Then they saw them break over the ridge that spanned the southeast of the village. There came a tide of screaming humanity encased in black steel and seated atop charging horses. From the backs of their steeds, the incoming raiders spouted nothing but the promise of violence and bloodshed from their mouths. The tips of their swords aimed to make good on it.

A horde of mounted warriors descended upon the people of Stonewatch. The ebon wave was followed closely by a score of foot soldiers that rushed in only a breath behind. They surged down the hillside to trample the tall grasses and fields of crops underfoot. The steel of their blades showed bright in the morning sun.

Those that lived on the most southerly edge were the first to taste death. They were given little warning or chance against what had come for them. Their homes were quickly overrun and brutally sacked, the lives of so many snuffed out in a blink before most ever realized what had struck. The invaders in black gave no quarter as they steadily pressed on. The pleas of the dying fell on deaf ears as all were swiftly put beneath their blades.

As those on the outskirts fell, blaring horns could be heard sounding from the center of town. The alarm called for all able-bodied men and women to pick up arms and defend their homes. Those that could, or weren't too frightened, came running with weapons in hand, ready to protect friend and family with all they had or die trying. But their efforts would soon prove to be of little use. The simple villagers had no hope of standing against such an army.

The invading column was led by a monster of a man that rode atop a massive steed of muscle and fury. Those that were the first to meet him quickly fled for their lives once they'd gotten a good look. He crashed into friend and foe alike as his great blade fell in a succession of vicious strokes. He spurred his horse onward with little regard for what lay in his path. Unlike the other warriors, his black armor bore no bracers or arm guards. His rippling flesh was covered in a spattering of red from those he'd already cut down. From behind his monstrous helm, he bellowed the cry of one that was lost in a blood frenzy. He did not even bother to shout out commands to the men around him. He let them indulge themselves in the thrill of the massacre just as he did, satiating their own bloodlust that spilled through the streets.

Not a person or beast that stirred across the land was spared from the terrible onslaught that had come. The decimation looked to be a thorough and complete cleansing. The women and children were put down just as swiftly as the husbands and fathers who fought to protect them. Mercy was a word that held no meaning, with cruelty being the order of the day. From the ridge the horde had poured over, a pair of stoic figures sat astride their own horses and watched the destruction below. A line of their personal retainers stretched out to either side of them.

"See how they scatter before us, Orrm," said General Zantz. His voice was a deep reverberation from within his horned helm. "They flee like sheep from a pack of wolves, seeking shelter wherever they can but finding none. How this bores me."

"Perhaps taking the field yourself may serve to enliven your spirits, sir," responded Captain Orrm. His eyes scanned over the carnage. "The past few months on the march have been enough to drain even the best us, including one such as yourself. It might do you good to loosen your sword arm."

"Warriors like us should not dirty our hands by disposing of such rabble, Orrm," the general responded. "No matter how appealing it may seem. I thought you would know that by now.

"Besides," he said, "that's what we have Boslog for. Just look at how he wades into them, like a magnificent butcher, seeing all around him as nothing but cattle to be carved into. He's the perfect sort for what we've been sent here to do. A merciless killer that shows not an ounce of pity."

"He's also unpredictable and crazed, sir," said Captain Orrm. "He's just as likely to strike down his own men as he is the enemy. Personally, I'd rather not have him in front of or behind me, no matter whose side he's on."

"Somethings are worth the risk, Orrm," Zantz replied. "I could loose him on a score of men and be sure than not a one would remain to trouble me. So what if a few of our own happen to fall at his hands. Pawns are there to be sacrificed are they not? But such is the beauty of Boslog, captain. You just have to know which direction to point him in."

"I'd still prefer precision over destruction, sir," Orrm said. "His methods are much too unsavory for my tastes."

"And that's why you're here, Orrm," remarked the general. "To help balance things out.

"But come, captain," Zantz said, booting his mount into a slow trot. "This is just the first of many villages to be razed to the ground here and we've wasted more than enough time as it is. Let us ride on while Boslog has his fun. He'll be along soon enough by the looks of things. Already with a taste for more blood in his mouth I'd imagine."

Captain Orrm wheeled his horse to follow behind the general's. The lines of men on either side of them fell in to take up the rear as the pair turned to leave. The captain could still hear the mad butcher's roars over the cries of the people below. Steel rang out upon steel as Boslog continued his unchecked rampage through the center of Stonewatch. Orrm shot one last glance over his shoulder to see the berserk killer plowing into a group of retreating villagers. He slashed them to pieces as they ran for their lives. He even cut down one of his own who was foolish enough to run over and join in. The other raiders were certain to give him a wide berth after seeing their comrade felled so readily.

For himself, the captain had never seen the use for such a murderous man in the several years since he'd taken up his post. He looked at Boslog as a liability that nowhere near justified the cost. But General Zantz was keen on the butcher's ways from time to time, pointing out that the best weapons were often those that were the most dangerous, to both sides if necessary.

"Already with the taste for more blood in his mouth," the captain muttered to himself. He eyed the brute as he whipped the reins of his steed to keep pace with Zantz. "I have no doubt about it," the man snorted. "No doubt at all."

II

The axe fell again as another log was cleaved in two. The sharp blade split the wood with all the ease of a warm knife through butter. He stood up to stretch his stiff back and roll his shoulders. His torso was bare despite the nipping chill. He'd been at it now since well before dawn, chopping his way through the large heap of timber that sat just behind his home. The mound had been nearly as tall as he was when he first began. It was quickly whittled down to two smaller stacks along with a scattering of leftovers. One of the piles was meant for himself while the other would be sold in town, an extra way to earn some coin when the game of the forests had been hunted too thin. Finally, the blade dropped once more. The thud that followed signaled the last of the logs had been hacked in half. He picked up the chunks and tossed one of them to the top of each pile. He undid the tie around his sandy hair to let it fall down his back.

"There," Asbjorn said to himself, "that should hold me for a while."

With a single motion, he planted his axe in the old stump he'd been using as a chopping block. He dabbed the sweat from his brow before slipping on a supple tunic to help chase away the chilliness. He took a moment to pick through the collection of scraps that were scattered at his feet. He made sure that no larger bits had been missed, tossing the usable debris over where he'd stacked the rest. He'd come back out later once he had a chance to warm up and recuperate, gathering the pieces of scrap that could easily be bound and sold as kindling. He would carry everything into town tomorrow morning along with a few spare hides he'd managed to procure over the past weeks. Hopefully he'd make enough to get some fresh honey, a bit of salt, and a few other essentials he was running low on. But for now, it was time for food. He quickly scooped up an armload of his own firewood to carry it back towards home.

It was hard for Asbjorn to believe that it had been nearly a year to the day since his battle with the great devil bear. His body still carried the scars across his chest and a few other lingering aches and pains from the encounter. It had taken him far longer than he would have liked to hunt the beast down after it had taken his father from him. He was finally able to find the demon's lair and call it to him after what felt like a lifetime. The bloody clash that followed had almost proved to be the end of him. The beast was a thing of pure fury that could easily make a meal of men such as he. But his desire for vengeance would simply not allow him to be beaten. He refused to let years of dogged pursuit go to waste. He drew upon a willfulness that served him well but just as often reared itself as a hindrance, relying on his sheer resilience to succeed where others had failed.

What followed was a horrific struggle between enraged Northerner and blood crazed beast. One that saw pure rage pitted against the anger of a single, driven soul. After nearly being done in by the thing, Asbjorn had finally managed to call upon his own fierce spirit, prevailing against his foe and striking it down after so many years. Once the score had been settled, he found that the demon's blood had stained his axe a deep crimson. Nothing had been able to wipe away the scarlet from the steel. With the beast dead, Asbjorn had skinned the flesh from its back, draping himself in its hide like a vindicating trophy. Its head had hung from his shoulder when he'd marched boldly back into town after it was done. The people of Brekka had silently stared at him as he'd returned to the village. Their eyes were wide and their mouths agape as they trailed behind him through the streets. Only a shocked few were able to utter more than a syllable.

Asbjorn had tried to refocus himself since then. It was a difficult endeavor to banish from his mind that which had consumed his days and nights for so long. He had to reset himself and look forward to a future with the need for vengeance no longer in it, along with one that possibly promised him more. For the most part, he'd been relatively successful in his attempts to at last let it go. But every now and again the thought of the hunt would still creep into his mind, unsettling his calm.

As he meandered back to his small longhouse, he once again wondered what his life would now be like without the bear to spur him on. The pursuit of the beast was all he'd fixated on as his childhood had passed and he'd moved into becoming a man. Despite his hard exterior, he was anxious about what would become of him. He was afraid of just drifting along with nothing but an unfocused temper without the beast to give him purpose. For a time, he had felt like a rudderless ship adrift on a wild sea. It was almost as if he were being pulled along by a strong current with no way to fight against it. He would have more than likely been lost if it had not been for one person, that being the young lady whose image was now at the forefront of his mind. She had always been there by his side through all of it. She'd comforted him through the troubles and the years of ridicule he'd experienced when he was younger. It was her who had pulled him back from the darkness he had found himself steadily sinking into. She'd soothed his turbulent soul more than either of them could ever realize. He had never seen just how much she'd meant to him when they were both children. But in recent days, he was beginning to see her true meaning to him. His feelings only grew stronger. He was just reaching the steps of his home when he heard a delicate sound call out his name. The soft words were like a song carried to his ears and then she was there.

"Asbjorn," her voice rang out. "Asbjorn, are you here?"

Magdalena came around the back corner of his home. Her blue eyes and warm smile shined brighter than the morning sun ever could. Her green dress swayed about her trim waist as she almost glided to where he stood. Her golden hair was woven into two long braids that followed the curve of her back.

The jarl's daughter was truly a vision to behold. She was the kindest and most gentle soul in the village. She had never been one to use her power or position to lord herself over others. She was a near perfect image of what one of noble birth should be. She had a way with those that her father governed over, an empathy to see life's trials from their point of view. It was Magdalena who had sat for over a week next to the unconscious Asbjorn after his father had died. Her gentle face and round eyes were the first things he'd seen when he finally came to. She had smiled an odd smile as she watched him intently then, her chin resting on her folded hands where she sat next to his bed. She had been by his side ever since that moment, always looking out for him whether he wanted her to or not. When Asbjorn saw her these days, he often had to be cautious of becoming lost in the girl's enchantments, wary of not doing what he had done just now.

"Asbjorn," Magdalena giggled. She looked at him with that same little grin. "Why didn't you answer me when I called out to you and what are you staring at like that?"

She put the question to him as if she didn't already know, giving him a chance to respond to spare himself from even more awkwardness. This was certainly not the first time she had extended him such a courtesy, and he was always thankful for it when she did.

"Nothing," Asbjorn replied sheepishly. He shook his head to chase away his flushed cheeks. "I was just thinking about my father again.

"You know," he said, stacking his firewood in a neat pile next to his door. "It's been over eight years now since he's been gone but it feels like so much longer. I think about him nearly every day still, wondering what would have become of me if he were still alive. Sometimes it's like it was just yesterday when I last spoke with him but most of the time it seems like a lifetime ago."

"Well, that's because you've done so much with yourself since he's passed," Magdalena said. She came to sit on the steps that led up to the house. "You're not the little boy you were back then anymore. You've grown into a man, made this place your own, and you even hunted down the great bear when everyone else thought you were crazy. Things have changed a lot for you. But to me, you'll always be the same old Asbjorn. And I like you that way."

"You've changed, too, you know," Asbjorn said with a laugh. He sat down to join her on the steps. "You're not that overexcited little girl I first saw when I woke up either. And that's a good thing."

"And what exactly is that supposed to mean?" Magdalena replied with a smile. She nudged him in the side with her elbow.

"Well, you know," Asbjorn said. He tripped over his words as he rubbed the back of his neck. "I was just thinking that I...."

"See," she laughed, "same old Asbjorn. Awkward and tongue tied as ever. You really need to work on your social skills, you know."

Asbjorn couldn't help but let out a small chuckle. He knew that what the young lady had just said couldn't be more true. He was indeed a man of few words, often feeling at a loss as for what to say around others. He was far more comfortable in letting the depths of his actions speak for him over anything else. He often found that even the most genuine of words could conceal a hidden meaning and he was not one for subterfuge.

But with Magdalena, the lack of speech was a very different thing. The young Northerner spent more time than he cared to think about trying to find the right way to say what he wished. Despite his efforts, he always seemed to draw a total blank when in her presence. He was far more accustomed to tracking wild game than professing his inner feelings to anyone.

But the more he thought on it, perhaps it had reached that point to just put his fears aside. It could only be now or never for so long, and no good thing ever came to one who waited.

"Magdalena," he said in the softest voice he could muster. He turned his gaze towards her.

"Yes, Asbjorn?" she replied, coming around to face him.

"You know," he remarked, summoning up all his courage. "What you said is true. I have grown and changed since my father was taken from me. I was only twelve years old then, a frightened boy who had no idea what to do with himself. Your father and mother always looked after me until I was old enough to do so for myself and no matter what happened you followed me everywhere. I've done so many things up until now," he said, "but there's one thing that I haven't that I should have long ago."

"And what might that be?" Magdalena asked. Her eyes shimmered like pearls as they looked into his.

"We," he began, hesitating as he struggled to find the words.

"Just say what you feel, Asbjorn," Magdalena encouraged him. Her hand came to rest on his. "I'm listening."

"We've been so close, the two of us," he finally managed to get out, "ever since we were children. Your family practically raised me when I had no one else to turn to and you were almost like a sister to me then, but it's so much different than that now. I've valued your friendship so much over the years, Magdalena, even when I didn't show it to you, and I'm sorry for that. But lately I've been wondering could there ever be something more between us?"

"More how, Asbjorn?" she half whispered. Her blue eyes fluttered as they stared into his. Her hand slid up the curves of his arm to rest on his shoulder. She pulled herself closer to him. She could feel the tension in his iron like sinews but there was also a gentleness there. His arm swept around her.

"Just more," he said, taking her by the waist.

Reflecting all of her sentiments, Asbjorn's eyes gazed into hers. He held her closer to himself more than he ever had before. They looked at one another for a long time in that moment, lost in the other's embrace and the feelings they had never made known until just now. Slowly, they drifted together. Asbjorn pressed his lips against hers. She was so warm and soft in his grasp. Her body trembled as she wrapped her arms around him to squeeze him tight.

Asbjorn held Magdalena near as his heart raced. He wondered how he ever could have missed this when he was younger. He cursed himself a fool for having never seen that the girl felt the same for him as he did for her. He wished that he would have been brave enough to express his heart's desire long before today, but that mattered little now. She was next to him and that's all he cared about. The unspoken things between them were made all so real in but a single instant. He had longed for something like this more than he'd ever known in the past, and now that she was his, he did not wish to let her go.

As the two held each other, a reverberating blast suddenly sounded through the morning air. The birds that perched in the trees took flight at the trumpeting of the noise. Asbjorn and Magdalena both sprung to their feet with a start when the tone hit their ears. Their heads instantly snapped back in the direction of the village. In all his life, Asbjorn had only ever heard that sound ring out once before. The last time the blare had assaulted his senses was the day his mother was killed in a bloody raid. It was not a welcome thing to hear it again. It had signaled death then, and it could easily mean the same now.

"That's the alarm horn back in Brekka," he said. His warm expression instantly shifted to severity. His eyes looked in the direction of town.

"What does it mean?" asked Magdalena. The concern was clear on her face. "I don't remember ever hearing it before."

"It means there's either an emergency, or," Asbjorn answered in hesitation.

"Or what?" she said.

"Or they're under attack," he replied in a grim tone.

"Come on," he said, taking hold of her. "We have to go. They might need our help."

III

Asbjorn and Magdalena moved hand in hand as they raced down the old path that led towards Brekka. They skipped over ruts in the ground and spreading tree roots that reached out to trip them up. The few small farmsteads they passed all had their doors open and windows ajar. The occupants stood out in the cold to gaze in the direction of town. Magdalena's thoughts swirled with a mounting fear. The girl had never been through something like this that she could recall. The village had seen its fair share of difficulties that she could bring to mind to be sure. She remembered several fires, brutal winters, and even a flood of the river. But all of those had been handled in due course and with Brekka's usual perseverance, the large horn that sat in the center of town not once having been blown to signal distress.

But this morning its call had broken the calm of the surrounding countryside, summoning all those of able body to make their way to the village square. She wondered if this truly could be an attack of some sort. The safety of her mother and father was all she could focus on. But in her panic, Magdalena looked to Asbjorn. She found that his expression carried not a bit of worry or dismay. He led her along as if he knew exactly what to do. She was sure that everything would be alright as long as he was near, but only if she could keep up.

Such was Asbjorn's pace that Magdalena was having trouble staying by his side. His legs carried them along quicker than the breeze. The young lady was panting for breath long before they reached even the outermost edge of town. She was thankful for the sight of the narrow lanes that she hoped might slow them down. They made their way through the dusty streets to the village square. A score of others had already gathered en masse by the time they arrived. Everyone in the crowd stared off in the distance to the southwest, looking at the pillars of black smoke that rose into the sky. The horn still sounded for a few moments more as all that were present came together. A low murmur spread through their number as the last reverberation faded.

"What could it be?" Asbjorn heard them asking. He and Magdalena snaked their way through. "It's coming from Westboar, I think," his ears picked up. "But what could have happened?"

Asbjorn's eyes scanned the crowd as he guided Magdalena along. He looked for any trace of the jarl in the masses. The girl stood on her tiptoes to try and see over the people's heads. If there was one person in the village that would know what could be going on it was Manus. The challenge at the moment, was spotting him amongst the packed bodies. There were so many clustering tight that it was difficult to pick out a single individual. Then Asbjorn heard Magdalena call out. Her arm repeatedly tugged on his sleeve as she pulled him in her direction.

"Father," she cried, waving her hand in the air. "Asbjorn, there he is. Father!"

The jarl stood near the center of the gathered townsfolk. He was doing his best to assuage the many questions that were being put to him all at once. The older gentleman looked somewhat flustered in the middle of a sea of discordant voices. His head snapped from one frantically talking resident to the next. When the village experienced difficulty, Manus was usually quick to pull in the reins and get a handle on things, lessening worries and putting minds at ease. But with this there were just too many inquiries coming at him at once, with no one quieting down long enough for him to sneak a word in edgewise.

Magdalena led Asbjorn over as she squeezed through the small openings between the villagers. His shielding arms kept the rabble at bay and from squishing in on top of her. She continued calling out for her father as they pressed on, but the jarl was unable to hear her voice until they were practically right next to him.

"Magdalena," he said. A look of relief came across his face. "I was worried when I couldn't find you. Thank the gods you're safe."

"We were out at Asbjorn's when we heard the horn blow out," she replied. She was just now able to regain her breath. "What's happening? Is it something bad?"

"We're not sure quite yet," Manus answered. "The watchmen saw the smoke rising not too long ago. They sounded the alarm to bring everyone in when they did. I've been trying to explain it to everybody, but no one will let me get a damn word in. If they'd all just hold their tongues for a moment, I'm sure I could sort things out."

"Everybody quiet!" Asbjorn's thunderous voice suddenly boomed out. The men and women that gathered around instantly fell silent. The big Northman looked to the jarl once they had all simmered down. He motioned toward the assembled villagers and for the other to proceed.

"Thank you, Asbjorn," Manus said. He and Magdalena both removed their hands from their ears. "I think I can take it from here." He handed the young lady off to the large youth, bringing himself up tall and straight to address the crowd.

"Now listen to me everyone," the jarl began. He drew their nervous attention to himself. "I have heard your questions and understand your fears, but as of the moment we do not yet know what might be transpiring in Westboar. I know that you are all very anxious, but I assure you there is nothing pressing for any of you to panic about. The watch saw the pillars of smoke rising this morning and sounded the horn as a precautionary measure only. Our present concern lies solely with our neighbors to the south. We may not know what has happened, but we can be certain that if it were reversed, they would be the first to send aid our way, the same as they always have.

"So," he said, "what I am asking for is a group of able-bodied men to make the journey out to our neighbors. To check to see if our fellows there should be in need of our assistance. I realize that it is quite the distance to travel on short notice but who will step forward to help when we need it most?"

There was a long pause after the jarl had finished his oratory. Many of the villagers cast a hesitant glance back in the direction of the thick black that drifted into the sky. The men of Brekka were by no means cowards but rising smoke in these lands often meant trouble. The comings and goings of bandits and raiders was not uncommon to hear of. The brigands were known to sometimes set fires to small settlements only to draw in a bigger quarry. It seemed that not a one would step forward to take up the endeavor. The torrent of voices that had come only moments ago was now reduced to a few whispers. But just when all seemed lost, the deep shout boomed out again, breaking the uneasy silence.

"I shall go," answered Asbjorn. Magdalena looked up at him as a hint of unease came to her eyes.

"I shall go as well," came another shout.

"And I, too," sounded one more, until no less than half a dozen men had stepped forward to volunteer.

"Good, then," said the jarl, nodding in approval. "Know that we are all indebted to you. Gather whatever things you might need and meet back here within the hour. It may be serious issues that our friends are facing. Haste is of the utmost importance and we need to be quick."

"I have to go now, Magdalena," Asbjorn said. He held the girl's hand in his as he looked at her. "Get back home with your father and stay safe, and watch out for your mother."

"I will," she replied, "but just be careful. I have a bad feeling about all of this. I don't want to lose you, especially now."

"And you won't if I can help it," he said, bending down to kiss her before departing. "At least not anytime soon. Now get home and I'll be back in no time. That's a promise."

Asbjorn and the other five who volunteered moved swiftly as they headed to collect their things. The large Northman ran like the wind to get back to his home outside the village. He took a shortcut through the forest to avoid the curving path that was his usual route, instead taking an overgrown foot trail that perhaps all but himself had forgotten about. It was not the easiest course, but it was by far the most direct, saving him a precious few moments he could not afford to lose.

He thought of the others who had stepped up to go along as he went. All of them were life-long residents of Brekka and he'd known them for most of his days. He could get along fairly well with the older men who'd spoken out. They'd been acquainted with his father and were willing to give him the benefit of the doubt despite his past. But one of the younger men was Dorn and it could be certain that neither he nor Asbjorn considered the other to be anywhere near a friend.

The big Northerner and Dorn were of roughly the same age. They'd been at odds with one another since both could even remember. Dorn had always been a spiteful and cutting young man, knowing full well the amount of wealth and influence his family possessed and never shy about flaunting it. The spoiled youth deeply resented Asbjorn, not only for the other's physical prowess but also for the relationship the big man enjoyed with Magdalena. It had all finally culminated between the two one day last year. Dorn ran his mouth and Asbjorn threw such a beating on him that it had taken ten others to pry the enraged Northerner off.

Asbjorn was spared from a harsh punishment only by the intervention of the jarl. Manus spoke up for him in front of the council as he'd done so many times before. It had not been the first incident between the rival pair, but the jarl made it clear that it would certainly be the last, stating that he would no longer intervene on the other's behalf. But that had been months ago and was well behind him as far as Asbjorn was concerned. He instead looked to the situation at hand and tried to put what had happened in the past out of his mind.

Asbjorn had managed to lessen a good chunk off his trip home by taking the forgotten path. He was hardly winded after his brisk run through the woods. Without losing a moment, he belted his large hunting knife around his waist, throwing on a light fur to help keep away the forest chill. Before heading out, he slung a quiver of arrows over his back and grabbed up his new bow. He checked to see that the string was in good shape and pulled tight.

Reflecting on it, he wasn't exactly sure why he'd come forward when the jarl had asked for men to make the journey to Westboar. He'd said the words before he could think about it too much or stop himself. While he'd always felt like an outsider here, Brekka and its neighbors were still his fellow Northlanders in need. As he made his way back toward the village, he could hear his father's voice speaking in his head, remembering how the man would always say that those that could help always should. Even now, he wanted to make his father proud. He knew that if the man were still alive, he would be doing the same thing, putting himself in harm's way for the welfare of another.

The others were already waiting for him by the time Asbjorn returned. None had nearly as far to travel as he did. As he came to join them, he saw Manus discussing something with one of the more seasoned men near the well at the center of town. Both had a look of concern on their faces.

"Alright, everyone," the jarl called out, seeing that Asbjorn had made it back. He and the other man came over. "After speaking with Gurson here, we both believe that it's best to proceed with caution. If you see that you can help when you arrive, then by all means do so. But if it turns out to be something more serious, I want you to return here immediately so that we can better organize assistance. I want all of you to be safe and smart," he said, "and whatever you do, do not put yourselves at any unnecessary risk.

"Gurson," Manus stated. He motioned to the older man. "I give them to you."

"We'll be cutting through the old trails and forest paths to reach Westboar," said Gurson. He was a thick, graying fellow who was one of the most experienced hunters in the village. "Taking the main roads and skirting the trees would take far too long and we don't know how urgent their need is. I know that the old footpaths can be treacherous at best, but if we stay alert and look out for each other we should be just fine."

"You don't have to worry about us, old man," chimed Dorn. He smirked at Asbjorn from where he stood with two of his friends. "Just make sure the ox there can keep up. I'm not about to slow down if he goes and turns a leg."

Always with spite in his voice, it was a rare thing for Dorn to pass up on an opportunity to take a shot at Asbjorn. Normally, the big Northerner would have found it within himself to try and ignore the slight. But something just hit him wrong this time. It was a concerning situation and no time for insults. He decided that he preferred not to take it.

"Watch your mouth, ass," Asbjorn snapped back. "Or I'll put you and your girls through a door again."

"You were lucky that day and you know it," Dorn spat in return. His face went red. "I'd like to see you try it when we're ready for you!"

"I'm game any time you are, pig," replied Asbjorn. "Just come at me and find out!"

"Both of you quiet!" interjected the Jarl. He harshly scolded the bickering youths. "This is more important than your petty grudges right now. If the two of you can't put it aside, then stay here. The rest would be better off without having to babysit a pair of squabbling children. Now what's it going to be, boys? Can you shut up for a few hours, or am I going to have to send the two of you home?"

Dorn answered after a short moment. "My apologies, jarl." A scowl lingered on his face. "I'm fine."

"Asbjorn?" asked Jarl Manus, glancing towards the other. He received a begrudging nod in return. He eyed the pair one last time to make sure everything was clear. They did not look up to meet his gaze.

"Good," he added in a sharp tone, seeing that he'd gotten his point across. "Gurson," he said, "please continue."

"I want you all to watch out for one another out there," Gurson went on. He cleared his throat and wagged a finger at the group. "And that goes for each and every one of you. There's no place for personal arguments or petty quarrels here. If I hear so much as a peep of a fight, I won't hesitate to crack your skulls myself and don't think I don't mean it.

"Now, we're wasting valuable daylight," he said, "and we have a long way to go if we're going to make Westboar by this afternoon. Remember to stay in eyesight of each other and call out if you need any help. Now let's move."

The six men headed out to leave the village behind. They fell in line behind Gurson as he led the way. As they departed, a pair of worried blue eyes was locked on the form of Asbjorn. Magdalena looked on from where she stood in the doorway of her father's home. A lump rose in her throat and a knot twisted in the pit of her stomach. She could not explain her troublesome feeling, but it made her want to rush after them before they could make it too far, begging for them to stay. She had just made her desires known after so many years of keeping them to herself. The thought of possibly losing Asbjorn now was just too much for the young lady to bear. A growing dread began to slowly build up inside of her, like a creeping shadow that stretches over a calm countryside. As she closed the door, she turned and leaned heavily against the cedar, unable to shake the notion that something terrible was coming.

IV

The men of Brekka raced through the thick trees of the Northern Forest. All of them kept stride as they ducked under branches and leapt over fallen logs. It would normally be more than a day's journey between their village and the distant Westboar but by skipping the main roads and cutting through the heart of the woodlands they were making the trek in half the time.

Gurson pushed the group along at a moderate pace, making sure that all were still within view of one another and avoided any foolish injuries. Asbjorn had to be told to slow down several times as they rushed through the dense underbrush. He was more than capable of leaving the rest far behind him if he'd wished to. Dorn snickered to himself each time the other was scolded but deep down he could not deny the envy he carried for what the big man was capable of. To his credit, Asbjorn did not let the shouts or the spiteful Dorn get to him. He forced himself to hold up and pull back for the sake of the others. He was secure in the fact that he could leave them all looking at his backside if he'd wanted, running circles around them as they struggled to match him.

As they drew closer to Westboar, they could still see the pillars of smoke from time to time. The twisting black reminded them of what might be waiting each time they glimpsed it. Gurson slowed them down to a near crawl about half a mile out, preferring the careful approach as they neared the outskirts. As they reached the edge of the woods, the older man brought up his hand to bring the group to a sudden halt. He stared out through the brush and into the clearing beyond.

"What is it, do you see something?" asked Dorn. He slunk up to crouch next to Gurson. Asbjorn followed on his heels. The older man brought a quieting finger up to his lips. He still scanned the open ground that stretched out before them and looked to the trees.

"There's no sound," said Asbjorn, following the other's gaze. "It's too quiet out here, especially for this time of day. There should be birds or even the odd animal or two but there's nothing."

"Right," Gurson replied, shaking his head. "In all my years I've never heard the forest this dead. There's not a thing stirring out here, not even up towards Westboar. This isn't right," he said. "Not right at all."

Gurson motioned all of them to fall in behind him again. The six men of Brekka anxiously crept from the cover of the wooded canopy and out to the clear. They moved inch by inch as they made their way towards the drifting spirals that still curled into the sky. They were wary of even the subtlest of noises or signs of movement but still heard and saw nothing.

As they came to a slight ridge that overlooked the village, their nerves suddenly peaked. The hairs on their arms and the back of their necks stood tall. They could feel it prickle through them long before they saw it, at last discovering why the air was so quiet and the land so lifeless. An icy shudder ran up each of their spines as they reached the top of the crest. They stared down at what none of them wished to find.

What spread out beneath them lay in smoldering ruins. The structures that were once the homes and farmhouses were now nothing more than piles of charred wood and ash. As far as they could see, it looked like a desolate wasteland. The six men proceeded carefully into what was once the home of their neighboring brethren as they took in the destruction.

The town that had stood here just the day before was completely razed to the ground. The thick smoke burned their nostrils and stung their eyes as they reached the outer edge. They wandered through the remnants of the once lively

Westboar. Not even old Gurson knew what to think or say as he took in the carnage. The ground was painted a dark red beneath their feet. The crimson soaked into the earth to become a churned mess of scarlet. They were all on anxious guard in case whatever had done this may still be lingering but none saw anything that might be prowling in the decimated remnants. Then an overpowering smell hit their noses. The stench of blackened meat that had been left too long on the fire wafted on the winds. The men gathered to where the horrific odor led them, coming upon what was left of Westboar's large feasting hall. The six of them stopped in mid step as they drew ever closer. None wanted to believe what their eyes fell upon.

The remains of the people of Westboar were stacked in a towering heap before the smoldering structure. Their seared corpses were tangled together in a mound of burnt death and indistinguishable bodies. Men, women, and their children alike had all been thrown in a mass here and inside the hall. Not a single soul was seemingly spared the wrath of whatever nightmare had descended. The men from Brekka loitered in front of the pile without knowing the words to say. None had ever encountered anything like this before, and never wanted to again. At last, Gurson spoke up, breaking the silence that pressed on top of them with a start.

"Spread out and search for anyone that may still be alive," he said. He almost whispered the words. "And try to keep your senses about you. Who or whatever did this might still be nearby."

The men drifted apart to comb through the rubble and slaughter. They searched through the ruins for what felt like hours, coming across nothing more than a lone mule with an arrow protruding from its haunches. The bodies that had not been dragged and stacked in the middle of town still lay where they had fallen. Most were buried beneath the remains of their scorched homes to cling to one another even in death. Save for the injured mule, the purge of Westboar had been complete down to the last inhabitant. Not even the stray dogs had escaped the massacre that had been brought. Asbjorn gazed over the desolate village as he roamed through the lanes. He wondered what could have been capable of doing such a thing and why. Then the cry of one of the others sounded out. The Northman's head snapped in the direction of the shout.

"Gurson," it rang through town. "Over here. I have something!"

All five of the remaining men of Brekka came running at the other's call. They found him kneeling in the roadway that led from Westboar. His hand lightly grazed over the ground. His eyes followed the trampled dirt into the distance.

"What is it?" asked Gurson, coming to a swift stop. "What have you found?"

"Tracks," the other answered. "Hoof and boot prints. Lots of them, too."

"How many?" Gurson replied.

"I can't tell," the other said. "They're all muddled together with those of the villagers. There's a hell of a good amount, though. Far more than the people who lived here."

"Where do they lead?" Gurson asked.

"Some lead back out towards the countryside," the other answered. "Probably chasing down anyone who tried to flee to the woods for safety. But most of them lead along the road to the northeast. Towards home."

"Can you tell how long ago they left?" Asbjorn suddenly interjected. "How far ahead are they?"

"Shortly after first light I'd say," the man replied. "They've got one hell of a jump on us, that's for sure."

Asbjorn turned to Gurson. "We have to move," he said. "On foot, it takes nearly a full day to travel between the villages. If they're on horseback or moving fast, it's even less. We have to go!"

"Try to stay calm, Asbjorn," Gurson implored. "We have no idea who this even is yet, let alone what they can do. We can't just go rushing off to battle like a bunch of halfcocked fools. Actions like that could get us all killed."

"I actually agree with him this time," interrupted Dorn. "Every minute we spend here is a minute we could be moving to help our friends and families back home. They may not have time to wait for us to come up with a plan. We need to get moving."

"All of you feel the same?" Gurson asked. He looked to the others around him.

The rest of the men answered with a determined expression and a nod of the head. The older fellow was expecting nothing less from any of them. He knew that it would be nearly impossible to rein in even a single one. No matter what he said or did he would not be able to stop them from running off to protect their homes. He still wished they had something more to go on, however, preferring to have a better idea about who or what his enemy was before racing off to meet steel with steel.

"Alright then," he said in a grim resolve. He dropped everything except for his short bow and the sword at his waist. "We travel light. Leave whatever you don't need here and try to keep up. Odds are some of us won't be coming back to collect our things."

With those words, the six men of Brekka rid themselves of everything that could not be used to defend kith and kin. They uttered silent prayers to whatever gods or spirits they believed in as they shed any excess burden. They tightened sword belts and secured quivers, plucking bowstrings to make sure their weapons were pulled taut. One by one they all took off into the forest like a shot, leaving the smoking remains of Westboar behind. Not a single man was still in view as the last pack hit the ground. They rushed to meet whatever awaited them head on.

V

As quickly as they'd made their way towards Westboar they raced for home even faster. The previous caution they'd shown in the forest was the farthest thing from their minds. The men hastily bounded over fallen debris as they weaved between the trees, tearing through the underbrush that littered their way. Asbjorn moved through the woods with all the grace of a wild animal. His muscled legs took him well out in front of the others. There were only a precious few in the village that the big Northerner cared deeply for. Those that he did hold close he was willing to fight like a savage beast to protect. The images of the devastation he'd just left behind burned at the front of his mind. The possibility of a similar fate befalling his home fueled him onward as he forced himself to go faster. His thoughts rested on the one that mattered to him most, Magdalena, and he would sooner push himself to death than let any harm come to her.

He did not know how long it had taken him to cover the miles between Westboar and Brekka, only that it seemed like he could not make the journey fast enough. The sun had already dipped well below the horizon by the time he neared the outskirts of home. The fleeting light dwindled in the sky as he began to pass a collection of familiar landmarks. Through the small stream and over the old stone wall that marked the southernmost farms he went. Asbjorn knew that he was at last nearing his destination. That's when he saw the flickering orange reflecting off the clouds above. The clash of battle suddenly rang in his ears as the forest began to thin.

"No," he whispered as he commanded his legs to go faster. "Gods, no!"

Asbjorn tore from the tree line to see that nearly everything was set aflame. The shapes of foot soldiers and mounted men in black armor swarmed through the streets to put down anything that moved. He did not know where the other five might be that he'd accompanied to Westboar, nor did he particularly care at the moment. All that Asbjorn could focus on were the dark forms that had come to attack his home. His anger was kindled to life much like the flames that now engulfed the village. It was unwise and foolish, but he could not stop himself from charging straight in. He streaked into the village proper as he readied his bow and took aim, sending the arrow at the closest thing he saw with deadly effect.

The first of the raiders in Asbjorn's path went down before the man ever knew what hit him. A sharp shaft skewered clean through the meat of his neck to drop him instantly. Before he could hit the ground, two of his companions followed shortly behind him. Both were dropped by flying arrows before they could make it more than a few steps.

With three dispatched, Asbjorn threw his bow aside and snatched up the sword from one of his fallen foes. He slammed hard into yet one more of the murderous marauders that was coming at him. He drove the point of the steel deep into the other man's abdomen, puncturing armor and ripping flesh as he picked the screaming wretch up and off his feet. He threw the flailing man aside and tore the blade free as he surged ahead. He did not break stride as the body clattered to the ground to be left laying behind him. Everywhere he looked he saw his fellow villagers being put to death by the ruthless killers in black. Their pleas for mercy fell upon deaf ears as the blades rose and fell without pause. But he ignored everything that was happening around him. He raced toward the center of town as the cries of the dying echoed in his ears. The welfare of but one person was his only concern now, and he would carve through hell itself if he must to reach her.

Asbjorn managed to fell yet two more of the invaders as he moved swiftly along. The amount of fight they put up was hardly enough to slow him down. He squeezed through the tight spaces between the trade shops that ringed the village square, avoiding the thickest clusters of fighting by veering from the choked lanes. The flames that crawled over the walls licked at his flesh. The heat singed the tips of his sandy hair and stubbly beard. As Asbjorn slid out into the open, he finally laid eyes on Magdalena's home. Despair came to fill his heart as soon as he took in the dreadful sight.

The longhouse of her father's was already covered in flame. The fire quickly consumed the whole of the dried timbers and roof thatching. In front of the place stood a circle of heavily armored warriors next to black steeds, along with who appeared to be Jarl Manus desperately struggling against the most elaborately adorned of them. Manus was doing his best to bring down his steel-clad foe, but the vast superiority of the dark marauder's skill was more than apparent. He almost toyed with the attacks of the lunging jarl. He stayed just outside the reach of Manus's arcing swings. Then the jarl came in with everything he had. He put all his strength behind the sword he swung overhead. But the dark clad warrior's serrated blade guided the other's weapon aside. Manus overextended himself with his final stroke to leave his guard woefully open. His opponent's steel wasted little time in finding its mark. The cold tip plunged through the jarl's chest to protrude from his back. The jagged teeth tore muscle and bone in a spray of scarlet mist. The jarl went lifeless as he dropped his sword and slumped to the ground.

Asbjorn heard a horrified scream ring out from somewhere within the house as Manus went down. He recognized all too well the sound of Magdalena's distraught cry. Without giving pause, he was off and moving again, plowing into the circle of armored men that surrounded the front of the home. They stepped aside just as he came in with several wild swings at the one who'd felled Manus. The warrior avoided the

Northman's blows as if they were nothing more than those of an angry child. He almost seemed insulted by the clumsy attacks, giving pause to address the incensed Northerner that'd rushed him.

"You have a lot of nerve coming at me like that, boy," reverberated a deep voice from within the skull faced helm. "What makes you think I'd soil myself by engaging an impetuous youth like you? I only fight men not children."

"I'll kill you for what you've done here today!" Asbjorn snarled. His teeth were bared like a wild beast. "All of you!"

"How dare you assault General Zantz in such a manner, you savage," spouted Captain Orrm. He stepped up to draw his own sword. "Please, my lord," he asked, "allow me to dispatch this fool for you."

"Then you fall first, you bastard," Asbjorn replied. "Come at me!"

"Enough," commanded Zantz, waving Orrm off. "Return to your place."

At the general's order, the captain re-sheathed his blade and backed away. His eyes stared a hole through Asbjorn from behind his deathly face guard. Zantz removed his own helm so that he could speak to the young man face to face. His grizzled features were set in an expression of cold disdain. The scars on his flesh spoke volumes of his many years on the field. His experience at warfare utterly dwarfed that of any who were nearby.

"You show much bravery, boy," the general said, "more so than the rest of the pathetic rabble we've put down since arriving here. I suppose I should admire that in you in some small way, standing up to us where others have turned and fled. But you still have to be dealt with and I've dirtied my hands enough with your like. I have something special in mind for you," Zantz went on with a smirk. "Something that might provide a bit of entertainment for my men.

"Boslog," he motioned with a flick of his wrist, "come."

A mountain of a man stepped from the circle at the general's beckoning. The others cleared well out of his way as he strode to Zantz's side. He was a giant when compared to the rest of the raiders, standing easily a head taller than even Asbjorn. His black armor was hardly able to contain his muscled frame. It almost burst at the seams if not for the buckles and clasps that held it together. The sinews in his arms tightened and tensed in anticipation for what was to come. The sweat glistening on his skin from the warmth of the fires.

"Are you bored, Boslog?" asked Zantz. The towering man nodded his head and almost growled in response. "I haven't been very fair to you today, have I?" the general continued. "I've kept you on the leash for far too long. I promised you blood but so far have given you none, but I do believe it's time to let you have your fun. Let the fury that lives in you consume this one, Boslog. Do as you like with him. He's yours."

At the general's words, the giant lumbered toward Asbjorn and pulled off his own helm. An almost blank affect was splayed across his marred features as the head piece clanked to the ground. Around his shoulders, hung a sword no less than six feet in length. He slid the blade from the sheath to toss the scabbard aside. One of his cohorts quickly scurried over to snatch it up, nearly falling over himself as he hastily cleared out. As soon the weapon was in his hands Boslog's expression and demeanor shifted. His knuckles cracked tight around the handle. His narrow eyes widened as his pupils constricted. The veins in his neck and arms bulged until they looked as if they would burst.

Asbjorn had heard about men like this from some of the older huntsmen who lived in his village, warriors that were so blood mad they would go completely berserk when confronted with the promise of battle. The big Northman had been in that state for himself on several occasions. He was aware of just how deadly his current opponent could be. As Asbjorn steeled himself to face the giant, he heard Magdalena call out his name from the burning house. He shot a quick glance in the direction of her cry and then went back to Boslog. And then the giant man charged in. He was salivating for a fight, and he was ready to have his fill of it now.

Asbjorn hardly had time to raise his sword before the other was on him. Boslog moved like lightning for a man of his size who was also weighed down in full armor. The Northerner's blade was almost torn from his grasp by the fury of his enemy's blow. His numbed hands were barely able to hang on. Boslog's strength felt immeasurable as he pressed in with the assault. He was a man, or perhaps beast, of pure physical power that was driven by rage. Asbjorn did his best to keep up with the berserk warrior. He fell back and attempted to stay just out of harm's reach. But his body was already fatigued from the long run to and then from Westboar. The difficulty of also dealing with such a formidable foe was quickly taking its toll.

Boslog was unrelenting when he saw Asbjorn reeling. The brute's greatsword came to within just inches of the winded Northman. The youth knew that he had to do something for himself or he would soon be all but finished. He took a reckless risk after a wide swing and dove straight in. He hoped to run the other through before the animal had a chance to regain his ground, but Boslog recovered much swifter than Asbjorn would have ever thought. The berserker brought his blade back and around to lock the two weapons together at the crossguards. He stopped the Northerner's would be charge before it ever got going. For a long moment, they stood like that and just glared at one another. Asbjorn's arms shook as Boslog foamed at the mouth. The young Northerner knew that if the battle crazed invader could get his sword free it would be over. He did the only thing he could think of in that harrowing instant.

In desperation, Asbjorn twisted his body with all the strength he had in him. The torque behind the movement wrenched the weapons free to send them both flying through the air. The act had cost Asbjorn and his opponent each of their blades, but unfortunately, the other seemed to not care in the slightest.

Boslog seized the Northerner by the throat. He squeezed tight as he smashed a balled-up fist hard across the other's jaw. A stunned Asbjorn hardly managed to snatch the hunting knife from his belt. He slipped the point between a gap in Boslog's breastplate and into the brute's side. The blood flowed freely from the wound and through the spaces in the black steel, running down the handle as the desperate Northerner twisted it in. But the vicious warrior did not even begin to register the pain. He instead seemed to let out a groan of enjoyment rather than one of discomfort. The monster responded by tightening his hold and ramming his forehead into Asbjorn's face over and over again. The dangling Northman at last went limp in the other's choking grasp.

The world spun around a groggy Asbjorn for a brief instant. He was no longer aware of where he was or what was happening. Through the spiraling haze, he thought he saw a familiar silhouette run from the door of the burning house, only for two large shadows to close in over it and throw it to the ground. It crawled toward him before it was violently yanked back up. It was dragged back to the home to once more be flung into the blistering flames. Then he felt a hard jerk as he was hoisted high into the air. Everything seemed to drift by in slow motion as he almost floated along.

"Magdalena," Asbjorn sputtered in a daze. He forced the word through the agony as his hand reached towards the house. Then there was nothing at all beneath him as his body suddenly went weightless. He was up and then plummeted into blackness as all went dark.

VI

The sun slowly rose as the smoke snaked its way into the heavens. the fires burned spotty in what remained of the now razed Brekka. The carrion birds were already starting to gather this early in the morning. They descended from the sky to peck at the fresh corpses that lay scattered over the earth. The wild dogs and roaming wolves were not far behind, drawn along with the other woodland scavengers by the stench of death to fight over fresh meat. It was a veritable feast for the more opportunistic predators of the vast Northlands, one they thought they could partake of without the threat of disruption, or so they hoped.

A single hand trembled as it rose from the mouth of the well at the center of town. The bloodied and scraped fingers pawed around the rim to try and find a handhold. At last, it managed to close over the edge. Another came from the depths to secure its own grip. With more effort than most could muster, Asbjorn hauled himself from the dank hole. He spilled into the light to lie flat on his back. His face was a swollen mess from the beating he'd taken at the hands of the berserk giant. His body was a throttled wreck of bruises and scrapes. It had taken every bit of him to claw his way from the waters at the bottom of the pit. He'd lost several of his fingernails to the rough stones on his way up. He was exhausted to the point of near death by the time he reached fresh air, but as injured as was, he still lived.

Asbjorn rest in the warming sun for a long while as he allowed himself to catch his breath. The feeling slowly returned to his numbed limbs. The rays of light shown down on his near broken form. A few of the braver creatures that lingered about attempted to creep his way. They scattered once he twitched and they heard him groaning, giving him a wide berth as they returned to an easier meal. After more than several moments, he finally found the reserves to bring himself up on rickety legs. He staggered through what little remained of his home.

The destruction of his village at the hands of the black armored raiders had been complete. Not a thing was left intact or allowed to remain standing. Asbjorn wandered through the bloodshed that was strewn as far as he could see. He passed by the bodies of his fellow villagers in a disoriented haze. The feasting birds flapped and took to the air as he drew nearer to the spots where they fed. They sounded protesting calls in response to having been so rudely interrupted. He saw what was left of old Gurson and several of the others that he'd accompanied out to Westboar. Their remains were stuck with arrows as they had seemingly tried to rush into town just as he did. He even noticed the corpse of Dorn amongst them, seeing that the unfortunate young man had made it only a slight bit further than the others. But still, the woodsman's son had been run through at the belly, split up the middle to let his insides spill out. In a way, Asbjorn envied them. They'd not had to see what was now left of their loved ones. He too would have preferred a warrior's death over this but for some reason he'd been fated to survive.

As Asbjorn shuffled along, he finally came to the charred rubble of what had once been the house of the jarl. The man was still lying face down where he'd been slaughtered the night before. He regarded the fallen Manus with a sorrowful expression. He mourned the other that had looked after him for so many years since his father died. And then he gazed over to where the house had once stood. Tears welled up to fill his chestnut eyes and rolled down his cheeks.

"Magdalena," he exhaled in a shaky breath. He wiped away the droplets from his battered face. He knew that she had left him now, lost to the searing flames and buried beneath the blackened ruins. The one that he had held the dearest and cared for the most was gone. A love that he had never fully realized until a short time ago was snuffed out. His heart broke with an emptiness that he never thought capable of feeling. Not even when his father had been taken from him had he endured such a thing. He'd never before experienced a despair like what came to him now. The world suddenly held no meaning for him since everything had been ripped away. And then something else began to stir deep within the recesses of his soul, something that he had not felt in quite some time, and it was not kind.

Asbjorn turned on the spot without so much as a glance back. He shut out the pain and anguish as he marched purposefully from the village and through the outskirts of the Northern Forest. It was like something terrible had been roused inside of him. It was a thing that had not been there since he felled the great bear. Part of Asbjorn hated that it was woken again. It was a raging turmoil boiling away that yearned to be vented. But another part welcomed its return wholeheartedly, embracing its furious coming like a long-lost friend.

Quickly, the big Northman reached his secluded home just outside the village. The wild dogs and hungry wolves proved wise not to give chase as he went. His small longhouse had been thoroughly ransacked and destroyed just as the others were, but fortunately, it was not burned to the ground. Asbjorn wasted no time in going for exactly what he wanted. He kicked the debris across the floor as he made his way inside. He found the well-hidden trapdoor at the far rear of the house. He flung the tipped table that impeded his way aside and flipped the latch that opened it. Thankfully, they had remained undiscovered by the marauding invaders, left just as they'd been placed here nearly a year ago, untouched and waiting for him.

The big man pulled forth what he had not cast his eyes on since last winter. His father's battle axe was wrapped in the cloak that he had made from the pelt of the great bear. Asbjorn draped the ashen fur around himself. The head rested on his shoulder as the polished ambers set in its eyes glittered in the interior. Already, he could feel his strength somehow returning to him, as if the beast's fierce spirit mingled with his own. It seemed to fortify his being and mend what had been broken. His lingering weariness slowly began to drain away.

With the darkened pelt around him, Asbjorn next took hold of the hefty blade. He stared into the steel for a brief moment. The etched head was still stained crimson from the blood of the infernal beast. A single drop of scarlet trickled from his thumb as he ran it down the edge. The weight of the weapon felt like nothing at all in his grasp. It was almost as if it were pleased to be back in his hands after so long. He tucked a sharp knife into his belt and walked from the house. He took nothing else with him but the crimson blade and a burning anger, never expecting to return.

At this point, the big Northerner was no stranger to seeking vengeance. He'd spent most of his youth heeding its damnable call, but never had it felt like this. The thing that had been ignited was something else entirely. It had awakened his darkest wrath that he preferred to keep hidden and buried. He feared what he might be capable of should he listen to it, but no more. It had been almost a year since the urge had left him, but the time had finally come for Asbjorn to accept it again. Today, after so long, he would hunt once more, and death be to any who stood between him and his prey.

VII

As the reds dipped in the west the men in black steel leisurely set about making camp. A chill wind gusted over the grassy flatlands that spread out around them. They gathered around their fires having their fill of pillaged food and drink. The sounds of their cruel jests carried over the plains and into the forest beyond. The invading men laughed about the lives of the many Northerners they'd snuffed out earlier today. They made light of the dead as if the fallen were nothing more than sheep that had been put to the butcher's block. Each bragged about how many he'd put down at the point of his blade, recounting the pitiful way in which some had begged for their lives.

It had been like this with all the scattered villages they had passed through since entering the far north. They'd swept in to bring terror and death with them while leaving only the corpses to tell of their passing. They had been determined to leave not a single soul once they were through, taking a twisted pleasure in wiping the existence of these people from the face of the world. But from the thick tree line, a pair of seething eyes watched as the dwindling light faded. Who they belonged to waited in the shadows for the right time.

It had taken Asbjorn most of the day at a hard run to catch up with the marching column. He'd pushed his body to the limits of his endurance to do so. He'd trailed behind them as they cut a path through the dense woodlands, staying within the cover of the trees as the raiders had moved into the open to lay their encampment. It took every bit of himself not to just rush out and wade headlong into them. The blade he carried almost begged to spill their blood. But he had managed to restrain his growing anger until the curtain of night could fully descend. He'd waited for the invaders to settle in and become comfortable before moving in. He knew that he was vastly outnumbered by the enemy he stalked. He held little hope of being able to take them all. But those that he could get to grips with he would make pay dearly. One of them in particular he was wishing to meet again.

As the sounds of their mocking laughter began to fade, Asbjorn could keep himself in check no longer. He moved from the woods to slink low through the tall grasses that swayed in the breeze. He quietly made his way to where the invading force's large supply wagons sat at the edge of the camp. The company's horses were corralled in a makeshift pen that had been erected nearby. The carts and animals were watched over by only two guards. The men looked to be doing anything but paying attention at their posts. They both slowly meandered to and fro, exchanging an occasional word or two when they happened to cross paths. Asbjorn crouched low for what felt like hours as he watched them amble about. His patience was put to the test as he anxiously waited for them to come together for long enough. His fingers itched and his eyes twitched as he cursed them. He was more than ready to have at things but still managed to hold his urges. At last, they finally came to a stop during a lingering exchange, grumbling to each other about how ready they were for this to be done with so they could return to the warmer climes of the south.

The crouching Northerner moved with all the swiftness of a striking predator. He slipped up behind the two with his knife in hand. One dropped immediately with a gash across his throat. The other felt a strong hand clamp tight over his mouth. He tried to call out the alarm, but it was of no use against the iron-like grip that held him. A sudden pain twisted in his back as he struggled to free himself. He writhed for but a brief instant before the life ceased to kick out of him. His body went limp in Asbjorn's grasp.

Once the two were dispatched, he quickly looked to see if any of the others from camp had noticed. He eased the dead guard to the ground to avoid the clattering of armor. Thankfully, he found that the drunken raiders were still sleeping away the evening's revelry. Some of their snores managed to drift to his ears on the night wind. He wiped the blood from his knife with a scowl on his face as he tucked it back into his belt, continuing toward the waiting wagons.

Asbjorn wasted little time in rifling through the carts once he reached them. He made sure to keep a watchful eye on the few forms he still saw wandering through the encampment. He had to rummage through two before finally coming across what he was looking for, a keg of oil along with a torch and the accompanying tinder box. He busted a hole in the top of the small barrel. He left a steady stream over the tall grasses as he hastily worked his way in a wide arc and up wind. He copiously flung the liquid over the dry vegetation as he went, saturating the brittle leaves that quickly soaked in the moisture. Once the keg was empty, he cleared well out of the way. He opened the tinder to remove the bits of flint and steel. A few struggling sparks later and the torch was lit. Asbjorn reeled back to fling the fiery stick high into the air. The men in camp that still happened to be awake all looked to the sky. A single speck of light rose and seemed to hang at its apex for a brief moment. The tiny flame floated against the nighttime shroud like a flickering star. Then it plummeted back down to earth like a stone. An odd smell came to the men's noses as their eyes followed it downward.

The moment the light hit the ground, the soaked brush burst into a raging inferno. The fires spread out to encircle half the encampment in a wall of blistering heat. In less than a blink, the calm night had been thrown into bedlam as the conflagration roared to life. Cries of panic called out as the armored men rushed to rouse their slumbering compatriots. The strong winds pushed the blaze toward the campsite at an incredible pace. The hungry flames devoured the dry grasses like a ravenous beast along with anything else that lay before them.

A noxious smoke began to roll over the countryside. The heavy shroud blotted out the moon and stars to cast all into a deeper blackness. Eyes burned and lungs choked as the raiders pawed to find a way out of the suffocating veil. Most only managed to become even more lost and confused. Many tripped and fell over one another and their own belongings. Some were taken so much by surprise they never made it from their bedrolls before being hit by the flames. Amidst the chaos, they could all suddenly hear the horses going wild in their makeshift pen. The heat of the fires began to draw painfully close to the creatures to send them into a frenzy. The animals tore from their confining enclosure in a tide of pounding hooves, stampeding through the middle of camp in an attempt to find escape. The frightened beasts trampled over anyone who happened to be in their way. They crushed chests and pulverized bone beneath their churning legs. It was a glorious display of unbridled carnage. The dancing flames and billowing smoke made the Northlands resemble the pits of hell. The distraught raiders scrambled about like so many damned souls that had been cast to the torturous abyss, trying to claw their way from the pain and back into the light. And then, from the blackness, a large shadow moved in, bringing with it another type of death entirely.

Asbjorn stormed through the fires like a raging demon. His whirling axe carved through whoever it could get to. He split skulls and cleaved waving limbs from bodies. He cut the invaders down with a merciless coldness, not caring if they were armed and armored or half-dressed from having just stumbled from their bedding. He showed not a hint of remorse for the lives that came to an end on the edge of his crimson blade. He weaved and darted between the wild horses to sow a terrifying turmoil. The men continued to yell out to one another amid the havoc and obscuring smoke screen. Their shouts were met with only screams as the winds forced the fires further in. An hour ago, the Northern Plains had been a calm, if not breezy, landscape. But now they had spiraled into an infernal slaughter ground, complete with wails of agony and soaked in red.

As the mayhem raged, a circle of sentries in skull-faced helms pulled back the flaps of a large tent. Their commander came forth to witness the scale of the upheaval. General Zantz coldly regarded the disarray in front of him. He scanned over the fiery carnage with a steely eye. He began barking out orders to his men left and right a second later, sending out his personal guard to attempt to rein in the disorder. The horses still ran unchecked through his encampment. The blaze blew in to consume his shaken forces even as they scrambled about. He had not yet noticed Asbjorn thanks to the pandemonium around him but the same could not be said for the furious Northerner, who had already drawn a bead on the general.

Asbjorn stalked towards him once Zantz. He did not even register the death cries of those that he'd already left laying. His mind was completely focused on his moment of sating vengeance. The hate in his eyes made the blistering inferno seem like a candle by comparison. The Northerner's thirsty axe would satisfy itself on the blood of his foe on this night, cutting the general down for the massacre of the men and women of Brekka. But just as it was to come, the time was not quite there. Another stepped up to block the Northman's path before he could have his way.

Asbjorn barely managed to avoid the giant blade that slammed to the ground just in front of him. His instincts took over to spring him aside at the last instant. Before him towered Boslog, the battle mad berserker that he'd been helpless to stop back in Brekka. Asbjorn had hoped to avoid the crazed man and slip in during the confusion, swiftly putting an end to Zantz and as many of his men as possible. But if the butcher wished to place himself between Asbjorn and his quarry then so be it. The Northerner was not about to back down from this fight.

The two men squared off and circled around one another in the raging flames. The heat rose to the point of being nearly unbearable. Sweat poured off both their bodies in streams as the air around them became heavier. Each found it a laborious task just to pull in breath. Asbjorn stared at the monster with a fierce gaze, showing not the slightest bit of fear or intimidation as he faced his enemy. In return, Boslog glared back at the resolute Northerner. His eyes were flushed with a furious scarlet as the savage already began to foam at the mouth.

"You're that pitiful dog I threw down the well, aren't you?" spat an incensed Boslog. "This time I'll put you down for good, pig!"

"You won't find me nearly so easy the second time around," Asbjorn coldly remarked. "Now shut up and die."

With that, the clash between the two warriors was on, a battle between near boundless fury and vengeful rage. Boslog charged at the Northman with reckless abandon. He bellowed a wild cry as the slaver flew from his lips. Bracing himself to receive the assault, Asbjorn planted his feet and dug in his heels. The muscles of his legs tensed like coiled springs. The monster brought his great blade down in an overhead swing that would have been powerful enough to split a boulder in half. The Northerner threw himself aside as the sword's edge found only hard earth to carve into. Asbjorn remembered well the raw strength behind the bestial man's blows, knowing that he could not hope to stand against the giant in a head on clash. He quickly recovered his footing and shot in from the flank, bringing his axe around to cleave it into the other's side. But even he could not expect what happened next. The massive berserker moved with a blinding speed.

Boslog whirled in place before the blow could hit home. He caught Asbjorn's axe in the guard of his gigantic blade. He brought his forehead down as he viciously pressed in, smashing it across the bridge of his foe's nose. Asbjorn staggered backward in a daze as the red flowed from his face. He was barely able to stay aware of what was happening. The blaze spun in the peripherals of his vision as the warm liquid stung his eyes. The outline of the crazed warrior stalked ever closer. But the Northerner was determined to not go down so easily this time. He was set on taking everything the brute could deal out and more. But more is exactly what the monster was making to bring. The fight in him was just as strong as his opponent's.

The berserker came roaring in with a savage bloodlust. His great blade swung in arcs of streaking death. Asbjorn flung himself back as the whipping steel passed just inches from his belly. Narrowly avoiding the powerful strikes that would have cut him in half. He kept his axe poised as he ducked and weaved in between the violent strokes. He was ready for the instant that he saw even the slightest opening through the smear of red in his eyes. But Boslog was like a wall of steel and pumping muscle. His overwhelming aggression made it nearly impossible to close in. He kept forcing Asbjorn back and closer to the edge of the flames. The heat was enough to nearly char the Northerner's flesh, but then it came.

The monster of a man overcommitted himself in a moment of heedlessness. His anger-fueled way of doing battle left him exposed for the briefest of instants. In a flash, Asbjorn slipped beneath the giant's blade. His crimson axe bit deep into Boslog's abdomen. To his frustration, though, the raging behemoth gave no indication of the slightest of discomfort. He seized Asbjorn's weapon with one hand while slamming the pommel of his sword into the big man's back with the other. Asbjorn collapsed to the ground from the force of the impact. He gasped to find the breath that had just been knocked out of him, his spine nearly snapped to bits.

Boslog tore the axe from his side as Asbjorn crawled. He dropped it in the grass as the scarlet streamed down his leg. The monstrous man slowly closed in on his prone foe. The other still sucked in wind as he attempted to put distance between himself and the giant. The Northerner knew that with only a dagger now there was absolutely no way he could fell the pitiless beast. He glanced to where his axe lay and then back to

Boslog. Then he felt something hot burning in his hand. There was a blistering heat between his fingers.

Boslog raised his hefty blade to drop the deathblow. Before it could fall, Asbjorn flung a fistful of smoldering ash into Boslog's face. The glowing embers scorching the wild man's eyes. He stumbled about trying to scratch away the searing coals, frantically swinging his sword at anything nearby.

Asbjorn shot himself up to slam a muscled shoulder into the staggering brute. He bought himself a few precious seconds as he dove for his axe. No sooner had his fingers closed around the handle than the berserker had recovered himself. His face was a blistered mess as his blackened eyes gazed towards his foe. The blood still pumped from the horrid wound that had been left in his side. The red seemed to come in a ceaseless cascade of crimson.

How much more does he have? Asbjorn's mind raced. His knuckles cracked as his grip tightened around his axe. *Anyone else would have surely succumbed by now. He must be more demon than anything else. No,* he thought again. *He's only a man. And I've killed far bigger than any man before.*

As he breathed heavily, Asbjorn steeled himself for Boslog's next move. He blinked away drops of ruby sweat and swallowed down a mouthful of blood. His heart pounded as he waited. The other once again came.

"Die, Northman!" Boslog howled. He raised his weighty blade over his head as he rushed in for the kill.

Asbjorn did not retreat or attempt to sidestep this time. He'd grown tired of giving up so much ground to the barreling berserker. Instead, he launched himself straight at the crazed Boslog. His powerful arms brought his axe swiftly to bear. In a jarring crash, the two warriors collided together amid the inferno. Asbjorn's crimson blade shattered the other's sword in two. Shards of steel glittered like stars for just a moment in the firelight. Boslog stared down at the broken hilt. The fury in him still continued to grow. And then the axe was buried deep at the base of his neck. Asbjorn's blow landed to nearly take the other's head off. In an instant, the Northerner brought the blade down yet again, sinking the steel even further into Boslog's body to paint them both red. But try as Asbjorn might, the massive man still refused to drop. He staggered forward to try and wrap his scarlet spattered hands around his enemy's throat. At last, Asbjorn swept the blade low. Its sharp edge severed one of Boslog's legs out from under him. With a thud, the giant berserker finally fell to the ground. The last signs of life twitched out of him before he lay motionless and dead.

Asbjorn's chest heaved as he pulled in hot air. He stood over his slain enemy in a hard-fought victory. The muscles in his body screamed in revolt at the strain they had just endured. He wanted nothing more than to just rest but he knew that he did not have that luxury. Already, the flames were beginning to die down. The men that had survived the heat moved on the other side of the fire that stood between them and Asbjorn. He saw their shapes closing in as they searched for a way through. Their shouts called out all around for his head.

Then Asbjorn laid his eyes on those of General Zantz. The two men's gazes locking together in the waving heat. They glared at one another for a long moment through the blistering conflagration. Both knew that soon their time would come but not tonight.

As they stared at one another, the general's remaining guard came to his side. The blood soaked Asbjorn gave a final, defiant roar before turning and disappearing into the blackness. The last thing that Zantz saw was what was draped from the big man's shoulder, the blackened head of a great bear. Its amber eyes shined bright in the scorching blaze.

VIII

The last wisps of smoke were being swept away on the gentle winds. The dawning rays struggled to filter through the remnants of last night's fire. The aroma of scorched earth and charred flesh carried for miles. The scent of death once more drew in the wary scavengers of the vast Northlands. Packs of hungry wolves circled around the outskirts of what was left of the camp, while avian opportunists alighted to the ground to peck at what was strewn across the plains. General Zantz walked among what was left of his decimated encampment. He stepped over the trampled and burnt bodies of both man and horse. He came to find the remains of the slain Boslog amongst the slaughter. He nudged the corpse with the toe of his boot as he cast a look of bitter disdain.

"This is quite an exceptional man we face," the general remarked to himself. His eyes rose to survey the blackened landscape. "Or perhaps he's more like a vicious animal. No matter, I suppose," he laughed, "it all has to end the same."

Never in his many years had Zantz seen a force be so devastated by but a single individual. The feeling of being taken so off guard was not something he was at all used to. Whoever this brazen warrior was, Zantz both admired and hated him at the same time. He imagined what he could do were he to have only a handful of such men at his disposal. The general was not one to know fear from many but continuing the pursuit of this Northerner sent a ripple of apprehension up his spine. But there was one that Zantz dreaded even more than any of the wildest men of the north and he was not about to return to that foul demon with nothing but empty hands and hollow excuses. He knew that he had to press on with his task, even if it cost him the lives of every man under his command. As the general's mind drifted in thought, a voice spoke out from behind him. Captain Orrm came to give his report.

"My lord," the captain said, bowing his head. "We have done as you ordered and gathered all the horses we could, sir, along with any of the men that are still fit for travel. All those that were beyond help have been put down as you said. Their equipment is being picked through now. Do we make to return south to secure reinforcements?"

"No," answered Zantz. His voice was laced with a terrifying resolve. "Our path lies ahead not behind."

"But, general," protested Orrm, "we have been scattered like ash on the wind. Our numbers are only a fraction of what they were just a day ago. Our supplies have been dangerously thinned as well, my lord. Shouldn't we-"

"Did you see the man that attacked us last night, Orrm?" Zantz interjected. His grizzled features were set like unmoving granite. His dark gaze pierced through Orrm like streaking arrows.

"No, sir," the other replied meekly. "My attention was focused elsewhere."

"I did," said the general. "He wore the skin of a great bear upon his shoulders. Its eyes shined like burning coals in the raging fire. He's the one we want, Orrm, the one that the demon has sent us so far to find. We'd be fools to tell our master that we returned without him."

"But, general," the captain implored, "we are in no condition to pursue anyone across these barren lands, even if it is only a single man. I beg that you reconsider. We are nearly depleted to nothing."

"Do you dare question me, captain?" General Zantz asked flatly. His fingers played across the pommel of the sword at his side. Orrm glanced down for but an instant. He knew full well the number of insubordinates that had met a swift end on the edge of that blade. He did not agree at all with the decision to press on, but he also valued the wellbeing of his own hide, not wishing to join the ranks of those that had been dispatched.

"No, sir," Orrm quickly responded. He again bowed his head to show subservience. "Forgive me if I implied so. Please, general, what are your orders?"

"Xiphactinas has sent us here to bring this man before him, Orrm," replied General Zantz, "and that's exactly what I intend to do. Saddle as many of the horses as you can, captain, and gather whatever can easily be carried. These lands are a chill hell but we're far from finished yet. The demon was right when he said that I would know who we sought once I saw him. After last night there can be no doubt. Tell the men to prepare themselves. Now, we hunt the Son of the Bear, and the beast's claws are sharp, and its teeth already stained with our blood."

The Bear in Shadow's Grip

I

The night birds flew from the trees as the black clad warriors stalked through the forest. The thrashing of the many wings blotted out the moonlight for the men below. Their dark armor scraped through the branches as they tried to move as quietly as possible. The squealing of twigs running along the steel caused them to curse under their breath. The pair drew their swords as they approached what they had so doggedly sought. The further sound of metal sliding against metal seemed to not disturb their quarry. They took it as a stroke of good fortune as they inched closer. The past weeks had been a nightmare game of cat and mouse for every hour of the day and night. The pale light glinted off their forged blades as they slowly closed in. A slight reflection played across the unmoving form that lie wrapped in the bedroll at their feet. They raised their weapons over their heads as they were careful not to make any more noise. Their eyes narrowed as they looked through the slits of their death's head helms. Without a word between them, their arms fell in unison. They pounded at the sleeping shape with their blunted pommels and stomped with wicked kicks. The warriors expected to bash into the soft flesh of their unmoving foe but instead they were met only by the rigid resistance of a hunk of timber. They flung the blanket aside to see the marred log lying before them. They cursed that they had so easily been duped in, but it was far too late to do anything now.

The large shadow suddenly came from the darkness. The gleaming death that whirled in its hands showed crimson in the moonlight. The heavy axe cut into the men before they could bring their swords up to defend themselves. Their ebon armor protected the invaders no better than if it were made of flimsy paper. The two collapsed in a heap with only a raspy groan. One of them tried to pull himself back to his feet from where he'd gone down. He lifted his sword to make one last attempt to ward off his oncoming attacker, but the weapon was effortlessly kicked aside with a heavy boot. The unforgiving axe then rose and swiftly fell again, snuffing out his life before he could have a chance to beg for mercy. The night once again became still.

Asbjorn yanked his blade free from where it had cleaved into the chest of his slain enemy. He spat on the dark armor as he stood over the fallen dead. His eyes burned with hatred as he stared at their broken bodies. He lifted one of them up to pull off the skulled helm so he could look in the man's face. It had been weeks now since the invaders had swept through Asbjorn's village, reducing his people to nothing but ash and a dying memory. They had arrived without warning to mercilessly slaughter all who had stood in their path. They'd left the slain corpses to rot in the sun and be pecked at by the carrion birds. Not even his precious Magdalena had been spared. The young woman had to watch her father be murdered and Asbjorn nearly beaten to death before she was condemned to her own end. The injured Northerner had pushed himself to near exhaustion climbing from the deep well that his body had been cast in, picking up the marauders' trail to where they made camp after their assault. He did not know who they were or from where they came. Nor did he particularly care about either. All he knew was where they were headed to next, and that the edge of his axe would send them there.

After they'd settled in, he had come storming into their ranks. He'd lit the surrounding brush aflame as he viciously put down any who stood to meet him. He had carved a path of destruction through their numbers in search of their leader.

He'd witnessed the merciless warrior skewer the jarl and burn the slaughtered man's family alive the night before. He was nearly to grips with the dog when he was cut off by Boslog, the blood mad berserker the commander kept as a pet on a short leash. After felling the crazed lunatic, Asbjorn had retreated to the vast countryside. Only his crimson axe and the ashen pelt of the great bear were with him. The long chase had been on ever since.

The warriors in black had pursued him relentlessly over the lengthy days that followed. He had managed to evade them at every turn so far to steadily pick them off a few at a time. He had dwindled their force to a fraction of what it had been upon first arriving, using his familiarity with the landscape to his full advantage, not to mention he was far more skilled than most of them. But they were once again closing in on him. The sounds of their horses and harsh shouts echoed through the darkened woods, heralding their approach.

Dammit, Asbjorn thought in frustration. He quickly scavenged what little he could from the two at his feet. *Do I get no more time than this?*

It had been like this ever since he'd charged into their encampment. His supplies were virtually nonexistent and came to him more infrequently. He had to get by on what little he could obtain from those he brought down or managed to procure from the wilds. He quickly cut the belts from these two as he wondered if they'd prove more fruitful than the last. He decided that it would be wiser to search through them when he had put some distance between himself and their incoming comrades. He turned to disappear back into the forest with the hope that at least one of them might be carrying a few scraps of food. If he were lucky, the night and the thick brush would buy him a few precious minutes from the notice of their trackers, but he was not holding his breath as he slunk away. The leafy darkness fell in to cover his exit.

Asbjorn had not been gone long when the lithe horse slipped between the branches. The lean animal gave pause when it came upon the slain men. Its rider quickly looked around to scan the surrounding foliage. He lifted a small horn to his lips once he'd made sure it was clear. A piping blast rang out through the dense forest. It was met a moment later by several other trumpets in return. One by one, the torchlights started to come alive in the dark. All converged towards the initial sound. As the ring of fire steadily tightened, there was a loud snapping of limbs and branches. A heavy steed tore its way through the trees.

General Zantz sat astride his saddle like a colossus of steel. The golden trim of his midnight armor just caught the rays of moonlight. Captain Orrm came into the clearing just behind him, bringing his own large mount to a halt next to that of the general's. From where they'd ripped from the brush, the other men followed the pair. All of them stood tall and unmoving before their imposing commander. Each one had his ears open and his mouth shut. Ready to receive the general's words as they sweated streams.

"What did you find?" the grizzled man asked. His deep voice resonated from his skulled helm. In response, the nervous scout went cold beneath his armor. He prayed the general be satisfied with his answer as he steadied his horse.

"Two of our men, dead, sir," the anxious man replied. He tried to keep his voice from quivering. "It was recently, too. Their blood still flows warm."

"I can see that, you sniveling idiot," the general said. "Have you found which way he went yet?"

"Not yet, sir," the scout answered hesitantly. "We still search for his trail."

"Then why are you all just standing here like a troop of brainless fools!?" exploded Zantz, roaring at his men. "I trust every man here knows of our lord's intolerance for failure. His twisted punishments spare not even one such as I. Find the Northman or I'll have your hides! Now move!"

Without another word, the men scrambled back into the forest. The firelight from their torches quickly faded and blinked out as they returned to the woodlands. The scout turned and galloped off to get ahead of them without adding anything further. Zantz's eyes bore into the back of his head as he went.

"It may be fruitless to continue our searching at night, sir," Captain Orrm suddenly chimed in. "With him knowing the land as he does, we might be better off to wait until daybreak to proceed."

"This man has evaded us for weeks now, Orrm," the general replied. "I will not relent when we are this close upon him."

"But he is far more familiar with this terrain than we are, my lord," protested the captain, "and we have already lost so many as it is. Even with the torches, we are nearly blind to his movements. And there are so few of us remaining to be spread so thin."

"And do you wish to tell our master that we let him slip away?" Zantz asked. The other quickly fell silent. "Xiphactinas wants this man that he calls the Son of the Bear brought before him, Orrm, and I am in no mood to disappoint such a being any time soon.

"We have both seen just how unforgiving the demon can be when he does not get what he wishes," the general went on. "How do you think I came about my position, captain? My predecessor proved to be a less than competent individual, and I do not intend to follow in his footsteps. Perhaps what our remaining men need is an example of better leadership from the front. Why don't you go and oversee their efforts personally. It may serve to inspire them."

"I did not believe that in voicing my concern I was volunteering to take the lead," Orrm shakily replied. He looked towards the imposing man in gold trimmed steel.

"Then you should not have spoken," Zantz said in an unnerving softness. "Remember that I tolerate cowardice even less than our Lord Xiphactinas, and that is very little indeed.

131

Now I suggest that you get your horse moving, captain. The Northerner puts even more distance between us as we speak."

"Yes, sir," Orrm said. He forced down a hard swallow. "As you command, general."

With reluctance, the anxious captain was off. The sound of his racing steed faded through the trees as he rushed to catch up with the men. Once alone, Zantz looked down at the dead warriors that were sprawled before him. His expression twisted to one of disgust behind his skeletal face guard. He had come to the northlands with no less than two full companies of black clad soldiers at his disposal. His warriors swept from village to village to wipe the existence of these people from the world at the bidding of his master. As expected, he had lost a number of his more expendable troops to the blades of the rugged folk of these lands. The sacrifice of a few frontline pawns was nothing new to him. But nothing had prepared him for what would happen after the razing of the last small village. It was as if the bloodshed on that day had awakened the vengeful spirit of the chill north itself.

The savage warrior that draped himself with the pelt of the bear was like no one that Zantz had ever encountered before. The big Northerner was more akin to a cunning beast rather than a human being. The man had the nerve to set fire to the general's own campsite, wading in through the flames to hack a score of Zantz's men to ribbons in the ensuing chaos. He'd bellowed a defiant cry at the general before slipping back into the shadows. The elusive foe now led the black warriors through the dense woodlands to bring them down seemingly at will. The three hundred soldiers that Zantz had started this campaign with were now reduced to a fraction of their former number. The ones that did remain were nearly driven to death by exhaustion and the mounting lack of provisions. But his scouts had informed him that the cover of the thick forest was fast running out. The hunters and their prey were drawing closer and closer to unobstructed flatlands every day. And once away from the concealing trees, this savage was as good as theirs. He would be no match for them over the clear expanse of unprotected ground.

"The Son of the Bear," Zantz whispered to himself. The general, at last, started to understand why the demon Xiphactinas feared this threat that he pursued. If truth be told, Zantz was beginning to fear what the man might be capable of as well. He did not wish to see firsthand the depths of savagery the Northerner might descend to. But the general also knew the terrible horridness that his master could wield, along with the torturous agony that was inflicted upon those that disappointed the demon. Zantz was not about to return to the south at all empty handed. No matter the cost he had to pay to do so.

As the moon began to dip, the general heard another horn blow out in the distance. His heavy boots drove hard into his horse's flanks to urge the animal to move. He galloped off into what remained of the night. The two that lay dead were left to the mercies of the woodland scavengers that were already beginning to gather. Zantz knew this hunt was far from being finished, with plenty of blood left to flow over the Northern Plains by the time it reached its end. Most of it would undoubtedly belonging to his own men, but he was determined to bring in his quarry, nonetheless.

II

Asbjorn's legs throbbed as he darted through the thinning trees. The orange glow of the sun was just showing through the clouds in the east. He gave pause to lean against a tall oak to try and catch his breath. The perspiration ran off his body despite the coolness in the air. If he could, he would have turned and headed back into the dense cover and the safety of the woodlands but even now he could hear the growing voices of the pursuing soldiers echoing behind. The last thing he wanted was to be caught out in the open being as drained as he was. He preferred to remain within the brush to give himself the best chance to fight on his own terms. But the enemy's numbers were quickly pushing him closer to the forest's edge. The constricting net of black armored men tightened to choke any chance he might yet have at victory.

Ahead of him, he could just make out the wide-open countryside. He weaved from trunk to trunk to spy through the vegetation while casting a cautious eye back. The plain's deceptive spaciousness seemed to welcome him with an unobstructed breeze and the promise of the sun on his face, but he knew that the exposed flatlands held a waiting death. They were a clear expanse for as far as he could see, with nothing so much as a clump of shrubs to take cover in should he have to. But either way he chose held its own share of dangers to tackle. At least ahead did not guarantee as much of a fight as behind.

Asbjorn crept from the security of the overgrown brush and out to the open. His eyes scanned from side to side as his hands clenched around the handle of his axe. He felt like a skittish deer making its way into an exposed meadow. The hairs on the back of his neck and arms stood on end. He was nearly clear of the forest when he heard the faintest of snaps come from his left. He dove aside just as an arrow pierced into the ground where he'd been standing. The three armored men came roaring towards him out of the overhanging leaves. A fourth stayed back to nock another shaft from where they'd been waiting in ambush.

Asbjorn was pulling his weary body back up before they could make it halfway to him. He moved to keep the approaching three between himself and the lingering archer that remained in the trees. He charged straight at the first of them that he could get to grips with, ducking under a wild slash to drive in. He picked the poor soul up and off his feet with all the ease of lifting a small child. The muscled Northerner used him to plow through the other two who rushed in behind. The man kicked and flailed helplessly as the pair streaked directly for the lone bowman. The unfortunate soldier was held in place like a thrashing shield. The startled archer managed to get off but a single shot as the wall of black metal and pumping legs barreled towards him. The sharp tip found its way deep into his compatriot's back. Asbjorn launched the man that he carried like an armored projectile. The flapping warrior crashed on top of the stunned bowman with a clattering thud. Before either of them could recover, the big man's crimson axe came slamming down. It split a steel helm and the skull it contained before cleaving through the pinned archer. Their suits of black armor did nothing against the biting blade. The ashen steel was no match for the edge of the vicious weapon.

Two down, two to go, Asbjorn thought. He came around to face the others that were just recovering. *But I know there're more, and I can't afford to be slowed down like this.*

Without allowing the pair to get their wits, Asbjorn pressed in with his assault. He snapped one of the men's heads back with a violent punt that connected just below the chin. In response, the other came at the Northerner with a feeble attempt of an attack. His swiping blade was easily guided aside by the big man's axe. As the blow went wide, Asbjorn came back around to carve into the center of the marauder's breastplate. A spray of red speckled the ground as steel screeched through steel. He kicked the already dead man from his blade to ready himself should the other be closing in but found that there was no one left as he poised himself. One of the black armored invaders lay at Asbjorn's feet nearly cut in half. The other was sprawled flat, his neck broken and his leg slightly twitching. In return, the Northerner's body was wracked with fatigue. His muscles ached and his stamina was nearly gone. He longed for just a fleeting moment's rest to renew himself, but it was simply unwise to drop one's guard when there was still danger lurking about. He may be tired but not foolish.

As his chest heaved, the tree line suddenly erupted in an explosion of broken limbs. The heavily armored rider streaked from the woods and into the coming dawn. The black warrior rammed his charging horse hard into Asbjorn's side. He brought down the blade of his broadsword as he galloped past. Thankfully, Asbjorn just managed to turn aside the blow. The mass of the steed and the strike from above were still enough to knock him to his knees. His eyes followed the rider in steel as the man brought his mount back around. The armored raider came to a stop just long enough to taunt the prone Northerner.

"So, you're the much-feared Son of the Bear," said a snide Captain Orrm. He put on a threatening air of confidence. "Forgive me if I'm less than impressed. The way you've been bringing us down, I was expecting much more. But perhaps it was too much for a savage from the north."

Asbjorn lurched to his feet as Orrm mocked him. He leaned on his propped-up axe as he did so. He did not know what it meant when the warrior in black had called him the Son of the Bear, nor did he truthfully care all that much. All that mattered to Asbjorn was that the man who sat in front of him was not the one who had killed the jarl and condemned

Magdalena to a fiery death. That is who he wanted. Not these pathetic pawns that kept coming at him.

"Spare me the waste of you," Asbjorn replied. He stood as the rising sun glinted off the ambers in his bear's head cloak. "And tell me where your lord is."

"Savages such as you are not worthy to face General Zantz," Captain Orrm responded. He clearly saw the exhaustion in his enemy. "You'll get by with me or you'll have nothing at all."

"Then you'll die before he will," Asbjorn spat. "Now come at me, and let's get this over with."

Asbjorn readied himself as Orrm whispered something within his skull faced helm. The captain spurred his mount in the sides to charge straight at the waiting Northman. He made to slam the armored horse into his opponent yet again, knocking the wind out of him or perhaps breaking a limb or two. But a weary Asbjorn was just able to slide out of the animal's path. The captain came down with his broadsword to once more miss as he tightly circled around. General Zantz had ordered that the fierce Northerner to be captured alive no matter what. The demon Xiphactinas desired to deal with the savage personally. But that had cost the black army far too many of its crack soldiers. The vengeful Asbjorn fought with every bit of the ferocity of the great animal whose head adorned his shoulder. Captain Orrm realized that if he were to attempt to seize such a dangerous enemy that it would more than likely be the end of him. He decided to throw caution to the wind and take the opportunity to put the other down for good. The captain knew that a more than harsh reprisal would most certainly come his way, but how was Orrm to help it if the Son of the Bear refused to be taken alive?

As Orrm continued to rain down blows, the spent Asbjorn was nearly sent reeling. He still refused to give in as he knocked aside the hammering strikes with the head of his axe. If the two were both on foot the harsh struggle may have been going much differently, but the mounted warrior held a considerable advantage at the moment, continuing to crowd in on the back of his steed. Asbjorn was not only getting beaten on by the man in the saddle, but he was also having to contend with being knocked around by the armored mount. The trained beast thrashed with its powerful legs as it rammed with its flanks and haunches. As he turned aside another strike from above, the animal lashed out with one of its hooves, kicking Asbjorn in the chest with a wicked snap. He stumbled backwards and fell to the ground expecting to be instantly trampled on, but to his surprise the rider did not close in to finish it. The marauder was taking his steed out to come around for what looked to be another charge. It was something that Asbjorn was not sure he could withstand again, but had to, nevertheless.

The captain pushed his mount to pick up speed. The galloping horse made a wide loop around the waiting Northerner. Orrm wanted nothing more than to run this primitive fool down and finally put an end to it. He aimed to finish this miserable hunt with a single, decisive stroke. Asbjorn wobbled on shaky legs as he stood and followed the rider's course around. The pumping steed came it straight towards him. Its pounding hooves were like a growing thunder as it rapidly closed the distance. The sound heralded the storm that was to come. The big Northman dug his feet in to brace himself and receive the charge. The black armored rider pointed his broadsword like a piercing lance. The tension in Asbjorn grew as sweat ran down his face. The approaching death at the tip of a sword was almost upon him.

Then, just when the oncoming animal looked to hit, Asbjorn bent low. He tore the helm from one of the dead warriors that rest at his feet. He flung it as hard as he could directly at the rushing horse's face. The skeletal visage of the hurled helm struck the animal between the eyes. As the headpiece hit home, the startled beast bucked and violently reared up. The sudden jolt took the racing Orrm completely off guard. The black clad warrior clutched at the reins to keep from being thrown from the saddle. His single-handed grip was simply no match for the power of the jerking beast. The steed's force and the weight of his own armor combined to wrench his fingers loose. The captain was tossed into the air to slam hard to the ground. He lost all the wind that was in his lungs as he came tumbling down. The impact left him momentarily stunned and more than a little vulnerable.

The surging Asbjorn was on him before Orrm could bring himself up. His crimson axe moved in a blinding haze despite the heaviness in his arms. For his own sake, Orrm's hand was still clasped around the handle of his sword. The captain desperately struggled to fend off his attacker's frenzy. The invader was a skilled swordsman without a doubt, more than capable of holding his own against most men. But there was no way he could come anywhere close to matching Asbjorn's fury, especially after the jarring impact of just being thrown from his mount.

The wild Asbjorn pressed in with his for teetering. He forsook any technique for the recklessness of raw strength. After two glancing blows Orrm's sword arm had gone numb. A third almost spun the man around in place. A fourth tore the limb from the socket to send his weapon flying. Seeing the captain unarmed, Asbjorn brought the axe back and around one last time. The blunt hammerhead on the reverse side caved in the steel of Orrm's breastplate. The wounded marauder was sent skidding to the ground like a toppling tree. An agonizing sputter came from the skulled faceplate of his helm. He stared up as he fought for the breath that would no longer come. Asbjorn's darkening shape and a dimming sky loomed over him.

"You can't win, Northman," Orrm rasped from within his helmet. A frothy scarlet came from his lips. "You have no idea what pursues you."

"If it's this Zantz then he'll be following close behind you," Asbjorn puffed. "But as for you, you're finished."

Without another word, the heavy axe came down again. The blunt side of the head snuffed out the captain completely this time. Asbjorn's lungs burned as he looked down at his slain enemy. His body reminded him once more of just how long it'd been since he'd known rest. He had finally learned the name of the man that he wanted amongst the cruel raiders. The bastard known as General Zantz was the one who had cut down Manus and overseen the razing of Brekka. But to seek him out now would be a fool's endeavor. The condition that Asbjorn was currently in was in no way conducive to a fight, and he knew it.

Asbjorn's head snapped back in the direction of the tree line as he gathered himself. The sounds of shouting men again came to his ears. He had allowed himself to become bogged down at the edge of the woods with this worthless rabble. It was time he knew he would be hard pressed to make up. He had to put as much distance between himself and the forest as possible or else he would be easy pickings once the black warriors cleared cover. That's when he saw Orrm's horse still lingering nearby. He realized that the beast was his only option.

He ran to the animal that instantly began to rear up and kick at him. Asbjorn slapped and fought to get a hold of the dangling reins. At last, he managed to yank the creature down and get a foot in one of the stirrups. He had to struggle to lift himself into the saddle. He was by no means comfortable on the back of the skittish thing. He'd never been one to enjoy the pursuit of horsemanship after an incident when he was much younger. He preferred to make his journeys under his own power, but sometimes desperate acts were required in certain situations, no matter how off putting they might seem.

Asbjorn had just gotten the stubborn creature moving when the men broke through the brush behind him. Their hate filled shouts faded in the distance as he swiftly raced toward the dawn. He did not know where he was going in a land that was so far from his home but anywhere was better than back towards the way he'd come. Then he saw the sun crest over the eastern horizon. Its reddish hue outlined the jagged peaks and towering cliffs. They were the Blade Mountains that sat to the southeast of the great Northern Forest, and if he could only reach them by nightfall, he may yet have a chance.

III

The Blade Mountains were a perilous range that lay far from Asbjorn's home, through the sprawling Northern Forest and across the bitter, windswept plains. Within their crags and gullies, countless Northerners and explorers had lost their lives. They'd either fallen to their deaths or been buried beneath the rocks, or sometimes worse. The sharp peaks rose to split the drab sky like giant daggers. They towered to overlook the chill land across the whole of the southern horizon. They were the last barrier between the rugged north and the more delicate people of the south, standing like stone guardians that oversaw the passage to either. And right now, they were also Asbjorn's last chance at refuge, but only if he could navigate their dangers in time.

His horse just managed to limp through the foothills and up to the base of the rocky mounts. It collapsed and was covered in a lathery sweat. He'd pushed the animal beyond its limits to cover the miles of open ground between the forest and the distant mountain range. He'd not relented in his pace from dawn to when dusk began to descend. The poor thing was nearly dead from exhaustion as it finally managed to reach the imposing cliff sides. Asbjorn's body felt every bit the same as he clung to the saddle. There were times during the day when he had nearly toppled from the animal's back but then he would glance behind to see the tiny specks that were the enemy scouts closing in. He forced himself to go on each time he was reminded of their presence but just how much further he could manage he was beginning to question.

Asbjorn quickly dismounted as the horse fell to the ground. He stumbled along on numbed legs as he made his way up the slopes. Close on his heels were the pursuing trackers of the black army. Their light steeds were able to swiftly make up ground as his horse lagged over the last stretch. He had worked hard to put the distance between himself and those that hunted him but that had all been eliminated as they brought their mounts to a halt less than a minute after he did. From their short bows, they unleashed a slew of arrows as they came down from their saddles. Asbjorn was thankfully too far out of range for the tips to strike home. As he heard metal hit stone, he rushed to climb even higher. He ducked within the mountain's rocky passes, dipping out of sight to quickly be lost from view.

If Asbjorn was beyond exhausted, then the invaders in black were even more so. Their arms shook as they struggled to pull back their bowstrings and maintain their aim. General Zantz had been merciless in his drive to bring in the Son of the Bear. The needs of his men had fallen on deaf ears as he pushed them beyond their breaking points. Not a one of them dared to be heard protesting him. All knew that whoever spoke out would swiftly be cut down for even thinking about voicing a second guess. And then there was the demon that the general himself was made to answer to. Not even the fearsome commander dared to cross Xiphactinas. It was that infernal being's will that truly pressed the warriors in ebon steel onwards. The men feared the power that such a devil could wield more so than the blade of any man. It was he who had demanded that the Son of the Bear be brought before him and it was General Zantz who had been tasked to carry that out, no matter how many he had to kill or sacrifice to do so.

The drained scouts cautiously pursued Asbjorn up the mountains as dusk descended. Their trembling bows were ready to send arrows flying at the slightest hint of movement. They crept through the sloped stones in tight groupings. They were ever wary of what might await them around any turn. The evening shadows played off the rock formations to keep their nerves on edge, making it look as if looming death lurked in every recess. As the search wore on, it seemed that their elusive quarry had completely vanished. There was no trace of him to be found. Then, just when all felt calm, the crimson blade came from behind one of the larger stones. It sliced through a bow and into the flesh of the man that carried it. He was dead before he could manage a scream or yelp of surprise. The one that walked next to him followed close behind. The others that stood nearby called out to one another as their fellow soldiers went down. They released their arrows as they just caught sight of Asbjorn. All of them were on his tracks as he shot up a steep incline.

The tired Northman's muscles knotted as he pushed himself ever higher. His fingertips were scraped raw as he clawed his way over the stones. If not for the fading sun, he very likely would have been pierced through the back several times over. His pursuers' aims were thrown off by the poor lighting and their own heavy fatigue. He knew that he had to find cover soon. He could in no way keep up his frantic pace and avoid harm for much longer. Eventually, the sharp shafts would hit their mark. The toll that the wounds would take along with his own dwindling stamina would be more than enough to stop him. But he could find not a spot nearby to safely take refuge in. He was surrounded by only the jagged stones that jutted from the mountainside this far up. In desperation, he dove behind the biggest one in his path. The arrows bounced off the hard granite to leave small nicks where they'd struck. He leaned heavily on the hard surface to catch his breath for just an instant. The sound of approaching voices and scrambling boots drew closer and closer. Then he felt the large bolder shift only slightly against his back. The notion of a risky idea burst into his mind if he still had enough strength to carry it out.

Asbjorn squatted low and braced his shoulders against the stone. He placed his hands on his knees to help himself push off. With all the might he could muster, he heaved the massive boulder back. He bellowed a savage cry to help him summon the will. With a rumbling crash, the giant rock gave way and toppled down the steep slope. It rolled like thunder towards the warriors beneath as they stared up in horror. They scattered for safety as the trundling boulder came toward them. Asbjorn skidded down behind to try and catch himself before he could slide too far. The marauders, however, panicked as they found themselves with nowhere to flee. The tumbling rock had brought down a small avalanche to follow in its wake. Those that were not crushed outright were buried beneath tons of stone and granite. The plummeting Asbjorn slammed down hard on top of the pile of rubble. He choked on the thick dust that had been kicked up when the slope had given way, wiping the stinging grit from his eyes as he gathered himself.

As the haze settled, Asbjorn could still hear and see the forms of several of his pursuers. They were in the midst of trying to dig themselves out. They worked with all they had to pull their bodies from the strewn debris. They moaned out in pain at their broken bones and the black armor that had been dented around them. Most had no hope of getting themselves free under their own power. The amount of rock that pinned them in place had crushed their extremities to a near pulp. Asbjorn staggered over on wobbly legs to where each of the enemy invaders still struggled to loose himself. His axe fell in successive strokes to put a swift end to each despite their pleas for mercy. For a brief moment, Asbjorn had thought about sparing the groveling men from the blade. He'd never been one to show outright cruelty to the totally helpless. But then he thought again of Brekka and the other neighboring villages. The people there had begged for their lives just as these swine did now. The marauding force had shown them not the slightest bit of quarter in return for their appeals. Asbjorn's anger came to push away his brief thought of compassion. He stared down at the injured like a pitiless hunter looking at a trapped rabbit. The sharp edge of his steel demanded vengeance, and that's exactly what he gave it.

He glanced back down the mountainside once the air was quiet. He knew full well that the footmen and General Zantz could not be far off. Those that remained of the black army were steadily making up ground on him by the minute. They would soon be on him just as the swifter scouts had been. He wanted to run and keep moving to extend his lead, but his dead limbs had finally reached the point that they refused to be pushed any further. They demanded rest whether the situation allowed for it or not, almost giving out on him in mid-step with only the slightest exertion. He had to find some kind of sanctuary to take shelter in, a hiding place to allow himself to reinvigorate his body. That's when he saw the opening in the cliff face that he had not noticed before. The narrow cave was almost totally invisible in the fleeting light. It must have been unearthed in the aftermath of the rockslide. The entrance was so small that he had to hunch over and nearly crawl on his belly to slip inside.

Asbjorn collapsed on the hard stone once he'd made his way into the interior. He found that it was pitch-black save for the dreary bit of sunlight that managed to sneak in through the entrance. The cover of night would soon descend over the jagged peaks of the Blade Mountains, bringing with it a heavy darkness that the ailing Northerner hoped would conceal his temporary haven. He knew that he should try to drag himself farther into the deepening shadows. He should move as far away from the mouth of the cave as he could. But now that he was down this is where he was going to stay. Gradually, his eyes drifted shut as he gripped his axe and tugged his cloak tight. An uneasy yet welcome sleep washed over him. He lay on the hard floor of the chill cave oblivious to the world outside. The amber jeweled eyes of his bear's head cloak came alive to glitter in the blackness.

IV

Asbjorn snapped awake in the darkness of the cave. It took a few seconds for him to recall just where he was. It was still night when he was roused from his shaky slumber. The shouting voices drifted in from outside. The men of the black army had, at last, made it to the mountains. General Zantz had sent them up the hazardous slopes with only flickering torches and the scant starlight to show them the way. Asbjorn pawed his way to the entrance to gaze over the rocks. He brushed aside his filth caked hair to spy the specks of fire that spread across mountainside. His pursuers were following the trail that their scouts had left behind to lead them here. The sooner they discovered the corpses of their men the sooner they would be guided straight to his shelter. If only he possessed the strength that he normally did, he would have slunk from his hidden refuge, moving amongst them to hack down while a bit of night still lingered. But he was still in no condition for a fight at the moment. His stamina was somewhat replenished thanks to his rest but by no means at its peak.

Asbjorn cursed to himself as he backed into the encompassing darkness. He let out a heavy breath as his eyes still focused on the faint outline of the entrance. He had crawled in here to find a place to hide and recuperate but now he was trapped like a skittish rat by those outside. To leave would surely be walking into their hands, while staying here would more than likely get him found within the hour. There were far too many of those that scoured through the rocks for them not to notice this place. Their torchlights were bound to show them the way sooner or later. With his body still protesting, he did the only thing he could think of. He retreated farther into the underground in hopes that he might find a pass that led through the mountainside. With luck, he would be able find his way back out and into fresh air in no time, or at worst, be discovered by the invaders or lost forever within a subterranean prison.

Asbjorn groped his way into the blackness that lurked within the Blade Mountains. He was not at all sure what he might find the further in he went. He was totally blind as he felt his way along the uneven stone. He stumbled and tripped as his feet were constantly being caught on the rock and his head knocked against the ceiling. He staggered through the dark for what seemed like a lifetime, not knowing if he was moving along a straight pass or in a horribly twisting circle. He tried to keep his confused bearings about him as best he could. He stayed against the same wall should he find himself having to retrace his unseen steps. He pawed and padded until he finally began to feel the slightest wafting of air. He saw thin slivers of light barely peeking through the cracks in the rock ahead.

Asbjorn felt over the sides of the tunnel. The granite was cool and oddly brittle to the touch. He ran his hands over the surface of the curiously smooth stonework. He detected a definite pattern beneath his fingertips where the bits once fit tightly together. As he applied even the slightest pressure, the cracks in the stone slightly widened, allowing even more illumination to sneak through as fragments flecked away to fall at his feet. He stepped back and held his breath to cautiously listen for the next several moments. He heard nothing but his own heartbeat coming in the black. Satisfied he was alone, he brought up the blunt hammerhead of his axe. He smashed away at the weakened stone to knock it down in crumbling chunks.

The light that came rushing through was still hardly enough to brighten the narrow passage, but it was a welcome reprieve from the pitch-black he had just trudged through. He stepped through the opening that he'd just made to set his feet on a rough stone landing. The stairs that were carved into the rock were barely visible in the dimness. He made his way slowly down the lofty flight that led even farther into the bowels of the earth. He carefully tested each step so as not to take a harsh tumble through the shadows. As he descended deeper into the mountainside, the stairway gradually began to widen. The plain stone of the catacomb walls gave way to an unexpected sight.

Toppled statues lay strewn across the plunging steps. The columns that had at one time served as their bases sat one across from the other to line the stairs. What the figures may have once been images of Asbjorn could not tell. The blackness was too thick to get a good look at them and everything was covered in a layer of dust. The cool air gradually began to stink of a musty dampness as he reached the bottom of the stairway, as if he were entering an age-old tomb that had not been opened since the dawn of time. As he passed through a high arch, Asbjorn could not believe what his eyes fell upon. His thoughts were awestruck to a stupor.

The enthralled Asbjorn gazed out over a vast subterranean chamber. The titanic cavern rose ever upwards to stretch far into the shadows. If forced to say, he would swear the entire mountain had been hollowed out. The light he saw came from openings in the rocks high above that looked to have been purposefully placed. The sun must have risen outside as he had wandered through the darkness. Its rays shone down in distinct pillars that swirled with a gentle drifting of dust. For the moment, Asbjorn had forgotten about his weary body completely. He did nothing but stare upward as he entered into the expansive space. The thought of his relentless pursuers had also been lost in his momentary amazement. Any urgency that he once possessed was swept aside by an undeniable curiosity.

He had only ever heard a handful of stories about the mysteries of the Blade Mountains before. They were mostly second or third hand accounts that were picked up from the rare trader or odd explorer that came through Brekka. The tales spoke of the far-off range in equal parts wonder and dread. They warned of the many beasts that roamed over the lonely slopes, but also of the majesty of the snowcapped peaks. But never could Asbjorn remember anything such as this being whispered of. The scope of such a place was not imagined possible in any Northerner's wildest dreams.

Asbjorn spun in small circles as he walked through the massive cavern. He tried to take in everything his wide eyes beheld. The place looked to contain the ruins of a lost village or even small city of some sort but what any of the fallen structures might have been he was completely unsure of. Most of the ruins appeared to have collapsed in on themselves over the passage of time, buckling under their own weight as the supports and ceilings had fallen into neglect. But there was a large section towards the center of the area that looked as if had been burned to the ground. The charred timber still poked from battered foundations and many of the walls appeared to have been bashed in. He could only speculate at what could have happened to the people that had once made this place their home. No one in his village had ever hinted that they'd heard of something like this. But then he gave pause once more at the far end of the chamber. His gaze slowly drifted upwards.

A gigantic fortress stood to reach to the very top of the cavern. The mighty walls and bulwarks were chiseled into the dusky rock of the Blade Mountains themselves. On each side of the entrance rose two towering statues. Both looked to be identical right down to their smashed faces and broken features. What remained of the figures somewhat resembled several of the toppled images that Asbjorn had seen when first descending to the colossal chamber, but like the ones previous, he could not glean much more. Large chunks of rock had been knocked from the effigies' heads and torsos to fall to the ground. The weighty rubble left shallow craters where it had landed. The wandering Northerner had to step over and around the piles of scattered debris. One of the pieces still bore an unblemished eye that stared coldly up at him. He followed a wide flight of steps to the citadel's front gates. He was still enamored as a young man from the isolated forests would be

150

when surrounded by such grandeur. Asbjorn was used to being around small structures cut from rough timber and felled logs. The jarl's home that had stood in Brekka was the largest place he'd ever seen until now. But here, under a mountain, he found himself in a very different setting, one that he was not at all comfortable in as his senses slowly returned.

The fortress's entrance stood open and waiting for him. Asbjorn's hand tightened around the handle of his axe. The doorway was nearly as tall as six grown men but the way inside was so narrow that only two could pass through should they stand shoulder to shoulder. Light filtered through the halls from unseen openings. The staleness that drifted out was even more pungent than when he'd first wandered into the cavern. Part of him screamed not to enter this place. It tried to remind him that he still had the warriors in black close on his heels and to continue to flee. But he was still somewhat captivated by the dread majesty that he had found. Another part urged him to push forward into the house of subterranean shadows.

He stepped across the threshold to tread over the battered doors. The wood beneath his feet was rotting away from its rusted banding. The puffs of dust continued to churn in the air with each of his footfalls. He passed into the confines of the stronghold's vaulted vestibule. Halls branched out in every direction as his eyes scanned the chamber. The wide-open spaces stretched into the darkness. Lacking a flame, he followed the direction the light led him. He snaked through the citadel and up stairways to brush past so many empty rooms.

Then he came to a long passage that took him to a set of double doors at its far end. Its walls were adorned with faded and peeling imagery. Portrayals of torturous deaths that he had never thought others capable of were depicted along the length. Men that were dressed in garb that resembled the large statues delighted themselves at overseeing the heinous acts. As he neared the closed doors, he came to one last image. He saw twelve thrones seated with the same robed figures that seemed to have been the ones who'd ruled this place. They were all shown gathered around the chair of a thirteenth who sat with six on each side. They drank and watched as one of their subjects burned in an iron cage that was placed over a raging fire. The malicious figure that sat at the center looked to be the master of all. He wore a many pointed crown upon his brow to lord over the masses. Asbjorn had never heard of who these men were or what this lost kingdom might have been, but he was pleased that he had not been here to see it when it thrived. A strong contempt came to him as he saw what those that had resided here were made to endure.

Turning from the final mural, he pressed on the heavy doors. They budged only slightly at the touch of his hand. He pushed again only to have to step back and put his shoulder into them. He, at last, remembered just how tired his body had become. He gave one more shove and heard something splinter on the opposite side. The doors suddenly gave way under the force his is weight. The wood scraped across the floor and the rusted hinges creaked as Asbjorn forced them open. The large beam that had been holding them closed fell to the floor.

The chamber Asbjorn found was a large, circular space, with another entrance straight across from him and one more at the far side to let the light come in. All three appeared as if they had been barred from the inside. The one at the far end had been beaten down long ago while the door straight across was still held in place. The interior looked to be untouched save for the fallen doors. Nothing was destroyed or burned as he'd seen outside the fortress or throughout the sprawling city. But what drew his attention most were the objects situated at the center of the room. All of them were circled around to reflect the last image he'd seen before entering.

Asbjorn slowly stepped into the inner arc of ancient thrones. The gilded seats were arranged around a blackened fire pit that was enclosed by five iron spires that resembled a spiked claw. Within the chairs, their long-expired occupants remained. The dry, sunken corpses were slumped over with an empty chalice clutched in their gnarled fingers. The bodies appeared to be unharmed as Asbjorn came around to the light. He moved in to examine the dead more carefully. Under a thick layer of grime, he could see that their tattered garb looked like that of the statues and the men of the paintings in the hall. The passing of unknown ages had taken a harsh toll on the once exquisite fabric. All of the lords he'd seen in the earlier images were here save for one. The absence of the brow the pointed crown would have rested upon was hard to miss.

The thirteenth throne that marked the beginning and end of the ring sat empty. Nothing more than a corroded cup lay on the floor a few feet away. The seat was the most grandiose of those in the chamber. Its armrests were carved in the shape of sirens' heads. Their unclothed bodies wrapped around the legs and their hair twisted up the sides to form a demonic visage at the top. Asbjorn stared for a moment at the hellish face that looked back at him. The air in the chamber suddenly became chill. Then he heard an echo from somewhere outside the fallen doors at the end of the room. The sound of faint voices and tumbling rocks drifted in. No sooner than it had come the cold was gone.

Asbjorn rushed from the throne chamber and through the broken doors. He exited on a high terrace with a line of arched windows that overlooked the city below. He held his breath and listened carefully until the sound came again. The call of the familiar shouts were barely audible. From the far end of the cavern, he saw their torches as tiny specks of flame. They were the remnants of the black army having finally found his secluded hiding place in the mountainside. They must have followed his tracks from the small cave and through the dark catacombs. He had been so overtaken by the scale of the forgotten city he'd let the thought of haste slip away.

He cursed himself that he'd been fool enough to let them make up the distance, knowing that they were now between him and the only way out of here that he knew of. The flames of their torches looked to be spreading out to comb through the ruins. They were more than likely searching through the structures to locate him. Asbjorn thought for an instant about trying to slip through their stretched line once more, leaving them to pick through the many rooms of the massive fortress to try and find his whereabouts. But then he realized that it would not take them long to discover that he was no longer here. They might even pick up his exiting trail before they could even reach the stronghold. After that, they would soon be on his heels again. They would chase him down to hunt him to the point of pure exhaustion, and then it would be over.

Asbjorn cracked his neck and rolled his shoulders. He tried to work out the stiffness in his sore muscles and chase away the weariness. His body still protested but this is where he would make his stand, turning the hunters into the hunted within the shadowy remains of the forgotten city. He would let these lonely ruins serve as their tomb. It would be a fitting end for such men to be slaughtered in an out of the way place as this.

Asbjorn pulled his fur cloak tight. He ran his finger along the edge of his blade, testing to see that it was still sharper than anything he'd ever held before. For a brief instant, he thought of Magdalena, but then he quickly pushed the sentiment from his mind. He knew that General Zantz must be down there somewhere. The merciless commander drove his men like dogs to bring in the elusive Northerner. Asbjorn would find the cruel butcher that now searched for him, and when he did, he would leave the man's broken body to rot amongst the rubble.

Asbjorn withdrew back into the ancient fortress as the torches reached the edge of the city. His legs swiftly carried him through the shadows. He hurried through the halls to once more reach the entrance. He slipped down the stairs to disappear into the sprawling ruins. With his blade in hand, he moved like a ghost through the collapsed remnants. Both he and his steel were eager to meet the soon to be dead.

V

The warriors of the black army cautiously entered the remains of the subterranean city. Sweat beaded off them from beneath their dark armor. They had all seen what the man they now hunted had left of Captain Orrm on the plains and their scouts on the mountainside. None held any desire to follow in their slain comrades' footsteps. Their quarry had been like an elusive phantom since they'd razed their last small village to the ground. He'd came and gone with the shadows to leave nothing but death to tell of his passing. If it had been up to them, they would have left these lands behind weeks ago, retreating back to the south to regroup and lick at their wounds. But the steel-clad hand of General Zantz kept them within his tight grip. He'd refused to relent in the push to bring in the prey they pursued. And then there was the demon Xiphactinas who ruled over the land they had come from. They had been ordered to bring the Son of the Bear before their dark master, dragging him back to be delivered at their Lord's feet. Failure was not an option for the black clad soldiers or their commander. Retreat meant a certain doom while pressing forward looked to promise much of the same. But some chance was better than none in their minds. A potential end at the blade of the northern savage seemed far better than an assured one at the hands of their ruthless lord.

The men spread out to search through the ruins once reaching the edge of the city. They jumped at any hint of movement caused their waving torches and the shafts of sunlight that filtered in from above. They tried to stay in sight of at least one of their compatriots as they stalked through the narrow lanes. The intervening forms of the derelict buildings made that difficult. They took their time as they looked through every structure they came upon. They were wary of not to miss even the slightest possible place where the big Northman might be hiding. They poked through what had been left and abandoned in the homes. Most found nothing of value but some came across an odd bit of silver or two they quickly pocketed. Many were beginning to wish the savage may not even be here at all, having slipped through their line or out another passage in the rocks to be speeding far away. The silence they encountered was both reassuring and maddening all at once. The not knowing if death surely awaited brought hope but also a tinge of fear at the same time.

Then suddenly, they heard the clash of steel and a short scream. Two of the nearest soldiers ran towards the horrible cry. They approached an open doorway of what looked to be one of the fallen households. They came around each side to find a dwindling torch flickering within. One of their fellows lay face down in a pool of red with his head split open. The back of his skulled helm showed a cleaved gash in the dark steel. They quickly scanned the empty space and then exchanged anxious glances. Both turned to leave when the black shape was upon them. They scarcely had a second to raise their weapons before they felt the crimson streak cut deep. It was a strike so swift that even the most alert would not have stood a chance against it. Through the massive cavern, the echoes of their final cries resounded off the walls. The shrill wails were perfectly fitting for such a setting.

The remaining men in black all forced down hard swallows as the sound slowly faded. Their shaky hands tightened around bow shafts and worn sword hilts. They came together in larger groups as they hesitantly made their way in the direction of the noise. Another pain filled scream burst out to be followed shortly by several more. One of the groupings was passing by what appeared to be a large shrine of some sort. Broken statuary and fallen markers lay scattered across the ground. As they crept along, one of the fallen sculptures suddenly sprung to its feet. A whirling axe took off limbs and carved into weathered armor. The few that were not immediately cut down scrambled to put up a fight. They brough their arms to bear against the unexpected attack. But their blades were quickly knocked aside by furious muscles as sharp steel bit in. One tried to drag himself away as he futilely clutched at the stump where his arm once was. A booted foot found the small of his back to pin him in place. His life was snuffed out less than an instant later. He was sent to join so many of his many comrades that had preceded him in death.

Asbjorn pulled his axe from the dead man's back. He kicked the body away as he flicked the blade clean. He breathed heavy and looked down at the slaughtered dead. He took just a moment to regain his wind that was becoming harder to pull in. But before he could take more than a few breaths an arrow whizzed inches from his nose. Another group came from the far end of the street. He quickly ducked into the remains of the crumbling shrine, trying to avoid them until he could close the distance or manage to slip away. But the enemy swordsmen proved to be faster than he thought this time. They roared in just behind him as their furious shouts called to summon the others. Asbjorn knew that this had to come sooner or later. He had hoped to avoid engaging them outright until he'd at least thinned their numbers a little more, but nothing could be done of it now. He positioned himself low just behind a piece of toppled masonry. He listened as the heavy footfalls came rushing his way. Just as they reached him, he shot up to bury his axe into one of their mid-sections. He tore it loose to swiftly dispatch another that was racing up behind. Despite felling these two, there were still more that surged towards him. Yet another arrow sailed just wide of its mark.

Asbjorn pushed himself to charge straight at the oncoming soldiers. His weary body was kept going by force of will and a lust to fight on. His brazen recklessness caught all that came at him off guard. His weight crashed into the nearest to propel them into the marauders that moved up behind. The mass of tangled humanity and flailing swords quickly went slamming to the ground. Asbjorn waded into the midst of them to work his axe in tight swings. The blade, hammerhead, and butt of the handle all struck in rapid succession. The edge rose and fell as those beneath tried to fend it off. Half of them were dead before the first could even hope to find his footing. Asbjorn thought at this rate the rest might yet fall. Then the big man felt a piercing pain in his upper leg. The wooden shaft that hit him skewered straight through the meat of his thigh. He bellowed in rage and threw himself at the archer who was desperately fumbling to nock another arrow at the doorway. The man was cut down before he could get the notch over his bowstring.

Asbjorn came back around to see those behind him were beginning to recover themselves. They were on their feet and swiftly closing in. Others that had been attracted by the melee were now making their way into the shrine, too. The black clad warriors came from all sides in a rush. A tightening circle of armor and blades pressed dangerously close. The big Northerner wasted no time in his retaliation. He charged into the men that he could see directly in front of him. He downed two before the ring of steel could completely converge on his back. But their superior numbers were finally taking their toll. His fatigued muscles were also not aiding him in the least.

The armored soldiers piled in when they saw him start to falter. The weight of their bodies and the dark steel they wore drove him to the ground. He could no longer wield his axe properly under their combined mass, but he could still fight like a wild beast, twisting limbs and reaching under helms to gouge at eyes. None of the invaders believed how much fight he still had left, but one man could not hope to ward off such a constant hail of blows. Eventually, the pommels of their swords connected against his exposed skull. Their heavy boots stomped and kicked at him to steal what little oomph he had left. In a last effort, he tried to lurch after the nearest he could get to. They backed away as his footing gave out thanks to the broken arrow still sticking from his leg. He collapsed in the center of their circle. He was at the mercy of men who he knew would have none.

"Slay the pig while we still have the chance," one of them spat, "and we can be done with this burdensome task!"

"General Zantz ordered him to be brought in alive," piped another. "I'm not fool enough to go against that. I prefer to have my head attached to my neck."

"As do I," said a third. "We have him down. We should bind him before he gets his breath back."

"Then if you cowards lack the courage," the first spoke up again, "I'll do it myself."

The dark clad warrior pushed the others aside. He stared down at Asbjorn as he raised his sword. The big man returned the look with hatred behind his eyes. His limbs quivered as he attempted to command his muscles to move. But try as he might, he simply had no strength with which to fight back. He was only able to wait for the steel to fall and end it.

"Burn in the hell where you came from, Northman!" the marauder said as he prepared to drop the stroke.

"Stay your hand!" boomed a thunderous voice before the final blow could fall. The deep shout seized everyone in place. The circle of armored warriors slowly parted like the splitting of the seas. The menacing figure of General Zantz strode through their number. The gold trim of his armor caught the torchlight as the flames danced over the steel. The horns of his death's head helm and his tattered cloak made him resemble a devil more than a man. He towered over those around him, if not in height, then by force of shear presence. He stopped before the soldier that stood poised over Asbjorn. The other trembled inside his armored shell.

"Did I not say to bring him to me alive?" Zantz asked in a raspy whisper. He waited for a response.

"Allow me to explai-,"

Before the sentence could be finished, the other man's head was rolling across the floor. The general's arm re-sheathing his blade in the same motion with which he'd drawn it. The lifeless body of the unfortunate soldier crumpled before Asbjorn. A stream of red flowed from the wound to spread across the stone.

"Let this be another warning to you all," bellowed Zantz. "My words are to be followed to the letter or retribution will be swift. I, nor our Lord Xiphactinas, will tolerate such insolence. From our own men or anyone else for that matter.

"And you," the general half growled. He ground his boot into Asbjorn's hand. "I've waited quite some time to meet you again. So, you're the Son of the Bear, eh? If I'd have known then, I'd have taken you back in that pitiful little village, but I suppose that was my mistake. But now here you are in front of me, and I will not take you so lightly this time."

The general reached down to wrap a gauntleted hand around Asbjorn's throat. He heaved the big man up to his knees to look him dead in the eyes. Asbjorn's cheeks and face were swollen and bruised almost beyond recognition. His sandy hair was a matted mop of red and filth. The big Northerner tried in vain to struggle against the general's constricting hold. His grasping hands clawed at Zantz's forearm. But the other was just too strong for him right now. The mailed fingers dug into his neck to cause him to gag and choke.

"Pathetic savage," Zantz said. He squeezed his grip tighter. His steel covered fist continued to put pressure on Asbjorn's windpipe. The big man's feet frantically kicked as he desperately tried to pull in air. The veins in his forehead bulged and his face turned a beet red. He gave one last try before his muscles and limbs went limp. The general, at last, threw his unconscious form back to the ground. He glared down at the wheezing Northman in contempt.

Zantz looked to one of his men. "Tie him," he commanded.

160

"Yes, my lord," the other responded. The soldier quickly moved to secure the big man as instructed. "And then what, sir? No more light slips in and the sun is close to setting outside. Do we leave to press on in the dark?"

"No," answered a stern Zantz. He gazed towards the towering outline at the far end of the cavern. "Drag him to the fortress when you're done. We shelter there for the night."

VI

Asbjorn slowly came back to consciousness. He could just hear the sound of coarse voices and wood crackling on a fire. The flames cast an eerie play of shadow and light through the room. He was on the hard floor of a large dining hall. His ankles were bound, and his wrists tied tightly behind his back. Many of Zantz's men sat at a long table at the center of the chamber. The top was strewn with an assortment of dusty relics and their scattered equipment. They ate of dried meat and stale bread as they conversed amongst themselves.

The general's forces had numbered many more than this when they'd first come to invade the lands that were Asbjorn's home. They'd been whittled down to no more than a handful thanks to the Northerner's efforts. He knew that if it were up to them, they would have dispatched him when they'd brought him down back in the cavern, but he had been spared by Zantz's intervening words. Asbjorn's chestnut eyes scanned the room for the imposing commander. He was not seated at the table with the rest of is men. Then he heard a grating chuckle come from just behind him. The sound of which was unmistakable.

"I didn't expect you'd be out for long," said General Zantz. Asbjorn struggled to roll over to come face to face with him. "Not even with you being wounded and so exhausted as you were."

The general sat away from his troop and close to the fire. He turned Asbjorn's crimson axe over in his hands to examine the blade in the waving light. The Northman's bear head cloak rest on the floor draped over Zantz's black armor and horned helm. Its amber eyes glittered slightly in the dimness. Asbjorn watched as the general ran his thumb lightly down the weapon's razor edge. A single ruby droplet came to the digit's tip like a jeweled bead.

"Quite a deadly thing, isn't it?" the general said. His eyes went to Asbjorn. "Especially in the hands of someone like you."

Zantz was a grizzled soldier who had seen hundreds of engagements over his many years of bringing war. His scarred face looked as if it were made of tanned leather. His hairless head glistened in the orange and yellow firelight. His dark eyes reminded Asbjorn of black pits with no bottoms. The general played with the weight of the axe as he shifted the weapon from one hand to the other, surprised that it proved to be as light as it was. With a single arm, he swiped the hefty blade through the air. He looked back to Asbjorn after taking a few swings.

"Where would a simple woodsman like you get something like this," he asked, "and whoever would have taught you how to use it so well? Perhaps you found it in a tomb like where we are now or did you steal it from a wandering warrior that you and the other savages managed to bring down? Well," said Zantz, "speak up, whelp."

Asbjorn stared a burning hole through the man in front of him as the two regarded one another. He did not utter so much as a word to the sneering general's annoyance. Even if he'd not had a biting gag in his mouth, he wouldn't have given the other the satisfaction, only the steely glare that was now set on his face. Zantz smiled wider as he placed the axe next to his armor and Asbjorn's cloak. He picked up a knife that was stuck in a small table where a hunk of salted meat rest. He came over to stand above the helpless Northman. He cut the gag loose after a long, tense pause.

"There," he said, returning to his chair to flick the knife back in the tabletop. "Now we're free to talk. So, I'll ask you again. Where did you get such a deadly thing?"

Despite receiving the same question, Asbjorn still did not respond. He once more only gave the other a silent stare.

"Very well," the general said. "If you're not in the mood to speak, then perhaps I'll have several of my men come over to help loosen your tongue. They've all been waiting quite a while to get their hands on you. I can't promise they'll show much restraint. I was commanded to take you back alive, but I think that you could survive quite some time without your eyes or fingers, wouldn't you agree?"

Raising his hand, Zantz made to motion two of his warriors over. He glanced back to Asbjorn before he did so. The Northerner let out a deep breath as the other stayed the gesture. He knew that the general wasn't bluffing with his threat.

"Why have you come to this land?" the big man finally asked.

"So, the savage can speak," Zantz remarked. "But still, he does not answer my questions. Should I ask him for a third time or does he have enough sense to remember them?"

Asbjorn struggled to sit himself up to face the general on a more even level. A sharp pain shot through his leg as he did so. He had forgotten about the arrow that had punctured his thigh from earlier. He looked to see that the shaft had been removed and the wound crudely dressed. But it still did little to lessen the lingering discomfort. The hurt that came with his movements prevented him from bringing himself upright. With his arms and legs restrained, Asbjorn had to content himself with remaining on the floor. He looked up at Zantz's arrogant smile as he lay helpless.

"It was my father's axe," he begrudgingly answered. "He taught me how to fight for the most part. Not with that one, but it was close enough."

"Then I must say he taught you well," the general remarked. He glanced towards the weapon. "It's a shame that you'll never get a chance to wield it again. No need to worry,

164

though. I'll make sure that it continues to be put to good use. In the hands of one of my more loyal warriors."

Zantz smirked at the big Northerner after his last comment. He took pleasure in the other's inability to do anything about it. Asbjorn's eyes continued to bore into him. The momentary silence was palpable with tension.

"What do you want with me?" asked Asbjorn after a long instant. His voice was deep and formidable.

"The one that I serve has commanded that you be brought before him," answered Zantz. "I have merely been sent here to ensure that happens. You should be grateful that you're still alive. My men demand your head, but my master has decided that he wishes the rest of you to be attached to it. Whatever the case may be, it has spared you a bit more time. But I doubt that it's time you're going to enjoy."

"Why did you kill my people, then," Asbjorn said, "when it was only me that you were after? Why not take just me alone?"

The general smiled his arrogant smile once again. He saw a growing frustration in the Northerner's eyes. Zantz was foremost a ruthless soldier before anything else but every now and again he did enjoy stringing along the occasional captive or two. He plucked the knife from the table where he'd previously flicked it, cutting a piece of dried meat for himself.

"Why not put down refuse when given the chance?" he answered dismissively. "My lord wanted them dead, so they were dead. We didn't even know it was you we were looking for until you set our camp ablaze. That's when I knew it was you that he wanted. The Son of the Bear he called you, a beast among the men of the north.

"But look at you now," Zantz went on. "A miserable heap tied like a pig at my feet, and me forced to haul your carcass south. It's such a pity when true warriors can't leave it between themselves and on the battlefield. It's so much simpler when it's left in our own hands, wouldn't you agree?"

"Who is this 'he,'?" Asbjorn asked. "And why did you call me Son of the Bear? What does that even mean?"

"It means that you were marked for death long ago, Northman," Zantz sneered. He took another bite of meat. "And 'this he,' is my master and you'll be meeting him soon enough."

"But I don't understand," Asbjorn replied in frustration. "That doesn't tell me anything. Answer my questions, damn you!"

"What makes you think I'm here to answer to the likes of you?" Zantz said. He came to stand over Asbjorn with a scowl on his face. "You and your people are worthless savages that are far beneath one such as I. It gave me great satisfaction to purge them from this world and if I had my way you would have followed close behind, but the choice was not mine to make. If I were you, I would shut up and content myself with the few moments I had left, however fleeting and uncomfortable they may be.

"Now I have grown rather tired of this conversation, Northman, and I wish to return to my meal in peace. Just know that I could be rid of you whenever the mood struck me, perhaps telling my lord that you preferred to take your own life rather than be captured alive. You are at my mercy now, boy. You would do well to remember that."

The general motioned for two of his men to come over. The group had been quietly watching the exchange from where they still ate at the table. The pair hurried to stand before the imposing man afraid to keep him waiting for even a second. They were ready to receive his instructions without question.

"Gag this scum again and then get him out of my sight," the general ordered. "I don't wish to see or hear him for the rest of the evening. When you're finished, relieve the two that stand guard in the hall. The night watch is yours."

The two men quietly nodded. They hurried to tie a dirty rag around Asbjorn's mouth. The cloth cinched tightly into the corners of his lips. He did not try to utter a word to Zantz or the black clad warriors that dragged him away. He merely kept his eyes locked with those of the spiteful general. His anger continued to grow as he was pulled across the floor.

Zantz watched silently as the other was removed from his presence. He took his seat back near the fire once he was left alone. He glanced towards his few men who remained sitting at the table. Their heads quickly averted from his stern gaze. He would never admit it but the savage from the Northern Forest had proved himself a worthy foe. The scant amount of Zantz's soldiers that were left was more than enough evidence of that. It was going to be a long road back to the south for the remnants of the black army, especially with such a dangerous individual in tow. The general reclined in his chair to finish off his salted meat in quiet reflection. He threw a particularly tough bit into the hopping fire.

What a shame we can't just leave it on the field, Zantz thought. He stared down at Asbjorn's axe and bear head cloak. *What a shame indeed.*

VII

The two who had been ordered to the hall stood in the lonely corridor outside the dining room. A solitary torch flickered in its sconce. The pair had been tasked with maintaining the midnight watch as their fellow soldiers slept just on the other side of the door. As the night plodded on, they both found it difficult to stay awake. At one point, they each began to slowly nod off. Their hearts jumped to their throats as they quickly snapped to attention. They glanced around worried that the general may have somehow noticed them. Thankfully, they still found themselves alone in the passage. They resigned themselves to make idle talk between each other to help keep one another alert. They recounted the looting and pillaging they'd done in the various villages they'd passed through on their way here. But both were running out of things to say as they'd heard so many of the same stories from their other compatriots. They could only take bosting of death and pleading peasants for so long. Now, they stood guard in a dull silence on each side of the dining chamber. One stared blankly at the wavering torch while the other counted the stones of the walls and floor.

"It's just our luck to be stuck on guard duty the first night we could actually get some rest," remarked the one that gazed into the flame. "I'd give anything to be wrapped up in my bedroll right now. I really hate that damn Northman."

"You said that half an hour ago," responded the other. "And you made me lose count again."

"Sorry," said the first. "But I'm just so damn exhausted. I don't see why we just can't get some sleep? Now we're going to have to trudge along tomorrow half out on our feet while we try to keep pace. Besides, it's not like there's anything down here. He's already gagged and tied up inside."

"If I had my say, he'd already be in the ground," the other responded. "But you know how the general is," he whispered, "overly thorough and paranoid to the last. Just don't ever let him hear you say that. Unless you don't mind having your head removed from your neck."

"You're right," said the first again. He kept his voice low. "I'm already short enough as it is."

The two men broke out in a muffled laughter. They choked back their snorts as they mocked their fearsome commander. Their fatigue and lack of sleep had caused them to both become overly giddy. They'd been dragging on the road for so long they took any chance they could get at for levity. Normally they would never say a word about Zantz no matter how many doors stood between them. The merciless warrior seemed to have a way of finding out if a disparaging remark was even hinted towards him. He'd killed men for less and sometimes for nothing at all but these two were far from heeding their better judgement.

They had become so oblivious in their amusement they'd both failed to notice that the hallway was becoming colder. A bitter chill was beginning to crawl its way down the passage. The stale moisture between the stonework frosted over and a web of fine ice ran across the floor. The men's laughter slowly tapered off as they finally realized that something was amiss. They looked as their breaths hung heavy like a puffing fog.

The pair of invaders shivered in their armor as the frigidness increased. The dark steel against their skin had become freezing to the touch. The men exchanged looks as a raspy whisper suddenly came to their ears. Each drew their sword with a shaky hand. A glow of sickly jade began to show from down the corridor. It crept inch by inch to usher in a feeling that neither had ever experienced before. The ghostly light grew brighter and the cold more piercing as they both stood petrified. The wavering flame of the torch abruptly hissed out, and then there was only shadow in the bleakness.

Asbjorn's eyes just barely cracked open. He scanned over the room through the thin slits. He'd been slid into a far corner. One of the soldiers sat just nearby to watch over his every move. He'd been feigning sleep for just over an hour now. He'd waited patiently and could see that his sole guard had finally dozed off. He glanced over and saw the unmoving forms of his other slumbering captors. Their cacophonous snores grated on his every nerve. Some were reclined in rickety chairs that surrounded the old dining table. A few others slept with their heads down and laying on the tabletop. He'd like nothing more than to smother them all or snap all their necks in their sleep. He struggled against his restraints, but he couldn't get them to budge. Then he just caught notice of something else that drew his attention. If he could get to it, it may well be his salvation and his foes' end.

Asbjorn squirmed his way across the floor as stealthily as he could. He paused every few feet to listen and glance around at the still shapes. Not a one of them stirred at the subtle sound of him wriggling over the stone. The soldiers were simply too deep in their much overdue rest. Not even General Zantz made a move from his place in front of the fire. The imposing commander put on a hard front but was also locked in sleep's embrace after so long on the move. It took some doing, but Asbjorn made the distance quickly and quietly for being tied on his belly. He pushed off with his legs and toes to skootch along face down. He tilted over to his side when he wanted to look around and make sure that he'd not roused anyone. The farther he got the less of a worry that became. Once at the table, he shut out the pain and forced himself up to his knees. He just peeked over the edge to spy what he wanted.

It was a small blade that stuck from a bit of bread barely out of reach. Even for other dull knives this one would be lucky to cut through butter that'd been left in the sun all day. But it was also his only hope to free himself. No matter how blunted it was he would slice off his own hand to be loose. He nudged himself up to try and stand. He could never reach it with his hands strapped at his back, but he may be able to drag it over if he could manage a few more inches. The ancient table juddered under his weight. He thought that it would give out at any instant to alert the men. He was so close that he swore the exhales from his nose fogged the tarnished steel. It was a hair away so that he could nearly touch it.

But before he could do anything more, he felt a sudden coolness. A shrieking cry came from out in the hall to blast through the dining chamber. With startled jolts, everyone within was suddenly awake. Asbjorn swiftly dropped back to the floor before they caught sight of him.

General Zantz and his men sprung from their rest. They came to their feet to swiftly snatch their blades from where they sat in their scabbards. The general quickly surveyed the room as he came to the center. He found all of his black warriors present and the Northerner in the corner where he'd been left. He gave Asbjorn a suspicious glare before addressing his men.

"What the hell was that shout?" demanded Zantz. He looked towards the man who he'd ordered to stay awake. "What's happened?!"

"I, I don't know, sir," the nervous soldier stammered. "All appears well here. It must have come from outside."

"What do you mean 'must have come from outside,'?" Zantz questioned. "I ordered you on guard duty, didn't I? Were you not awake?"

The angered general's eyes burned into the man who was in front of him. Zantz's knuckles cracked around the handle of his sword. The anxious soldier visibly trembled before his frightening commander. He knew that his life hung by the thinnest of threads. Thankfully, the general seemed to relent at the last instant. His grip relaxed from around the blade's hilt.

"Find out what it was," he half snarled. "And don't ever let this happen again."

"Yes, sir. Right away," the other swiftly responded. He choked back his meekness as he turned to hurry off. He made it only a few steps toward the door before he stopped in his tracks.

"General," he said in an almost breathless whisper. "I think...I think something's out there."

Each of the men looked to the door. They could all see a dim glow of pale green beginning to slip inside. Everyone in the dining hall stood unmoving as they stared at the entrance. The flickering light slowly grew more intense as it crept from the floor and up the other side. It bled through the large spaces between the rotted timbers that were held together with rusted banding. A biting chill unlike anything that the men had ever felt spilled in. The bitter air assaulted their exposed flesh with needle like pricks. The flames in the fireplace dimmed to little more than candlelight. The temperature plummeted as the bit of water that remained in their drinking skins began to freeze.

Asbjorn watched from the corner as the scene played out. The old wood of the door bowed as the fibers creaked under the strain. The rivets in the iron banding began to groan and pop out. The corroded metal wrenched apart under the force that was being exerted. The men's hearts all pounded in their chests like racing steeds. Their nerves were stretched with an insufferable tension. At last, the ancient wood and rusted metal gave out against the torturous stress. The door breeched inwards to let the spectral light pour in, as well as the fleshless horror that followed it.

It was a terrible thing that entered the great dining hall, a ghostly being that looked to have come from the pits of hell itself. It floated along just above the floor. The tips of its bony toes dragged over the stones. Its face was that of a skeletal phantom. Ghost lights burned in the hollows of its empty eye sockets. Tattered robes and the remnants of a mangy beard wisped about its gaunt frame. A frigid aura of terror and chill rolled off it. In each of its gnarled hands it clutched the throat of one of the men that had stood watch in the hall. Their flesh was withered away, and the blank death stares were frozen on their faces. Asbjorn saw that upon the specter's brow rested a many pointed crown of iron. The thing more than resembled the lord that had been depicted in the circle of thirteen in the faded murals.

The deathly king heaved the two expired guards up by their necks. It flung their rigid corpses at their compatriots who all stood transfixed with terror. One of them flew over their heads to crash through the long table and send bits of clutter scattering everywhere. The other sailed straight towards Zantz. The sight of the incoming body was enough to snap him from his stupor. He dove aside to let the corpse slam to the floor. The dead man tumbled over to come to rest limply before the fireplace. The general came back to his feet shouting at the top of his lungs. He screamed at his men to snap them back to their senses. He came over to shove several of the warriors towards the undead lord. They gave out a deep battle cry to help reclaim their courage.

The soldiers charged at the hovering shade. Their broadswords were raised high over their heads for a haphazard assault. The blades carved into the cold body of the deathless king with ruthless swings. The powerful strokes were more than enough to drop any living man where he stood. But the sharp steel seemed to do nothing but pester the floating spirit. The men backed away as the hideous specter regarded the insolence they dare have. And now they found themselves far closer to the thing than they would have liked. The aura of cold coming off it was already causing their flesh to become frostbit.

Jagged fingers shot out as the undead being seized a pair of men by their faces. Its chill grasp was pure agony to the touch. They thrashed and convulsed as they desperately tried to pry themselves free, but their struggling was of little use against the shade's grasp. Their bodies began to quickly waste away as their kicks and spasming jerks died off. The whole of them shriveled and their joints became rigid and stiff as if death had set in long ago. The dead lord dropped their lifeless forms at its hovering feet. The eyes of pale emerald now turned towards General Zantz and those who remained. The men's expressions were now of pure fright. The corner of Zantz's lip twitched with uncontained dread. His own master was a demon of the highest of power, but Xiphactinas was far to the south, unable to do him any good against the foe that had arrived.

Asbjorn looked in shock as the horrifying spectacle went on. He had never witnessed something such as this. He watched as the deathly king of the forgotten city easily dispatched the initial group of men. It now slowly closed in on the general himself. Zantz and his remaining troop hesitated for a brief instant but then the instincts for sheer survival seemed to take hold. The remnants of the invading warriors all charged at the horrifying shade. Their commander forced them forward to take up his own position at their rear. Then Asbjorn saw it again just out of the corner of his eye, the knife that had been on the table edge and scattered along with the rest of the clutter. He knew without a doubt that this would be his only opportunity. He had absolutely no more time to lose to take advantage of it.

He heaved his muscled frame over the stone, trying to quickly make use of the hellacious slaughter at the center of the room. He could hear the men screaming and the general's brash voice barking out orders. He did not waste an instant to dare an upward glance. The bits of rubbish that had been strewn across the floor were knocked aside in Asbjorn's wake. His bound hands that were tied at his back pawed for the small blade. At last, his fingers closed around the knife's handle. He fumbled to cut the coarse rope from wrists. He struggled to work the blade in small, sawing strokes. As he feared, its edge was beyond dulled but its point was still sharp enough to find its way into his forearms just as it did with his restraints. The piercing shouts were fast dying off as the strands of rope were gradually being split. He knew that he was quickly running out of time to free himself. Finally, the fibers gave out enough that he was able to tear his arms loose. He turned over to pull the gag from his mouth and begin to cut his ankles free.

Only a few of Zantz's men remained but they were so taken with fear that none had an ounce of fight left. The spectral lord crowded their backs up against the wall. Asbjorn continued to cut as chill hands found their throats. The rusted blade had just broken through the binding around his legs when the last of the black warriors fell. Only General Zantz remained to face the shade. The once imposing commander visibly shivered as the deathly king approached him. He somehow summoned the will to force a defiant yell and a last-ditch lunge. But it did him no good against such an enemy. The living that had come to the subterranean citadel had no hope against its undying ruler. Asbjorn saw the general's sword drive into the thing's midsection. The phantasmal lord only stared down at the man. The dots of light in its eyes flared bright. It drew the blade out and tossed the steel aside. It dug its fingertips into the sides of Zantz's head. The general convulsed as he was hoisted off the floor and his flesh started to dry and crack. Asbjorn knew that as soon as the other was dead the ghostly thing would be on him.

He darted across the room as the general's dying form continued to jerk. Asbjorn's legs took him over the fallen dead and scattered rubbish in a burst of speed. At the moment, the deathly king was between him and the door. There was but one option left for him, and it gleamed in the firelight.

He went for his crimson axe that still rested next to his cloak. The blade shined even in the chamber's dimness. He was nearly there when he felt a heavy weight slam across his back. The body of the limp general drove the wind from him as it knocked him to floor. The sickly glow grew brighter over him as his exhausted muscles fought to push Zantz off. The harsh cold that came with it stabbed to his core. He heaved the general aside and crawled towards the axe. His fingers came less than a hair's length away when he felt the freezing needles around his ankle. It was a paralyzing pain that shot through him. It jolted up his leg to hold him in place. The spectral lord pulled him in with a strength that belied its boney frame. The Northman felt the life draining from his body and the frigidness spread through his veins. But there was far more to Asbjorn than there was to the black warriors. He had been forged in the great forests and rugged hills of the north. He fought through the agony that shot through his bones. He dug his nails into the stone to claw with his hands and push off with his legs. With a thunderous cry, he lunged for his waiting weapon. His hand found the handle as if the thing belonged there, and the blade was more than ready.

The crimson steel arced up to bite deep into the right shoulder of the deathly king. It cleaved halfway through the specter's clavicle and into its ribcage. The emerald light in the skull's sockets flared again. A scream so piercing erupted out to nearly split Asbjorn's eardrums. The tight grip that was on his leg eased as he managed to shake off the grasp. He pulled himself away to come to his feet and knock aside the advance of the jagged fingertips. The red blade streaked its way into the flank of the lord's midsection. Another shrill screech burst out that was even more earsplitting than the first. The howl sounded as if it were made up of a chorus of wrathful souls. Before the cry had a chance to die out, the heavy axe came around again, then once more on the backswing to strike with incredible force. The greenish blaze streamed from the cutting wounds that were left in the body of the king of the lost citadel. The floating horror collapsed in a dusty heap. Gradually, the light faded away. The iron crown clanked to the floor as the fleshless remains went motionless.

Asbjorn's chest rose and fell in the swirling dust. Every inch of him shook as his legs gave out and he sunk to his knees. He tried to gather himself in the quiet of the chamber and the warmth of the once again burning fire. The cold that had shot through his body slowly began to dissipate. The needle-like numbness that had nearly paralyzed him was replaced by the tingling return of sensation. He began to ease up for a moment, but his rest was a short relief.

General Zantz rammed into him with a hard forearm to the face. The vicious man rode Asbjorn down to the floor. Asbjorn had thought the general dead but there was still a bit of life in the persistent commander's veins. He came clawing at Asbjorn's eyes with nails that had grown long and brittle. The invader's skin was now wrinkled and spotted. The already deep creases of his face were even more pronounced. Asbjorn seized him by his wrists to keep the general's hands just inches from his flesh. With a quick twist, Zantz managed to slip one hand free of the Northerner's grasp. He dragged over the axe that rest just next to the struggling pair. He picked up the blade and tried to force it into the other's throat. His cloudy eyes were locked with the chestnut orbs of Asbjorn.

"Die, you accursed Northman!" Zantz savagely growled. Specks of foamy spittle sprayed from his mouth. He pushed back against the axe handle and the general's weight. His muscles burned like hot fire under the exertion. The sharp steel continued to inch its way down despite his struggling. The razor edge just cut into his neck to draw a fine trickle of scarlet. Zantz leaned even harder into the weapon as he began to feel Asbjorn faltering. He was determined now more than ever to take the other's head off before it was done. Then he felt himself being hefted upwards. The veins in Asbjorn's arms and chest bulged to the point of bursting.

Asbjorn clenched his teeth and pressed with all his might. The perspiration rolled from his forehead to sting his eyes. In his mind, he saw the faces of all of those that had been killed at the hands of the black army. The image of his lovely Magdalene and Jarl Manus came to him, along with the jarl's wife and even the spiteful Dorn. Deep inside, he could feel it come alive. It was the anger of a seething vengeance and the rage that had allowed him to slay the great devil bear just a year ago. His senses were alight and charged like a scorching inferno, and when Asbjorn was like this, none could stand against him.

The pinned Northman heaved the general into the air. Zantz's feet came up and over his head before he slammed down with a heavy thud. He staggered up to see Asbjorn arise like a spirit of pure vengeance. He could swear that the other's eyes burned red in the firelight. The Northerner stalked towards the backpedaling general. His knuckles cracked around the handle of his axe. Zantz's foot brushed against the hilt of a sword that had been thrown wide in the fight with the deathless lord. He picked up the blade to put the point between himself and Asbjorn.

"Back away, you savage!" threatened Zantz. "Come near me and there'll be blood!"

"I know there will," Asbjorn responded. "All of it yours." And then the big man charged.

Asbjorn's muscles exploded with ferocity. The general's arms were nearly ripped from their sockets as he desperately tried to fend off the blows. Zantz was by far the superior swordsman of the two. He'd weathered years of hard campaigning and fought more battles than the enraged Northerner would ever know. But the icy touch of the deathly king and Asbjorn's power were taking their toll. The Northman was being fueled by a driving bloodlust that the tiring general was unable to match. The crimson axe and Zantz's sword clashed together in the dining hall. Shards of metal were torn away from the general's weapon to glitter as they went flying. Then the chipped sword shattered with a final stroke of his foe's blade. The heavy axe carved through the thing as if it were nothing but a twig. Zantz made a final, listless effort to throw the broken hilt at the bestial Northerner but the other simply bobbed his head to avoid the projectile. The general's strength had long deserted him as the duel had dragged on. He was left defenseless against his foe's vicious retaliation. Through his weariness, the spent commander still managed to hold himself proud and tall, however. He might be broken and defeated, but he was still proud.

"You may kill me, you filthy pig," Zantz puffed. He tottered on his feet. "But my master will have your head by the end of it. You can't win against him."

"Not before I have yours," Asbjorn responded. "For my people!"

The Northman's axe arced one last time in the firelight. The general's shadow that was cast on the wall was one head shorter as it collapsed to the floor. After the final blow, Asbjorn found himself the only living thing left in the lonely chamber, surrounded by the fallen men of the black army and the dusty remains of the once deathless lord. The southern invaders had been put down to the last man. Zantz lay slain along with the rest. Asbjorn was overcome with a relieved shock after so many weeks on the run. He was at last able to rest his exhausted body.

He staggered over to pull his bear's head cloak around his shoulders. He kicked the gold trimmed armor and the death's head helm of the expired Zantz aside. The amber jewels that were the eyes of the ashen beast glittered as he settled in on the general's bedroll. He did not care in the least about the corpses that were slowly going rigid around him. Then he saw something in the warming light that he had not noticed a moment ago. He held out the messy strands of long hair that hung down in his face. They were matted and filthy from the nonstop days he'd been on the run but there was no mistaking the stark difference as they hung between his fingertips. Even through the grime, Asbjorn could plainly see the change. His once sandy mane had been streaked with a silvery white.

VIII

Asbjorn sat in the feasting hall. He rummaged through the few packs he hadn't gotten to yet. He tossed aside the worthless bits that were of little use to him. He'd spent the last two days resting and scavenging what he could from the dead of the black army. He'd dragged their corpses down the hallway so he might be spared their frozen expressions. He had slept away most of the first day wrapped in his warming cloak. He was able to feel the immense fatigue in his body fade away little by little. He'd risen only twice during those initial hours, first to pull out the bodies and then to find a small well in the massive cavern to wash away the filth. His long hair and coarse beard had indeed been marred by a deep streak of silver. It was a stark reminder of the terrible touch of the spectral king. How long they would carry such a marking Asbjorn did not know, nor did he really care if truth be told.

The tired Northerner had returned to the dining hall after cleansing himself. He rekindled the fire and then fell asleep without giving thought to food or drink. Strange dreams came to his mind as he slumbered in the lost city. He saw visions of his father walking calmly through the mists of the Northern Forest, and then of Magdalena being lost somewhere in the dark in search of him. Then he was amongst the stars in the infinite heavens. The specks formed the shape of a great bear that looked deep into his eyes. He floated in the blackness as he stared at the massive animal. The beast seemed to be warning or possibly urging him of something that awaited ahead. And then the shining dots were scattered in all directions. The image was crushed by the outline of a clawed hand that came from deep within the void. Despite the vividness, the dreams were not unsettling or tormenting. They rather brought an odd calm that often falls just before the night of a great battle. He still did not rest as soundly as he would have liked after being chased across the landscape for so long. His body and spirit both needed much more time than they'd gotten. Up and about now, Asbjorn's empty stomach was reminding him of just how hungry he was. He hoped that one of the dead might be carrying something more than he'd already found.

He rifled through several more of their packs. His growling stomach urged him to be quick. He, at last, came across a good portion of dried venison along with two flats of hardened bread. The discs had to be thoroughly soaked to make them anywhere close to eatable. Asbjorn waited patiently unit the rounds had taken in enough moister so they wouldn't crack his teeth. He wrapped the tough meat in the now softened dough. All the meal tasted of was bland mush and bits of coarse salt. But it was food and it filled him up well enough, and that's all that mattered for the time being.

Asbjorn rested in front of the small fire as he chewed a particularly stubborn bit. He was lost in his own thoughts and tried to put the tastelessness and foul texture out of his mind. He wondered what he should do now that General Zantz and his marauders had been slain. All those that had slaughtered his people and razed his village were dead with none that he knew of who remained. He had no idea of who the vicious commander's master was, nor did he have a clue as to where the invading army had come, aside from a land to the south. Zantz had only said that it was his lord's will that the people of the north be put under the blade, but never did he utter the name of the merciless power he served. Asbjorn was divided between returning home or perhaps pursuing whoever it was that Zantz served, but he truly had no notion of where to start with either. He was lost just as he had been after killing the bear, only this time with no one left to pull him back. He had just finished off his last bite when he suddenly heard a soft sound. He sprung to his feet with axe in hand.

It was an odd noise for down here in the stillness of the lost fortress. It was like wind blowing through the chimes the people sometimes hung from their homes back in Brekka. Asbjorn's eyes drifted around the room searching for the source. There was no one besides himself in the dining hall. Then the subtle chiming came again, followed shortly by yet another ring.

His notice was, at last, drawn to a small bag that sat with the others he'd not picked through. A dim glow snuck from under the flap of General Zantz's own pack. Asbjorn lifted the worn leather and undid the small clasp that kept the satchel shut. He was hesitant at first to have a glance at what rest inside. The bag contained only a single item within its lining. A perfectly smooth crystal the size of a ripened fruit.

Asbjorn took the translucent sphere in hand and tossed the pack aside. He held it up to turn it in the light of the flickering fire. He could see the details of his fingertips on the opposite side of the surface. His digits appeared slightly elongated thanks to the orb's curved contours. He examined it with the curiosity of someone who had never seen its like before and then the sound came again.

More and more rapidly the tones started to emanate. They were followed shortly by a dark cloud that began to spiral within the pulsating globe. Asbjorn watched as the indigo mists swirled in a tight vortex. Two burning lights suddenly flared from the center to startle him so much that he hurled the sphere across the room. The orb shattered as it impacted the far wall. The dark shadow that was once inside now rose to spread across the chamber. The twisting blackness looked to be made of the very stuff of the night sky. A void of twinkling lights took the shape of a great horned head. The lights that had burst in Asbjorn's face hovered in the midst of the darkness like two eyes of burning gold. They stared intensely at the shocked Northerner.

"You," said a resonating whisper that shook the chamber. "I can only assume that if you live, then General Zantz has failed in his task, Son of the Bear."

Asbjorn backed away from the waiving form. He kept the crimson blade of his axe between it and himself. He had never previously encountered such sorcery as was now on display. The very presence of it was nearly enough to force him to his knees. But with all he had, the Northerner willed himself to stay on his feet. He showed defiance despite the near suffocating evil, refusing to be pressed down.

"Who are you, demon?" he growled. His limbs shook. "And why did you call me that?"

"I am Xiphactinas," the deep voice responded, "and you have but to look at what you wear upon your shoulders to know why I called you that. I have been wondering what you would look like, Son of the Bear. It pleases me to finally know the face of my enemy."

"I am Asbjorn of Brekka," the big Northman said, "and I know nothing of you. Why do you hunt me? And why did you kill my people?"

"Because the stars have decided it to be so, Northman," Xiphactinas coldly answered. "And I knew not exactly who you were until this instant. All of the people of the Northlands had to be put under the blades of my warriors in order to find you. Consider it a long overdue cleansing that the world sorely needed. But it appears that I have grossly underestimated your tenacity, Son of the Bear. Do not expect it to happen again."

"To find me?" Asbjorn snarled. "You killed all of them, everyone that I ever cared about, just to get to me?"

"Of course," the star flecked shadow responded. "All the more likely to ensure I found who you were. And here you are still holding on, aren't you? And now with the knowledge that your very existence has destroyed all those that you ever cared for. It's good that you still remain Northerner, so that I can take my pleasure in breaking your spirit for myself, before I do the same with your body."

The golden eyes that floated in the void glowed as the faceless form almost smirked. An echoing laughter filled the room from wall to wall. The unsettling mockery of the star flecked being cut straight to Asbjorn's core. His already simmering anger now overflowed in a tide.

"I'll make you burn in hell for what you've done." the big man said. His fingers cracked around his axe handle. "I swear by everything I am, I'll track you to the ends of the earth if I have to. By my word, I'll kill you!"

"Then fall now, Asbjorn of Brekka!" the hissing voice bellowed. The fiery eyes of the horned head exploded into multicolored flames. "Die where you stand, Northman!"

The hovering void spread out with the furious utterance. The endless space streaked at him like a curtain of pure night. He cried out in a bold daring in response. He charged straight ahead to bring down his crimson blade. He cleaved into the void directly between the searing eyes. Every muscle in his body tensed as he carved into the horned blackness that felt all too solid. His axe split the shadowy shape just as it had with the dark armored warriors, but instead of a spew of red, there was a flash of light. As the steel struck home, the darkness burst into a thousand twinkles of starshine. An abyssal scream of wrath and hatred faded as the specks fell. The entirety of the dining hall was illuminated by the dazzling show for a brief instant, and then Asbjorn was once again alone, with not a thing stirring.

The big man glanced around as the last of the sparkles died out. He tried to make sense of what had just occurred. Whatever this demon was, it had been the one responsible for the slaughter of his fellow villagers, along with scores of others that had all called the far north their home. It had sent the armored men that had taken Magdalena from him and that alone was enough to provoke his enmity, regardless of whatever else had transpired. But now, Asbjorn knew the thing's name, and he would let nothing stop him in his search for his renewed vengeance, nothing.

"Xiphactinas," he said in a voice that dripped with venom. "Prepare yourself, demon. For as you called me, the Son of the Bear is coming for you."

To Kill the Stars

I

The scarlet rocks rolled down the side of the steep incline. The stones crashed at the base to break into countless bits. The Crimson Cliffs were known for being one of the most perilous landscapes of the sprawling south, given their name for as much blood that had been spilled here as well as the deep hue of the rock. The hazardous range was as sheer as daggers across most of it. The plunging gorges had claimed more lives than many could count. But the deadly slopes often proved to be the least of some men's worries. The shadowy crevices held things that would make a plummeting fall seem welcome by comparison. The tales of the beasts that made this desolate place their home were not often repeated. The descriptions invoked terrible images and conjured nightmares that were best left unsaid. Worse yet, was what was whispered to rest on the opposite side of the lonely peaks. It was a true hell given form if there ever was one.

Tomek Antal struggled to pull himself up the last few feet of the rock face. He'd been at the climb now since just before dawn. His fingers and the palms of his hands were nearly rubbed raw. His arms and legs ached with fatigue thanks to the ascent. He squinted as even more flecks of grit fell into his face. His gaze remained locked on the edge above despite the dust. With his teeth clenched, he made the last few pulls towards the top. He heaved his body up and over the ledge to find level ground.

It took Tomek a few moments to find his breath. The drab shape of the sun was nearly halfway across the sky. He rolled his sore shoulders and cracked his back to work away the stiffness. His cramped fingers were the last to be flexed and stretched out.

Tomek glanced back the way he had just come. His eyes of dark blue traced down the drop off and over the rough plains beyond. It was nothing but a rocky landscape and empty earth for as far as he could see. The distant cities further to the north were several days ride at best. The featureless expanse made the man think about just how far he'd come to reach here. Not only of the many miles that he'd travelled but also of the harshness that he'd been put through over the years. The past had never proven kind to the sullen Tomek. He'd endured more at his young age than many would in a lifetime. To look on him outwardly would be to see a hardened body riddled with its share of scars. But the taxing toll the abuse had taken had forged his mind into a deadly instrument, one that he had been quick to put to use.

Gradually, Tomek's thoughts drifted back to when his village of Marsax had first been attacked. He remembered the morning that the men in black steel had come storming from the hills to bring fear and bloodshed with them. The people of his home had scarcely been given a chance to put up a fight. The ruthless invaders cut down any who dared to wield a weapon against them, and even some that didn't. Men were driven from their homes and women dragged by their hair to the center of town. The children and the younger adolescence were kicked by armored feet to be herded along with their parents. Once rounded up, the remaining townsfolk were all held at sword point. The tips of arrows were trained on them to ensure their compliance.

The amassed villagers were surrounded by a wall of ebon steel. Each of the townsfolk were more than aware that none of the murderous marauders would hesitate in putting down an unruly captive or two. The fathers and husbands that wanted nothing more than to protect their families were forced to stay their hands. The promise that their sons and daughters would be the first to die kept them in check. Then the circle of blades parted to allow what the young Tomek thought was the devil himself to come through. A man that was clad in gold trimmed armor and rode atop a massive steed trotted into view. The death's head helm he wore made him look like the personification of evil itself. The young boy was able to do nothing but shudder in the dark warrior's presence.

Tomek could not recall what the man who rode upon the horse said on that day. His youthful mind was simply too overcome with fear to remember most of it. What he could recollect was that his people were to be made into slaves, forced to serve the whims of the black army and excavate the hills that surrounded his home. They were made to dig deep into the earth night and day, cutting cavernous shafts that plunged into the ground to haul up the precious ores the invaders needed to craft their sharp blades. Underground cave-ins and deaths within the haphazard mines were commonplace over those first months. The threat of harsh punishments hung over their heads to keep them in line. Tomek was more than once subjected to the malicious penalties imposed by his captors. On one instance he was nearly beaten to death for having kicked up too much dust on the boots of one of the guards. Those that did die or were killed off were quickly replaced by a fresh collection of bodies. The mines were made to be dug deeper and the precious minerals kept flowing. The cost that it took on the once peaceful lands and the people that lived there was not given a second thought.

Nearly two years dragged by as Tomek endured such conditions. He was a boy barely in his teens wondering if he would ever survive long enough to make it out of them. His people were thoroughly broken in spirit by the coming of their wicked captors. They were left to the fleeting mercies of those that possessed little to begin with. But then, late one evening, his father and rebellious uncle began planning something, a dangerous plot to free the enslaved villagers and liberate the oppressed Marsax. For months, they made preparations for their surprise coup, stealing what few weapons they could and hiding them away with the mining implements they'd fashioned into lethal tools. It was an agonizing time as they waited for just the right moment. They observed the occupying invaders to learn their movements. Then one night, Tomek's uncle announced that it was finally time. He planned their uprising for the morning after next. The outcome would hold their lives in the balance.

As the designated day arrived, it started out like any other over the past months. The townsfolk were awakened with the dawn to trudge into the tunnels and relieve those that had worked the night before. Both Tomek's father and uncle knew that a load of ore was leaving for the far south this morning, thinning the number of guards until more arrived to retrieve another haul. They knew the depleted ranks would give them their best chance at victory and all those involved aimed to take advantage of it.

After being chained and secured in place, the villagers in the shafts waited for the guards to return to their posts. They undid their locks with a key they'd managed to palm from one of their less attentive keepers. Once they were free, their patience was pressed even further until the shipment had left and the word was given. The men in the tunnels acted with a swift vengeance once the signal was received. They struck with sharped pickaxe and the short blades they had smuggled in and planted in the mines. They showed the warriors in black the same amount of mercy that had been paid to them, which was none.

The initial wave of guards went down easy for soldiers that looked to be so well armed and armored. The invaders were taken by surprise by the sudden assault. Pickaxe, shortsword, and heavy stone alike all found their marks. The guards' own broadswords were added to the hands of the rebelling villagers. The task to push up and out of the mines was far more arduous than expected. The townsfolk of Marsax and the outer countryside lost no small amount of their own as their captors had scrambled to regroup. They, at last, broke through to the openness of fresh air. They hoped to see their fellows above locked with the reeling marauders, but that is not what they found.

The men's friends and families were all circled around the mouth of the main shaft. They had been betrayed by carefully planted spies that had come from their own number. The guards they'd easily dispatched in the tunnels had been nothing more than expendable footmen. The more hard-bitten soldiers remained up top to be bolstered by the charging return of the feigned ore shipment. The dark armored men held the women, children, and the remaining villagers at the tips of their blades. They commanded those that led the revolt to immediately throw down their weapons and surrender. But Tomek's uncle found himself lost within his own anger at what he saw. He had no intention of giving in or going peacefully. A handful of the more overzealous spat at the invaders as they refused to relent, and from there the slaughter commenced.

Tomek could only hazily remember what happened next. The young man that he was then had blocked much of it from his mind. He recalled that the ones that had been forced to their knees fell first. His uncle and the few others that had rushed in were quickly cut down as more followed. Bodies in tattered rags and black steel all tangled together in the few images he could bring back. The forms that were swathed in filthy clothes dropped away as the ones in ebon armor remained more numerous. Then he was being forcefully pulled along by the arm, dragged through the woods faster than his legs could keep up with.

Tomek's father yanked him onwards in what felt like a whirlwind. The two streaked through the forest just outside the doomed Marsax. The sounds of battle and the painful cries of the villagers gradually faded as they went, replaced by the angry shouts that were already beginning to close in. Tomek could have sworn that the length of his arm was steadily being soaked with a wet crimson. The scarlet droplets left a steady trail over the woodland floor. In their haste, he could not recall that he had ever been wounded, but he could not speak for his father who still hurried him along.

The pair finally came to a jutting ledge that overlooked the river that ran close to their home. Tomek couldn't remember if he protested or not when his father had yelled for him to jump. But that mattered little when the incoming shafts struck the other through the back. Arrows pierced through the man's shoulder and lower midsection. The sharp tips entered into one side of his body to protrude from the other. The young man tried in vain to help his father up, but his hands were quickly knocked aside by the elder's strong arms. Then the flailing boy was up and off his feet. He felt a forceful shove and saw his father's grimacing face moving steadily away. Gravity took hold and he plunged to the foamy waters. He pulled in a deep breath just as he splashed down, and that was all.

Tomek let out a long breath as his thoughts came back to him. He adjusted his belt and bootstraps and looked away from the stretch of flatlands. The dull ache in his arms and legs had gradually dissipated as he took what little rest he could but this was not the time for mournful reflection. He picked himself up and brushed away the bits of grit that clung in his hair. He gathered back the raven strands to tie them in a long tail. His shifted from one side of the cliffs to the other. The emptiness of the flats was replaced by a haunting view.

What Tomek looked upon now was an accursed landscape that could have come from a nightmare. The entire valley was saturated by a waving heat and a dark cloud that hung low. Black smoke billowed from forge and foundry chimneys as gouts of flame followed. He was only able to guess what he might come face to face with once he was amongst them. Then in the distance, he saw his destination awaiting him. Its shining form stood in sharp contrast to the dullness of the rusty peaks. It was the obsidian citadel of the demon himself, taunting Tomek to make his way across the blasted landscape and pass through its gates.

Brushing his fingers across his dagger, he pulled the hood of his old cloak over his head. He made to slide down the opposite slopes and through the drifting smoke that obscured the land beneath. His quarry was so close that Tomek could practically reach out and touch it. It was just the position an assassin of his caliber wanted to be in. In all his time of dealing death, none of his prey had ever seen him coming until it was far too late. He liked it that way and took pride in his skill. In a puff of dust, the clifftop was left void. The killer swiftly descended to do what he did best, snuffing out whoever stood before him.

II

The way down was not nearly as difficult as the climb up. The path Tomek took was a much gentler slope to the valley below. Halfway to the bottom, he managed to get a glimpse at the black pass that was the only way that cut through the Crimson Cliffs. He'd not thought about trying his luck at that dread gorge. The pass was little more than a slim ravine that had been carved into the rocks long ago. The soldiers of the black army used it to move horses, troops, and equipment to and from the obsidian citadel. Thanks to their dark master, the men generally did not have to fear the things that lurked within the gap. The lord they served had been the one to fill its nooks with all manner of wicked things. But sometimes not even that was enough to stop the hungry beasts from picking off a man or two. The poor fellow's comrades would find nothing left of him but crushed steel that was covered in red, if they dared to look for him at all. Tomek had heard too many accounts of the horrors that were said to dwell within the mile-long stretch. He chose the lengthy course of going up and over rather than risk the way of the straight and narrow.

Tomek had to work between the massive boulders that dotted his way. His eyes spotted the remains of those who at one time had the same idea as he. More than one skeletal arm poked from beneath a large stone that had crushed the miserable soul beneath its weight. The skull and what had not been flattened had been picked clean by who knows what. He paid the sight of the strewn dead no mind. The fact they had expired in their actions spoke only of his own talents and their lack of such. He casually passed by the many bones that littered his path, strolling along as if he were very much at home in the bleakness.

Moving away from the jagged ground, Tomek saw that the flatter land would no doubt hold its own perils. The earth beneath his feet was cracked and completely devoid of moisture. He had to step over deep crevices that crisscrossed the land. He was wary of not turning an ankle or twisting a knee over the hazardous terrain. He even had to stop short and backpedal a few steps at several points, getting a running start to leap across the wider fissures. He thought for a moment about the collection of corpses he'd just seen when first descending, wondering how many more might lie at the bottom of the rough gouges that marred his way. At last, Tomek began to see the first signs of what could be called life since here. His sense of alertness heightened the closer he drew to the shifting shapes.

The assassin tugged his hood further down as he began to wander past small groupings of men. The oppressed locals stood next to pushcarts and shoveled dirt into pits that appeared to contain the remains of hundreds. Tomek snaked around countless mounds of earth with his hand on his dagger. The further he pressed the more dismal his surroundings became. The sprawling burial ground was dotted with makeshift markers of skulls that rose high. He finally left the mass graves behind to come to the edge of what might be called a village of some sort, or at least as close to that as the scattered dwellings could be.

The first thing to hit Tomek was the horrid smell that hung in the air. The stench of innumerable pigs was unmistakable to his nose. A sea of swine yards and rudimentary farms spread out around him. The animals feasted on a mixture of mush and what looked to be butchered corpses. In all directions, a maze-like web of troughs and hog pins sprawled. The squeals that emanated from the enclosures came in waves of disharmony. The pigs were packed in one on top of the other. The beasts were round and fat to provide ample meat to the forces of the lord of this land.

Tomek finally weaved his way to one of the mud-churned paths that traversed the landscape. He stuck to the far edge to avoid getting slogged in the filth that saturated the middle. He ambled by several meandering farmers that tended to the troughs and the yelping livestock, cautious of being spotted or recognized as an outsider. But then he saw that his own tattered cloak nearly perfectly matched the apparel of the natives. His tensions eased as he doubted that any would notice him should he walk in plain sight with blades on display. Not a single upward glance was cast in his direction. Everyone here knew their place, and it was with eyes down and tending to the hogs.

Tomek was thankful that the path he followed finally took him out of the squalid farmland. He was not at all sorry to have the stench gone from his nostrils. Then he saw where it was leading him to next. He knew that he would have to be completely on guard with where he was headed.

The stacks of the fiery foundries stood tall to welcome him. The black smoke spewed high to drown the valley in a haze that choked the air and dimmed the sun. This was the first time the assassin had glimpsed the men in ebon steel since entering this land. The guards patrolled between the smiths to keep the slaves that worked the bellows in line. He also noticed more men here that hauled the pushcarts that he'd seen near the burial mounds. Their wagons were loaded with the bodies of expired workers to be taken and carved up for swine feed and the leftovers thrown in the dirt. The scene once more harkened him back to the years of hell he'd lived through in Marsax. His ire began to rise but his resolve kept it in check.

Tomek darted amongst the roaring forges. The sound of metal striking metal came to his ears as steel was pounded into murderous blades. Over the endless clanging, he could also pick up the rough growls of the taskmasters. The snap of leather followed by painful cries could be heard between the drops of the hammer. As the assassin slunk through the shadows, he could not help but wonder how much of the ores from his own village had passed through this place, and also of how many instruments of death they were used to create to support the army's crusades.

Tomek came to the end of the forges and had hoped that more light would be able to sneak through the cover of smoke. The rays of the sun tried but were simply not strong enough to penetrate. The only illumination was from the flashes of fire that sporadically spouted from the foundries' stacks. It bathed the landscape in a hellish glow of orange and red. The assassin had finally come to stand just before the dread fortress. He took in the malevolent majesty of the place as he lingered in the shadows. Walls of ashen stone rose above as the only gateway arched like a waiting maw. The closed doors on the far side of the drawbridge were adorned with spikes and jutting studs. Braziers of burning oils topped the ramparts. The guards in their dark steel walked to and fro along the high battlements. But standing at the very center is what commanded Tomek's attention most. The gleaming tower of pure obsidian rose like a sword to split the heavens. The multifaceted sides reflected the flames of the forges over the land. The flashes played over the black glass in a dance of hot colors. The assassin knew without a doubt that the quarry he sought was somewhere inside, but the challenge was getting in undetected.

Tomek checked his back for an instant and then observed the roving sentries that patrolled the parapets. He noted their sauntering patterns before readying himself. In between two of the flashes, Tomek sprinted like a tiger. He hurried to the edge of the tall drop off that encircled the citadel. It would have been a troublesome time for even the most seasoned to make their way along as stealthily as Tomek did. The seconds between the bursts and the soldiers' gazes passed by in a blink. But for a man such as he, it was all in a day's work. The time between now and when he was a boy had been put to efficient use.

Ten years had nearly gone by for Tomek since his village had been taken. The things he'd been put through since then were enough to break most. He had been a scared adolescent when he first pulled himself from the river that his father had flung him to. He was nearly dead from exhaustion when he collapsed in the forest a few yards from the banks. He'd been found miles downstream by a small trade caravan that had wandered by to water their mules. He was taken into the vagabonds' numbers and made one of their own, but they did not often treat him as such.

The next few years were a cruel trial for him. The lashings he was made to endure made him weep every bit as those he'd received in Marsax. But gradually, there came to be no more tears to shed for the tortured Tomek. The sorrow he felt was slowly replaced by a strong hate. Soon, the end of the whip held no fear for him. The promised pain helped to forge him into something much harder, and he'd become very dangerous because of it.

Then, one evening, the caravan master thought to lay a harsh punishment on him during a drunken moment. He quickly found that Tomek had a much different plan on this night. The young man wrestled the lash away from his fat assailant, stringing it tight around the other's neck to choke the man to death before fleeing into the nearby city. That was the first time that Tomek had ever taken a life with his own hands. He'd felt the exhilaration of it through every bone in his body. He'd never had power like that before that he could ever remember. He almost rejoiced in the act of slaughter, and he knew that he could do it again.

In the years that followed, the young man from Marsax had fashioned himself into a merciless killer. He had only taken to murder for food and what coin he needed to survive at first. There were times when he nearly became the victim to be sure, but as his skills improved, so did the helplessness of his targets.

197

Soon, Tomek began to kill purely for profit. He became one of the most sought-after assassins in the lands to the north by those who knew where to look for him. One evening, he was having a drink in a small tavern after a particularly dull and uninteresting contract. The doors of the place had swung open as a group of men that wore the black steel strode in. He remembered well the ebon armor as soon as he saw it, as well as what the men that wore it had done to him so long ago, and he was no longer a frightened boy.

The patient killer watched as the three in dark steel cursed and bullied the other patrons and tavern workers. His boiling blood was kept in check by nerves that had been well tempered to such happenings. He cared not a bit for the harassed tavern goers or the serving women that had to put up with the crudeness of the soldiers. His eyes and thoughts were focused solely on the men in black and what he wished to do to them.

Tomek waited in his seat for several hours as the men ate and drank their fill. The three took turns running their hands up every inch of their serving maid as they accosted other patrons. The old keeper was more than pleased when the threesome finally grew bored and took their leave. He had wanted them gone since the second they walked in, but he was too afraid to speak up and raise their wrath. Tomek quietly followed the group as they stumbled back to the stables of the small roadside village. He cut them off as they went to retrieve their horses to ride back to their encampment a few miles away.

The conversation that followed proved to be short and sweet between the three men and the assassin. Tomek demanded to know where they came from and who their lord was. He received no small amount of boasting and threats in response. The swords of the black armored warriors were drawn as a slight smile came to his face.

In fewer seconds than there were men, it was all over and done with. There was a flash of steel followed by a swift movement and a pair of soldiers fell dead. The third's nose was crushed and his mind struck into unconsciousness before the other two could hit the ground. The assassin wiped a bit of blood from his dagger and slipped it back into its sheath. By the time the battered man came to, he was in the darkened woods somewhere outside the village. He was stripped bare and tied to a tree with coarse rope that bit into his flesh. Tomek rested next to a small fire that burned nearby. He came over to again ask who the man's master was when he noticed the other stirred. Once more, he received nothing but rudeness. He was pleased that the other had refused to comply, now having the perfect excuse to extract the information the harsh way.

The torture that followed was over far too quickly for the assassin's satisfaction. Tomek had only to remove a few fingers and stab a fistful of burning sticks into the other to learn what he wished. Despite a promise to the contrary, the killer slowly dispatched his pleading captive, setting out the next morning before the sun could rise to begin his trek south. He had a long overdue appointment with his far-off quarry, a prey that he had only ever heard whispers of but otherwise new nothing about.

Tomek skidded to a stop at the bottom of the drop-off. He used the light of the bursting fires to make his way along. His back was pushed flush against the fortress walls where the stone met the ground. He slithered across the rocks like a venomous viper. The guards that patrolled along the bulwarks still had not a clue to his presence. He followed his nose and a reflecting glimmer that showed just in front of him. He finally came to what he'd been searching for in the darkness.

Tomek pulled off his dirt-stained cloak and flung it to the shadows. His dark leathers beneath made not a sound as he waded into a pool of water that trickled from the fortress foundations. The stinking puddle came just above mid-thigh by the time he reached the grating on the opposite side. He had to work to pry the rusted bars free from where they were set in the stone. Fortunately, the rock was brittle near the bottom of the interlaced steel. The granite had been worn away after years of enduring the stagnant flow. The assassin was able to wedge it aside with the tip of one of his knives, just enough to slip through and then let it slide back to leave not a trace of his entrance.

Where the killer found himself next was a foul and disgusting place. The stench made the odor of the hog fields seem like a sweet perfume by comparison. He squirmed through the tight sewer on his hands and knees. His face was just inches from new and ancient filth alike. This was certainly not the first instance that Tomek had found himself in such an unenviable spot, but it had been quite some time since he would not be getting paid for it. But this was a personal vendetta that he sought to settle and not business. Money meant nothing to the slinking assassin for once. This kill was for himself and himself alone. It was one that was long past its due and not to be denied.

Xiphactinas, Tomek thought. The tiny speck of light at the end of the drain faded behind him. *Get ready for me, you bastard. This is your last night on this world. I swear it!*

III

The ripples spread out as Tomek passed from the drain-off. He came to a large chamber with snaking spillways that ran from a wide pool at the center. The foulest of muck dripped from a rusted grating that was set in the ceiling. A few torches burned in their places along the walls. He had paddled for what felt like days through the many drains that twisted beneath the obsidian citadel, wondering if he would ever find his way from the murky sewage. His eyes stung and his throat burned thanks to the amount of refuse that he'd found himself in. He'd lost track of how many times he was left gagging for breath. He was beginning to think that he would never make it out of the subterranean hell that he crawled through, but finally he had managed to catch the faintest wafting of fresh air, following it to where he emerged.

Tomek remained half submerged as he continued to paddle through the filth. Only the top of his head was visible as he hugged the sides of the sewer and carefully scanned the dimness. His eyes picked up no signs of movement in the flickering torchlight. He paused for a moment just inside the drainage mouth to listen and confirm the emptiness. Satisfied, he eased himself up and out of the drink. His dark leathers were soaked, and his boots were full of sludge. He drained the dripping muck from his footwear and wrung the stink from his hair. He did his best to ignore the way his skin crawled at the vileness.

Somewhat decent, the assassin crept out into the chamber. The steady stream that dripped from the ceiling combined with the torches to cast an eerie air over the room. The large pool looked to be a central sewage hub for the whole of the citadel above, collecting every bit of the waste that was put down the garbage chutes and funneling it here. Tomek marked it odd at first that there appeared to be no guards stationed in the lonely place. Perhaps having a room so well-hidden and riddled with stench made them feel that securing it better was not necessary. Then he thought that maybe those that watched over it might be waiting just outside the doors, avoiding the smell while poised to pounce on any who came through.

The assassin had to be wary of his precarious footing as he pressed on. The thick scum that was caked over the floor made it a slippery go. He was more than careful with his footfalls, purposefully stepping over the many channels that drained away from the main hub. On the opposite side of the chamber, he caught sight of a short set of steps. The stairs led to what looked to be the only door out of here. He gave a long breath of relief as he thankfully headed for the exit. He was ready to leave what still assaulted his senses far behind, but then a sudden splashing came to his ears.

The killer whirled and instinctively snatched his dagger. He gazed over the room and waters as he readied himself for whatever might come. He still saw nothing as he came around. The few torches that dotted the walls were hardly brighter than a candle flame. Then something began to rise up from beneath the ripples of the central hub. It was an odd round glow that strangely bobbed and swayed a few feet above the water. The pale yellow reflected from the steady dripping that rained from above. The color played through the surface and off the ripples to almost lull him into dropping his guard.

Without warning, the surface of the mire suddenly erupted. A long tentacle shot forth to dart straight toward the assassin's head. Tomek threw up his off hand to catch the incoming appendage by reflex. Its forceful jerk towards the pool yanked him across the slimy floor. With a glimmer of steel, he severed the tip of the sinewy whip with his dagger. A creamy spew came from the end that somehow smelled fouler than the waste. The rest quickly slithered back to disappear into the filthy water. The globe fell with a splash to follow suite.

Tomek tossed the wiggling end aside and looked to see a smearing of red running from his hand. The blood seeped from several small wounds where the boney hooks at the tentacle's tip had dug in. He stared back toward the settling filth when the pale orb again appeared just beneath surface. The soft light lingered for just an instant before Tomek was bathed in a foamy spray.

The pool exploded as the slime covered beast burst from the run-off. Its rotund body was propelled forward by long spindly arms and a pair of squat legs. Its bulbous form appeared to be made of mostly mouth and limbs. The teeth that lined its maw were as long as a man's forearm and came to needle points. Tomek back peddled as the creature came snapping towards him. The spry killer swiftly side stepped to avoid its clumsy charge. Small beady eyes watched him as he gracefully moved away. The glowing globe dangled back and forth from a fleshy stalk that protruded from its head.

Tomek set himself for a lunge after gliding aside. The tension in his legs tightened as he saw what was an unguarded opening. His muscles coiled like compressed springs ready to strike. Then the thing's jaws opened to nearly split its head and body in half. Its many forked tongue lashed out in a bundle of licking scourges. The assassin had to stop short and retreat even further in less than a second. His ears picked up the harsh ticks as tiny hooks scraped across the stone where he'd just stood. He could now plainly see why there were no guards on duty down here.

The long tentacles slithered back into the creature's mouth. The ribbons of slime that dripped from its lips nearly hung to the floor. The sides of its head pulsated just behind the hinge of its jaws. Its film covered eyes twitched up and down and side to side as it still tracked him. It stood motionless save for the occasional turn of the head and the wiggle of a clawed finger or two, almost as if it were sizing up the man as much as he did it. Perhaps it was wondering if something that proved so elusive was worth pursuing as its prey, but then it had been quite some time since an intruder had passed through its lair, and it was beyond hungry.

Tomek inched back as the thing still followed his every move. The heel of his boot hit where the wall met the floor. He stood with his back just inches from the unyielding stone. He slowly twirled his dagger end over end as he watched it watching him. His heart thumped in his chest as he waited for the thing to make its next move. He knew that he would have to be fast when it finally did. Then its mouth gaped open once again. The many tips of its tongue streaked straight at him for another try.

Tomek managed to duck aside with less than a hair's width to spare. One of the creature's fleshy lashes came so close it took off a portion of his sleeve as it zipped by. Missing their mark, the hooks at the end hit the wall with enough force that several stuck fast. The assassin saw his opening and wasted little time in taking it.

Tomek came down with the blade of his dagger in a swift slash. He severed the two soft appendages that were stretched taut and caught in the stone. The creature gurgled in pain as its tongue whipped back into its mouth. A viscous fluid pumped from the ends of the severed tentacles. The assassin followed behind the retracting appendage to quickly press his advantage. The reeling beast halfheartedly came at him with its gangly claws. The hardened killer avoided the rakes with more ease than would be expected, leaving retaliating gashes along the thing's forearm. In desperation, the wounded creature shot out with its tongue again. Tomek seized one of the ends that was still intact to give it a forceful tug. The bulbous beast stumbled towards him on squat legs that should not have been able to support its weight, bringing it dangerously close to the poised assassin, which is just where he wanted it.

Tomek's dagger struck with a flash. The dangling orb at the end of the head stalk was sent flying. Glowing ooze spattered the floor as the fleshy globe sailed through the air. Tomek released the slimy tentacle as the howling monster made a swift retreat. It splashed down back in the central pool to be swallowed up by the stinking sewage. The surface of the murky water slowly went still save for the ripples from the dripping above. Then the chamber was quiet.

Tomek went to one of the branching run-offs. He kept an eye on where the creature had submerged and rinsed the glowing gunk from his dagger. He was still wary of whatever else was lurking nearby, not knowing what other things were swimming in the cloudy drink after his encounter. He half expected the door of the chamber to come swinging open and a handful of guards to rush in, hurrying to investigate the gruesome howling that had just sounded out. But then he supposed that no man would wish to see such a beast that dwelled here enjoying its latest meal. He relaxed somewhat as he slipped his blade back into its sheath.

Tomek went to the door that was still closed. He listened with one ear pressed against the wood. Thankfully, he picked up nothing of notice. He gave a slight nudge but found the portal to be firmly locked, just as he thought.

He plucked out a few tools of the trade from one of the small pouches at his waist. A turn of his wrist and the click of a latch and the lock was opened. The expert killer cracked the door just enough to quickly poke his head out and then back in again. He saw nothing but a single torch that burned in the passage. He wondered what else he would come across as he ventured further into the black citadel. He knew that he would have to maneuver past the armored guards and others that would likely be roaming through the halls. But what mere men were capable of held no fear for him. Tomek was more than apt and ready to deal with their like. But having already encountered one beast he knew there were bound to be more. The gods only knew how terrible those might be, or perhaps worse. With the grace of a slinking predator, he slipped from the chamber to lock the door as if his passing had never occurred. His nerves were steeled and his quick striking dagger at the ready as the latch clicked shut.

IV

The shrill screams echoed through the halls as Tomek slunk past another doorway. The agonies of the poor soul within were apparent in the cries. The assassin carefully poked his head around the corner of the chamber. He saw two brutish men drenched in sweat that were gleefully at work on a third. A fire pit crackled at the center of the room. The pair of merciless torturers replaced one poker into the flames as they pulled out another. They scraped the glowing tip across the inner arms and raw chest of their manacled captive. The words they snarled were inaudible as the prisoner shouted and thrashed on the table. Tomek could swear that the utterances were something about this being the price for failure, but he couldn't be sure over the piercing shrieks. Whatever it was mattered little to him.

Tomek glided past the door with the two tormentors distracted. He continued through the twisting corridors that ran beneath the fortress. He had made his way by dozens of barred cells and smaller chambers as he'd come up from the undercroft. Some rooms were empty, but most were crammed to the brim with doomed wretches and the sadistic jailors that were all too eager to ply their craft. Brawny men in black hoods all roamed through the dungeon halls. The wily assassin had to think fast more than once to avoid detection. He ducked into niches and slipped behind doors to keep from being spotted. At one point he even suspended himself between the walls with feet and arms as a group walked just beneath him. The further Tomek managed to sneak, the more choked the citadel became. The cunning killer had to constantly be on guard. But this is what it had been like ever since he'd entered the south, having to watch his back even more than usual since beginning his trek.

The assassin had managed to procure passage with a small trade caravan after his interrogation of the soldier in the woods. He moved along with the peddling nomads and learned all he could of the black army along the way. He picked up bits and pieces of information at every stop they made, discovering that the forces of Xiphactinas were steadily on the move and expanding northward every day. It was not until the convoy managed the long journey across the Glass Desert that Tomek learned anything useful about his reclusive target. He left the caravan behind once they'd reached the far-off city of Shavar, the last bastion of what passed as humanity before reaching the Crimson Cliffs.

Shavar was a place that was said to be a hell to some and a heaven to others. All manner of pleasures and dark vices were indulged within its walls. It was ruled over by the hedonistic King Murat. He was a man that had grown much in power and riches thanks to his bargains with the master of the obsidian fortress. From people who meddled with things best left unspoken, Tomek heard a series of contradicting accounts. Some swore that Xiphactinas was a demon in the service of dark gods while others thought he was nothing more than a concocted myth. Whatever the case may be, it was known that Murat had made a deal with the devil of the far-off tower. He provided an endless stream of slaves and other goods in exchange for wealth and the assurance the black soldiers would let Shavar be.

It was after hearing this that Tomek's risky idea came to mind. The assassin staked out the routes of the slave trains that left for and came from the Crimson Cliffs. They arrived and departed at the exact time every other day. The caged wagons and cruel slave masters would pick up a new load of servants and head out just after dawn. Tomek observed their comings and goings from atop the city walls for over a week. He decided on the perfect spot along the roadway where he would make his move. He set his position late one night when the moon was low, digging a shallow pit and covering himself with the loose sands. He then waited patiently until the morning arrived. His unwary target passed just over the top of him right before daybreak.

The killer latched his hooks to the slave wagon's underside. He pulled himself up with a pair of straps and cinched them tight to hang against the bottom. The sand that had covered him immediately fell back, flattening out in such a way that none would have known he was ever there. He then settled in to endure the jostling ride that was to come. He was uncomfortably strapped below the swaying carriage to feel every bump in the road. For nearly two days, Tomek listened to the slaves' pleas and their appeals for mercy. Their requests were met in return with the pitiless response of the cruel wagon masters that raked their prods across the cages. He also had to listen to the accompanying soldiers speak of the black pass that waited ahead. They lamented that there was no other way around and warned one another to be alert once they reached the gorge. It was thanks to these comments the assassin thought that he had best not try his luck in the hazardous narrows. He freed himself from the cart and slipped away the night before they reached the cliffs.

Tomek took all the next day to shelter in a small cave at the base of the peaks. He rested his aching muscles and indulged in some food and water he'd managed to procure from the slavers. The assassin began his ascent up the treacherous mountainside before daybreak the morning after. He chose a spot that appeared the easiest but still held its own share of risks. A short while after noon, he laid his eyes on the lands of Xiphactinas and the bleak citadel at their center. The radiance of the obsidian tower rose above the smoke of the spreading foundries. He was within the halls of that dread fortress now, just leaving the lower confines, but there was still more than enough danger ahead.

Tomek eased the heavy door open to glance through the crack with one eye. A bit of fresher air snuck in with the dimmest of light. He immediately pushed it closed again as two robed figures swathed in violet walked past. Their hands were folded in their baggy sleeves and their hooded heads bowed low. He held his breath and readied his dagger for just an instant. He was fearful that his presence had finally been detected. But nothing ever came as he still seemed to go unnoticed. The men's footsteps faded away as they never broke stride. He eased the door open again to make sure they were gone. He slid out to find himself in a long open hall with one side overlooking a central courtyard. The creeping assassin nudged the portal shut and hugged behind one of the support pillars. He took in the view below and what lay on the opposite side.

Hundreds of black steeled soldiers exercised in the sprawling expanse. They were surrounded by groupings of the men that wore the purple robes and tended to their every need. Footmen went through drill after drill with their blades. Their commanders barked out a strict cadence and harshly corrected any errors. Across from them, others were lined up to practice with bow and arrow. The archers sent wooden shafts one after the other into targets that were all peppered with projectiles. It looked like the ebon army of hell itself preparing to bring death to the world, made all the more fearsome by the setting sun and the fires that burned in the surrounding braziers. But on the other side of the teeming throngs is what drew the assassin's eye most. It was the obsidian tower that waited for him. Its entryway was lined with fiery basins and the gates gaped wide. The sight brought a twinge of doubt to Tomek for the first time since entering here. He wondered how he would make it across the no man's land of dark armored men. He was certain of not being able to just blend in as he'd done back in the swine fields. Then his gaze was drawn to what was almost right below him. A risky notion started to enter his mind.

Pairs of black steeled soldiers vigorously clashed with one another just beneath him. Their comrades that waited for their own turns circled around to jeer and goad them on. Tomek had seen men in various militia spar and face off together many times before, but never had he witnessed two go at it with such an apparent mindset to kill each other. It was a violent training session with the blunted blades they wielded. The combatants fought like men whose very lives hung on the line. Sword banged against shield as they crashed together. The stiff shoulders they threw were more than enough to cause serious injury. Then one of the soldiers took the unsharpened steel hard to the side of the head. His helmet flew off in a spray of red as his eye was bludgeoned from the socket. The men that stood watching erupted as his limpness crumpled to the ground. His opponent soaked in the moment to strut and revel in his superior prowess. One of the overseeing commanders came to nudge at the unconscious man with the toe of his boot. He motioned two of the robed figures into action when he was met with nothing but a groan, and Tomek knew this was his chance.

The two men in violet dragged the motionless soul into a passageway that was only a few paces down. The killer hurried through the open hall and the door at its end. Down a twisting stair and through another corridor Tomek slipped, moving with all the haste he dared to but not so recklessly that he would be discovered. He could only guess that he was taking the right path to where the robed men were headed. He was still completely unfamiliar with the interior of the fortress and going on pure instinct. But the sounds that came to him told Tomek that he was indeed heading on the correct course. He followed the muffled voices and the clanking of steel.

The assassin came to where the two robed men were in the process of stripping the unconscious soldier down. They showed no regard for the injured man as they tossed his armor to the corner of the room. He breathed raspingly as they yanked the last of the steel plates away. His bleeding head was

211

jostled against the table where he lay. Once naked, he was taken under each arm and again dragged away. The pair in purple pulled him along like nothing more than a limp sack.

Tomek followed as they hauled the man into the recesses of the stronghold. He trailed through the dark halls and down steep steps until they came to a large chamber with a deep pit at its center. The pair left the soldier resting while they both worked a chain hoist that raised the cage that covered it. A chorus of hisses and shrill croaks emanated from below as the lid was lifted. The assassin crouched by the door and watched as the half-dead man was picked up by the wrists and ankles. He was swung back and forth like a pendulum to be thrown into the pit. With a crunching of bone, he was torn apart by whatever it was that dwelled at the bottom. The killer knew it was his moment, and he struck.

Tomek rushed forward in a blur of silent motion. He planted a foot directly in the back of one of the men and struck the other across the throat with the edge of his hand. The unfortunate fool he kicked went sailing into the hole. His cries were quickly cut short once he reached what lurked below. The other writhed on the floor clutching at his windpipe. The assassin put a single foot over his neck until his movements ceased. He slipped off the man's robes to put them on over himself. He rolled the former owner over the edge of the pit to join what was left of his comrade. He dared a glance down only to make out vague and horrifying shapes that feasted in the shadows. He thought it was perhaps better not to get a full view as he glimpsed a fleshy appendage covered in barbed suckers. The confrontation with the sewer beast was still fresh in his memory. He was able to go the rest of his days without seeing anymore of Xiphactinas's pets. Tomek left the chamber just as it was when he had first arrived, with the caged lid closed and the door shut. The sound of tearing flesh still came to his ears as he departed.

With his disguise in place, the assassin felt more at ease walking through the halls with little threat of being detected.

The few men he did pass gave only an odd sniff here or there at the strong sewer stench that still clung to him. He went back out the way he'd come. The dark soldiers were just finishing their drills as the sun finally set. Tomek strode straight across the courtyard as the commanders still bellowed at the assembled men. He followed a few others that wore the violet robes as the line passed between the flaming basins and into the tower. For only an instant, he gave pause and stared skyward. His gaze traced along the hard facets and sharp edges of the rising obsidian. As he narrowed his eyes, he bowed his head as he'd seen all the other hooded men doing, folding his hands within his sleeves to seem just as they were. He knew that Xiphactinas lurked somewhere within the dreadful citadel. He tapped at his dagger that wished to meet the lord of the black tower even more than he did.

Tomek passed between the fiery basins and through the doors. The image of a horned head with a five-pointed star emblazoned upon its forehead adorned each. He entered into the dark spire with nothing but vengeance and death on his mind. He knew his steel thirsted for the same thing.

V

Tomek stepped into the citadel to be welcomed by a cacophony of strange intonations. The words flowed into one another to make all of it incomprehensible to him. Once they'd passed through the doors, the line of robed men he followed split off in all directions. Some turned to adjacent antechambers while others continued down the long hall that stretched on. The assassin fell in and trailed in the steps of those that went straight forward. He walked down a tall passage that towered far above him. The walls of black glass rose up to seamlessly merge into one vaulted archway after the other. The pointed apexes ran the length of the lofty corridor. It felt to Tomek like being swallowed down the gullet of an immense beast. The midnight arches surrounded him like a boney ribcage after being devoured, never again to see the light.

He began to see other rooms and branching halls that diverged from the main passage. The small side chambers were all filled with the hooded attendants that knelt low and gathered around similar effigies. They bowed and prostrated themselves before a featureless horned head of indigo marble. A pair of horns crested from the thing's brow and two orbs of the finest gold were set in its eyes. Tomek noted the similarities of the depicted image to those that were displayed on the main doors. He supposed it must be the likeness of whatever dark god that Xiphactinas and his followers had come to worship.

At the end of the corridor, the killer came to what could only be described as a cathedral of the most blasphemous order. The interior was filled with scores of the men in violet that all gathered around yet another depiction of the dark deity. This image was a full figure that stood nearly twenty feet tall. The statue was seated upon a marbled throne that its contours flowed elegantly into. A single man stood before the likeness of the being with his arms wide. A five-pointed star of shining ocher adorned his robes. Tomek made to kneel and join in with the rest of the worshippers. He did his best to repeat the chanting his ears took in. But then he saw a curving stairway half hidden behind the base of the terrible idol. His instincts pressed him in that direction to leave the minster behind.

The assassin was across the floor and his feet on the steps before any could notice him. He left no more trace than a shadow chased away by the coming of the sun. Up the stairs and through the halls above he went. He wandered past the many chambers that were the dwelling places of the robed men. Behind most of the closed doors he heard nothing but silence, but concealed by others he could just pick up the muffled traces of rapturous, and sometimes painful, moaning. The voices and whispers of men and unseen woman alike could barely be made out on the opposite side. What deviant acts were being indulged in the skulking Tomek was only able to guess. He stopped not once to take a look inside. He continued onward to take a winding stair he saw at the end of the hall.

The further up Tomek went, the quieter and more deserted the citadel became, until only his own heartbeat came to his senses. He crept down lonely corridors and up even more flights of steps. The tower was a seemingly unending expanse of halls and stairways. It marveled the assassin at the sheer volume of black glass that was used in the construction. The amount of obsidian that made it up and how it was able to support its own weight was an almost unfathomable thought. It was whispered by those who were believed to know that Xiphactinas was some kind of godly thing in his own right. Perhaps such a being's power had something to do with keeping the mass of the tower standing. But the assassin had never met a god or demon in the flesh before. The prayers and pleas from his many victims had certainly never invoked such a thing to manifest. In Tomek's mind, Xiphactinas was nothing more than a man or group of men, commanding the most foolish and fanatic of followers with everything else an exaggeration. Soon, the word would be nothing more than a memory in the minds of those who cared to think of it, if anyone would ever recall it at all.

At last, the assassin came to a wide set of stairs that seemed to stretch the width of the entire tower. The muscles of his legs already burned from how high he'd climbed. At the top, he followed a path of lush indigo that ran over the lustrousness beneath his feet. He approached a tall set of doors that went from floor to ceiling. On either side stood men that wore the black armor. Theirs was trimmed in gold and their eyes watched him from behind the thin slits of their skulled helms. The pair crossed the shafts of their glaives as he stopped halfway down the passage. The killer was surprised that there were only two guards to watch over a place that he thought this was.

"Just where do you think you're going, wretch?" one of the dark clad men asked as Tomek lingered. "You know very well that initiates aren't allowed above the lower levels. Well," he demanded, "speak up, fool."

"I'm going through the doors that are just behind you," the assassin whispered. "And there's nothing that either of you can do to stop me."

"How dare you speak to a guard of the sanctum in such a manner," the sentry responded. "You clearly forget your place. Who the hell do you think you are?"

"Your death," the hardened killer remarked. "You and your master's."

Tomek tore off his robe and flung it forward before either of the men could react. The billowing fabric flew over the head of the guard he'd just conversed with. The assassin pulled two small knives that were tucked into his belt. He pitched the blades at the other sentry that was fast moving to meet him. The tips found their way just between the top of the man's breastplate and the bottom of his helm. The points sunk deep into his neck to drop him in mid charge. By the time the other had rid himself of the blinding cloak he was on his own. His eyes went wide as he tried to pick up the assassin's position. The killer was already less than two steps away. Which was ample distance for the adept murderer to deal with even the most armored of foes.

Tomek hit in a dizzying display. His dagger plunged into the guard's body and flailing extremities like the stinger of a scorpion. Through the elbow joint, up under the arm, and into the back of the knee the blade sank. The overwhelmed sentry had no chance against the attacker that was now well inside his guard. He crumpled to the floor just a short distance from his motionless friend. The assassin's blade dropped one last time to make sure it was all said and done, and then Tomek was alone.

The killer wiped the red from his steel as the guard ceased to sputter. He stepped over the corpses to stand before the rising doors. The slight nervousness he'd felt when first approaching the tower suddenly crept back in. The twinge made the hairs on the back of his neck stand up to remind him of his discomfort. Tomek normally enjoyed the anticipation that took hold just before drawing in for the kill. The sensation typically signaled the one thing in the world that made him feel truly alive. But this time it was disturbingly different for the hardened man. The tingle was like an approaching dread that reassured him this was no ordinary target.

Tomek pushed the lofty doors open after taking a steadying breath. He slipped through the space between them when it was just large enough for him to fit. What he found on the opposite side was something that even his seasoned eyes had never beheld, a wonder that hung above his head and seemed to exist in an endless dream of black, or was it more of a nightmare?

Celestial shapes churned and moved in the void like expanse that existed within the chamber's confines. The perfectly polished walls of gleaming obsidian reflected a sea of stars and the heavenly bodies that floated along. Planetoids circled around a central sun that shown dim. The dark oblivion twinkled with burning dust and was split by the trails of streaking comets. Along the floor, the runner of deep indigo continued to stretch from the hall outside, leading the way to a raised dais whereupon sat a throne of oxidized bronze. The metal of the seat looked to have been pulled and worked as if it were made of a malleable liquid. The top came to a spire that resembled outstretched claws. Tomek's thoughts almost refused to comprehend what it was that he looked upon. They were hesitant to accept that something like this could even exist, and then came a haunting voice.

"I was wondering when you would finally make it through my citadel," said a disembodied whisper. "Welcome to my inner sanctum, assassin. It pleases me to have a guest after so long."

"I'm no guest," Tomek growled in response. "I'm your executioner. Now show yourself!"

"If that is what you wish, assassin," replied the whisper. "I am only too willing to grant you the request you ask. But know that such a thing will only hasten your own death, Tomek of Marsax. If the time you have left means so little to you."

"How is it that you know my name and where I'm from?" asked the bewildered killer. "Just who the hell are you?"

"I am the emptiness of the void given form," the voice answered. "The chief servant of those who dwell beyond the stars. They have told me of your arrival since the moment you left the cities that lie to the north of here, and I have watched your coming as you crossed the Glass Desert and ascended the slopes of the Crimson Cliffs. I saw you as you tread your feet across my blasted land, and how you wounded my pet in the sewers and dispatched my disciples to feed their remains to the beasts in the pit. I must say that you are an exceptional talent, assassin. A rarity to even my age-old eyes. Why not join me in what you do, Tomek? I would put you to so much better use than you've done with yourself."

"The only thing I'll do is leave you dead on your own throne," spat the other. "You killed my village and my family. I'll never follow you."

"Curious that one such as yourself would suddenly care about life," replied the whisper, "when you seem to find so much pleasure in taking it. Why still concern yourself with things that happened nearly a lifetime ago, especially since they have forged you into the deadly thing that you have become today? You should be thankful to me and for your many hardships, Tomek, and revel in what you are."

"I don't care a damn thing about life," responded the assassin. "I've killed more men and women than I can even remember, what's a few more in the end. But what I do care about is seeing a score settled, and if you know me then you know how much I hold a grudge and what I'm capable of to carry it out. Every day I've thought about what I'd do if I ever found the one responsible for the destruction of my home. I won't deny myself the satisfaction of taking your head now. Now enough with your hiding and long-winded talk. Come and face me and we'll see if what they say about you is true, or just bloated exaggeration."

"Very well, assassin" whispered the annoyed voice. "It seems you have chosen your road, as much as it disappoints me. Prepare to receive what you asked for, Tomek Antal. And we shall put your considerable talents to a real test."

Two stars suddenly flashed bright in the darkness. The specks descended to hover just above the seat of the empty chair. The pair of burning orbs flared a brilliant gold as they settled and drifted together. The star flecked form of a man materialized around them. The dark thing that came into being was a featureless shape of the blackest night, strewn with the same cosmic heavens that swirled in the heights of the chamber. Its fingertips ended in needle like points. A pair of horns swept from its brow to resemble the many statues throughout the tower. It sat upon the bronze clothed in a draping of deep violet. Its shining eyes focused on the killer who stood petrified before it. His cool confidence deserted him in a sudden chill.

"Greetings, at last, Tomek of Marsax," the figure said as it rose from the throne. "Am I not all that you thought, or am I more?"

"Xiphactinas," the killer uttered with a wispy gasp. He backed away. "The rumors were true, weren't they? You really are a demon."

"The worst kind, assassin," Xiphactinas responded in a soft voice that hit like thunder. "And you are about to find out just how horrible I can be."

"And you're about to be dead!" the killer snarled, trying to summon up his courage. "I'll not fall to you!"

With a bolstering shout, Tomek hurled himself straight at his waiting foe. The dagger that had ended so many countless lives was poised to take the most sought after one of all. It marveled the assassin that the demon would leave himself so defenseless when confronted by such a threat, especially with knowing just how deadly the apt man was. But before he could make it more than a few feet, he found out exactly why. A clawed hand came up to casually wave him off. An unseen force slammed hard into his chest to send him rolling across the floor. Xiphactinas stepped down from the dais to follow slowly behind. Methodically, the demon stalked after the other as Tomek attempted to regain his breath. Scarlet drops came to the killer's lips as he spat out a mouthful of red. Several of his ribs were broken from the impact of the invisible blow, but there was still plenty of fight left in him.

Tomek saw the demon closing in. The star flecked being stopped as their eyes met. Xiphactinas's golden orbs went dim for a fraction of a second, then a glowing brightness came from their very core. They flashed like searing stars as the assassin barely threw himself aside.

Two jets of burning fire shot from the demon's eyes. The flames left a trail of scorch marks and bubbling glass across the floor just where Tomek had been. The killer came to his feet and ran for his life. He circled around the outside of the chamber to stay just ahead of the blasting heat. In a desperate dive, he threw himself behind the throne. The tarnished bronze shielded him even as the top was cut in half and nearly melted to slag.

"I must say that you do impress me, assassin," laughed Xiphactinas. The spouts of flame abated. "It's very few that can avoid my power the way you just did. What else do you have?"

Tomek crouched behind what was left of the seat and clutched his dagger. His heart truly raced in his chest for the first time since coming here, or in many a year for that matter. Despite the many tales and warnings, he had expected to find nothing more than a living man or group of such, not the star speckled darkness that had just spewed fiery death at him. He plucked a small vial from a pouch at his belt. He popped the cork with a steady hand to coat his blade with the thick green that oozed out. The substance was a vile fluid brewed by only the most wicked and depraved of individuals. He had been saving a small amount for just such an occasion. Even the slightest drop that entered a wound was enough to kill over a dozen in less than a minute. Tomek emptied the whole of the container over his steel. He readied his saturated dagger and pulled several other small knives from his waist. He held one between each knuckle of his fist and then he moved like lightning.

Tomek darted from behind the half-melted throne to deftly avoid another blast. He weaved left and then quickly back to the right to keep his enemy from drawing a straight line. Another streak of flame came just inches from his bobbing head. The intense heat blistered his cheek and singed his raven hair. He flung his three small blades directly at the demon's face. The fires again subsided as Xiphactinas motioned with a hand to throw the projectiles off. The starry being had spared himself the sting of the incoming steel, but the act had grossly opened him up to other perils, just as the assassin had hoped.

Tomek charged in with his full weight behind him. He plunged the tip of his dagger directly in the demon's chest. He expected to crash into the darkened being and hear a painful scream. What he was met with was something that felt as if it was not even there. His cutting blade carved through a black void that seemed no more solid than thin air. In his astonishment, he was struck harder than he'd ever been hit before. He was again sent rolling. Xiphactinas's swatting backhand put him down like he was nothing but a fly.

"What's the matter, assassin?" the demon asked. "Were you perhaps expecting something else to happen? I believe you'll find that I'm so much more than the usual rabble you're used to dealing with. Surely there's more fight in you than this."

Tomek vaguely registered the words as he came to his knees. He spat out several teeth from his cracked jaw. His head swam as the walls of black glass spun in his peripherals. He looked up to see Xiphactinas towering above him. The demon's horned shape and golden eyes stood in hellish contrast to the stars and planets that churned overhead. The hardened killer had never faced a foe like this in all of his days. His deep seeded arrogance and overconfidence in himself were broken. Many of his bones could say the same.

"What are you?" Tomek slurred almost incoherently. He struggled up to his feet to sway back and forth. "Why won't you die?"

"Because you are not the one that is fated to kill me," Xiphactinas coldly responded. "Nor were any of the others that came before you. That distinction belongs to someone else.

"But you have proven to be quite impressive nonetheless, Tomek of Marsax. Ever so much more than those that preceded you. Most never make it past my guards or manage to survive the cliffs that ring my domain, let alone come all the way to my throne room. I was going to end you here but perhaps I can still make use of you after all. It would be such a shame for your talents to be snuffed out before they could be made to serve me. Wouldn't you agree, assassin?"

"I've already said that I'll never serve you," Tomek sputtered. "I may be a killer but I'm no dog of a demon."

"You no longer have a choice in the matter, Tomek," Xiphactinas replied. "You belong to me now."

The assassin gave a look of hateful defiance at the thought of being oppressed under the demon's thumb. He remembered well the years of servitude he'd spent in the mines that were once his home. He would not let himself be subjected to such forced bondage again, preferring death over once more being made into a slave. He launched himself forward in a wild charge. His barreling assault was met by a foe that simply awaited with open arms. His blade sliced and stabbed through the air again and again. A poison dipped edge that would have been more than enough to drop anyone slashed in tight strokes. But the nothingness of the star flecked form still remained unharmed, almost welcoming the pitiful attempt to end him.

In response to the attack, Xiphactinas simply seized the assassin with a claw tipped hand. The strength in the demon's grasp was monstrous and far too much for the killer to overcome. Tomek plunged the dagger deep into his enemy's chest in a desperate effort. He was shocked to find that unlike as before the blade stuck firm. A force that he could not fight against suddenly began pulling him into the demon's blackness. His arm was sucked up to the shoulder in less than an instant. He tried to kick away only to lose his legs as well. His lower half was enveloped up to his waist before he could manage anything further.

Slowly, the void overtook the writhing killer. It came to cover his chest, neck, and gasping mouth before finally robbing his whistling nose of air. Soon, all that remained of the horrified assassin was one flailing arm and his eyes that stared wide into Xiphactinas's golden orbs. The nothingness spread steadily over his head as panic filled his gaze. The last things to be overtaken were Tomek's outstretched fingertips, and then the stars moved in and the assassin was gone. The demon was the solitary figure in his inner sanctum.

Xiphactinas strode over to stand before his broken throne. He brought up his hand as he regarded the melted bronze. At his unspoken urging, the metal became of liquid, flowing and knitting itself back together to spiral up into the outstretched claws just as before. The demon sat even as the scorch marks and the trails of his fiery gaze began to fade away. The walls and floor of smooth obsidian renewed their luster to appear as if they had never been touched. It had been far too long since someone had penetrated so far into his imposing stronghold. Xiphactinas found it entertaining and a welcome reprieve from only hearing the murmuring of his masters and observing the heavens. But it was a fleeting pleasure and there were still matters to deal with that were unsettled. The coming of another from the Northlands who sought an audience with the lord of the citadel still loomed.

The demon looked to the turning cosmos above and reclined in his chair. The stars came together to show him the image of the great bear his masters had warned him of. The constellation of the beast soundlessly roared as it met the gaze of the golden orbs, promising Xiphactinas a far harder battle than the one just had.

With nothing but a stare, the demon dismissed the threatening image. He did not have to be reminded of the man who had killed General Zantz and the rage he'd seen displayed behind those chestnut eyes. The Son of the Bear was still drawing nearer by the day, and the ruler of the obsidian tower was determined to be ready for him, no matter the lengths that had to be taken to do so.

The Chronicles of the Bear series will continue in the next gripping adventure,

The Bear in Red Webs.

About the Author

Remy Morgeson began his writing journey in 2016 determined to take on the world of sword and sorcery head on. A longtime lover of fantasy and pulp fiction, Remy found his inspiration in the fantastic settings and larger than life characters he has shared adventures with. His influences include authors such as Robert E. Howard, John Jakes, Lin Carter, Michael Moorcock, and Fritz Lieber, as well as a handful of other talented individuals too numerous to name here. Remy's work has been featured in publications such as Savage Realms Monthly and his debut series, Chronicles of the Bear, being released in February of 2021.

In addition to writing sword and sorcery and dark fantasy, Remy enjoys a variety of other interests, including vintage RPGs, retro video games, weight training, and binging the occasional anime or two. He currently resides in Danville, Illinois with his wife and daughter, whom nothing would be possible for him without.

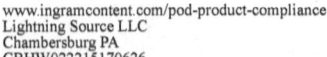